CW00661763

Heather currently lives, works and writes; fuelled by tea, spite and disapproving looks from a cat.

For my family, friends, thornbacks, Cleo, and the wonderful colleagues I have had the pleasure to work with.

Heather Jephcote

THE GOLDFISH BOWL

AUSTIN MACAULEY PUBLISHERS™

LONDON ∗ CAMBRIDGE ∗ NEW YORK ∗ SHARJAH

Copyright © Heather Jephcote 2023

The right of Heather Jephcote to be identified as author of this work has been asserted by the author in accordance with sections 77 and 78 of the Copyright, Designs and Patents Act 1988.

All rights reserved. No part of this publication may be reproduced, stored in a retrieval system, or transmitted in any form or by any means, electronic, mechanical, photocopying, recording, or otherwise, without the prior permission of the publishers.

Any person who commits any unauthorised act in relation to this publication may be liable to criminal prosecution and civil claims for damages.

This is a work of fiction. Names, characters, businesses, places, events, locales, and incidents are either the products of the author's imagination or used in a fictitious manner. Any resemblance to actual persons, living or dead, or actual events is purely coincidental.

A CIP catalogue record for this title is available from the British Library.

ISBN 9781035827312 (Paperback)
ISBN 9781035827329 (ePub e-book)

www.austinmacauley.com

First Published 2023
Austin Macauley Publishers Ltd®
1 Canada Square
Canary Wharf
London
E14 5AA

Special thanks to my dad, Bob, for proofreading my terrible spelling x.

Table of Contents

Any similarities herein to persons (living, accused, convicted or dead), entities or events (existing, dissolved, bankrupted, etc.) are entirely likely due to the inherent nature of corporate culture and the society we inhabit at large.
Any recognition by any individual or company of any individual or company that is depicted in the following story is acknowledgement by that person or entity that their existence imitates art inspired by life.
Get over yourselves.
Do better.

Chapter 1
This Could Have Been an Email

This is not where I saw myself in five years. It's not where I said I'd be either. When I was sitting in that airless cubby being interviewed and quizzed over intents and direction I didn't have (and still don't), I didn't have the heart to them I just needed a job and I couldn't care less what it was doing so long as it paid enough to keep a roof over my head. Didn't have the heart? Or, didn't have the courage? It may have been the latter. I was worried and panicked at the meagre provisions in the redundancy packages that were being handed out left, right, and centre at my last job, and knowing that being qualified and experienced was as worthless as the degree I had forked out for, I had gone into a long series of interviews in which I regurgitated the same old answers.

Yes, I am trustworthy. I am a hard worker. I am willing to work overtime. I am meticulous with detail—but I don't get lost in it. I can prioritise my work to ensure that all work is done in a timely manner. What am I looking for? A role in which I can establish myself within a company, but a position with the opportunity to grow as an individual within my chosen career path. Why, yes! I *am* a team player who is able to take responsibility and work independently.

Did I hit enough buzzwords for you there?

Every so often in these interviews there would be a curveball. A question conceived in the whimsical pits of a burnt-out mind specifically designed to throw a candidate off their game. I guess in some interviews they are presented as lively little ways to express yourself and have fun, but I assume all the interviewers I spoke with used the random questions purely to panic the interviewee. They probably all skim read the same corporate HR interview techniques booklet.

What kitchen utensil am I? One that can follow instructions but use my common sense and good judgement to find a suitable route to my desired outcome[1]. I would fight neither a giraffe-sized rat nor a hundred rat-sized giraffes—as a natural leader who can take the initiative; I would ride the giant rat into battle followed by an army of tiny giraffes. How much would I charge to wash all the windows in London? Depends; is this a government contract and how many friends do I have there?

Of course, I didn't actually say that in my answer. I can't remember my actual answer—my brain wasn't in charge of my mouth at that point.

Do I work well under pressure? Big red flag there. The biggest of red flags flapping about trying to warn off all applicants. How often are there urgent stakes in this position? What kind of pressure is put on people? Are managers brandishing whips and locking doors? Is this a common occurrence? Is it due to poor management? Underfunded departments, or a resistance by corporate to employ the necessary quantity of staff?

Of course, I didn't actually say that in my answer. I said yes. And followed it up with examples of times I had worked well under the mis-management of other companies.

At one point, unsurprisingly not an interview I got a call back for, I was asked how many marbles I could fit into a car.

Seriously?

Seriously.

I'd had enough. It had been a long and tortuous journey cross-Pennines to have the interview. There had been multiple modes of transport involved, delays at almost every station, a lost ticket, and a drunk stag-do singing in one of the carriages who had split half a can of beer over my new suit. I smelt as though I belonged in a brewery, or a pub, or outside a football stadium having lost my ticket to enter.

So yes, at this point, I had had enough with their stupid questions.

With pencil, paper and the power of a search engine, I googled my way to an answer.

Assuming that there is a reason you want to transport the marbles (and therefore need the car to be driveable) a quick google informed me that my own car's boot capacity (with back seats folded down—I'm not a moron) was 1,069 giggle litres. Though rough and dodgy, I think it's safe to say that the majority of these litres can be viewed as 10×10×10cm cubes for the purpose of this

---

[1] Spatula? I think I'm a spatula.

hypothetical situation in which I, a grunt interviewing for low level office work, would need to transport the big man's marbles.

Assuming a standard marble size of 12mm diameter (as per the British Marbles Board of Control's British and World Marbles Championship—who I can only assume is the authority on these matters[2]), and with a perfect packing density (where all marbles sit uniformly on top of one another, tessellating in order to reduce gaps between the individual marbles) the number was in the hundreds of thousands. I don't remember the exact number I came to—I wrote out the maths long form.

Again, this was all under the assumption that the marbles needed to arrive in a functional form and so crushing them would be inappropriate.

I'm not sure how you would reconstitute a crushed marble.

Heat?

And pressure?

But, and it's a fairly big but stop giggling the weight of the marbles mustn't hinder the manoeuvrability of the car. I'm not an idiot. The weight of these competition marbles is somewhere between 4g and 5g—which begged the real question of this farcical endeavour—do I play it safe? Take fewer marbles to assure these miniature glass orbs all reach their fictional, intended destination, or do I risk it? Do I assume that the marbles are all in their lightest forms, and go big and risk it all.

At this point the interviewer tried to intervene. Unsuccessfully. I was on a roll.

A handy blog I came across while boring the now-concerned interviewer to death with my precise workings out on a clearly meaningless and ultimately regretful question, commented on not being able to take ten 20kg bags of cement in one go due to the pressure on the suspension. I ended up with somewhere between 40 and 50 thousand marbles.

I could have stopped there.

I should have stopped there.

The interviewer, who was already marking down that I should under no circumstance be hired by this company, clearly expected me to stop there.

I did not stop there.

See, the thing is, either the word 'marbles' was being used in this question as euphemism for some form of illicit substance or some form of non-

---

[2] Footnoted to show my workings

transportable goods with a ban or expensive tariff (blood marbles, perhaps) **or** I had clearly underestimated the value of the humble marble, and the business to which I was applying knew something I did not about the current state of the global marble market and lucrative (though secretive) investments available therein. So, I would of course be expecting at least some of my pay to be made in marbles, and would therefore be using the glove box for my own personal stash of marbles (euphemistic or otherwise).

I do wonder how people did interviews before the advent of the internet in your pocket. Maybe they just weren't asked stupid questions.

Unsurprisingly, I didn't get that job.

I got this one.

Which is why I have been sitting in this station hotel function room for the past three hours being addressed by all and sundry from the London office who have wondered north for a couple of days on expenses and allowance to lecture us on the state of business in person rather than sending us the updates in the weekly email blast from… Bill? Or is it Mike?… No, Bill… I'm fairly sure it…—I don't care. It doesn't matter. It comes through as a link on a mass email and they never bothered to give us access to the programme the email links to so none of us can open but that we're all expected to read their blog enthusiastically.

I'm sure in some organisations this works well enough. Maybe if the blogger were interesting or entertaining—someone personable who is able to make lasting impressions on his subjects. Underlings? Employees.

"You have to think of Ieso Financial and Wealth Management like a giant turtle," the head of some department or other enunciates clearly with his hands open to cradle the imaginary corporate turtle. This is going to be one strained and tenuous metaphor. Simile? I don't care. He's already moved onto an anecdote of the time he was working on a beach in some far-flung stunning island *gratuitous holiday photo* he thought about how, like the turtle, we need to protect ourselves with a hard shell, to make our way out of our sandy beach birth and down towards the sea without getting distracted by the big, bright lights of the city and race against the hare; knowing that if we keep it slow and steady, we can win the race.

Last one there was a tortoise, mate.

You don't care.

I don't care.

I could be doing actual work right now. Getting on with all the stuff they are going to berate me about tomorrow. I can feel my queue of work grow with every tick of the clock. More emails flooding my inbox. Requests to return phone calls from contacts annoyed and disappointed I wasn't available for them, threatening to pull business because of my lack of availability even though there are dozens of people willing and able to assist them[3]. More letters that will be turned around a day late.

It'll be nice to get a day out of the office, my manager says.

Sure, Jan. But it's not as if the work that needs to be today is just going to magically disappear. I'm still going to be expected to finish this in the same time as attending this mandatory, self-aggrandising pat-on-the-back circle-jerk of titans of industry.

They're paying you for this, I remind myself. Like a theatre company paying an audience to watch them. You even get both fizzy and still branded water to share with the colleagues at this table as they lecture you on all the wonderful things they've done this year. Little mints to stave off hunger as we are shown their lovely holiday on which they decided to found a charity to encourage business in pre-industrial villages.

Yes, we get it. you are a wonderful human being, but stick it in the weekly news blast like everyone else.

One of the skivvies is placing pens and paper on each table. They are going to make us brainstorm, or worse—have **fun**.

At least we could choose where we sat today. That's better than last year. Last year they wanted to have an even spread of departments and roles across the tables in order to build cross-department relationships and collaborate— always collaborate—to create solutions in a pre-paid think-tank.

I was one of the last to arrive last year, due to my bus having a hissy fit and having to wait on the verge of a dual carriage way until another bus happened along and picked us up. In the end I was sitting with the dregs of the office who other tables had skilfully, apologetically, managed to avoid. It was like being stuck at a singles table for a distant cousin's wedding reception in one of Dante's purgatorio terraces. I had to make small talk with accountants and trainers as someone from HR 'directed' our conversation.

If they ever actually bothered to listen to the comments we make in the never-ending stream of surveys we are *encouraged* to complete, they would know what

---

[3] 'Willing' might be a bit of a strong word…

we think and they would maybe even act on it. Ideas swirl around the ground floor for years before the higher-ups spontaneously produce the idea themselves. I've been here long enough now to know that they'll be congratulating themselves for something one of us put in a suggestion box years ago.

That's what happened when Brian left. A few months after he retired someone went through all the ideas he had submitted and picked out half a dozen. They were praised. Brian got nothing.

I look up and catch Megan's glance across the table. She widens her eyes so I can see the whites all around her dark brown irises. She's trying to keep herself awake, jotting down notes in a small notebook, trying to appear engaged with far more effort than I am. She spent some time on her hair this morning, curling the ends under so the layers are defined.

She had it cut last week, though I'm not sure if she did that specifically for this event. She gets it cut on a regular basis. She has also put on a little more makeup than usual. To make a good impression, I imagine, on those who are only here for a day or two. Although she finds this as boring as I do, she has aspirations and she is willing to play their game.

I smile and nod and stifle a yawn by swallowing it. I haven't stopped yawning all morning. I know my manager has seen a couple, but the little psychopath hasn't yawned back once.

Oh, goody. Time for another video.

I'm pretty sure the music they are using skirts perilously close to a copyright infringement lawsuit. It sounds like a song that was popular a decade ago, though I can't for the life of me remember the song's name. Which is really frustrating. It's right there, right on the tip of my tongue and I just can't quite grab it.

The lights in the room go down so we can more clearly see the happy lives of our customers flash by with the pulsing music. like we are sitting in the more depressing nightclub.

Is this hell? I think this might be hell.

The managers and team leaders seem to be into it. Shoulder dancing at the table to my left a few rows closer to the stage.

Yes, let's do our best for our customers—let's ignore that 1 in 5 people in the office are working as delivery drivers in the evenings to make ends meet.

I'm not making that up. The union did a poll. A smaller though growing and more concerning number are members of pyramid schemes. Mostly hair and beauty, some weight-loss, some clothing, and I keep getting the generic messages from them on Facebook asking if I want to join them.

It is incredibly creepy when the twins from the mailroom both send messages at the same time, shilling out shining-twin vibes

Come join us, creepy smile, dead-eyed stare. *Come join our MLM.*

Crying face laughing emoji ×3. Red heart emoji ×3. Makeup emoji ×3.

I've met you in real life, ladies. I know neither of you has that range of emotions. You know I don't wear makeup unless I'm desperate.

I wander off into a daydream, and the station hotel function room bursts into flames. Fireball across the ceiling. The screen crackles and curls up as it is consumed. The fire doors are locked—an oversight by the visiting senior staff. The emergency team from the office don't have their high-vis jackets, the station hotel function room is not their domain. Stampede to the main doors—also locked. Trapped. No windows. Burnt to ashes. Put out of my misery.

Deep breath.

Positive thinking.

Go to your happy place.

Cross a wide desert and find the oasis that only you know the location of. Your sanctuary from the world. No matter how maddening the outside world, the oasis is a constant place, A place of true rest. Cool breeze through lush palms. Sweet air. Dip a toe in the cool water. Drink straight from the coconut.

I really need to find a real life equivalent of this and then lose my passport. I could live off coconuts and the occasional scorpion, right?

Shit. People are raising their hands. I've missed the question. I look round at those responding, trying to keep a blank expression on my face. I see Megan hasn't raised her hand. She shakes her head a little. I don't need to raise mine.

Whatever that was about, the CEO looks content with the response.

"Great," he says. "Excellent."

Slip back to the oasis…

Oh, never mind; it's question time. I should actually pay attention to this. Questions have been submitted via the app throughout the event, not that I ever got my app to work. I never do at these events. I don't know whether it's my phone that won't link up to the Wi-Fi and the app, or whether the app recognises me and actively rejects connection.

I understand, app. I wouldn't connect with me either.

Frustratingly, it means I never get to vote on the question either. But I really should pay attention; there is usually important information in this part of the session.

Oh sure, sure. Start with the questions that begin with positive, flattering comments. Why not. Which ego-stroking lackey is moderating this. It would be a shame if you didn't get through all the questions and need to get back to us at a later date because you took up all your time thanking people for their kind words and low-ball questions about pet projects everyone above a certain pay-grade is excited about.

I pull my bingo card from out of my trouser pocket, surreptitiously tilting it so only I can see it. I've made notes of the other side, legitimising it to the others at my table and any manager who cares to glance over. Lee in admin support made them for us. He printed off the templates and gave us a list of options to put in our squares. I'm pretty sure I've covered almost every square in my box.

Drum-happy music over stock images of happy, happy people having fun	MC makes inappropriate joke that falls flat about a speaker's age/appearance/clothing	Technology fails (except Wi-Fi)	Our lord and saviour (CEO/CFO/etc.) appears via video conferencing
No Wi-Fi available for 'participation' via app	Music copyright infringement	Call and answer fail	Cringe. Just, so much cringe.
Weird metaphor	Overly enthusiastic, meaningless alliteration. e.g., Live Life Large!	Nonsensical title of even delivered as though event is a music festival	Audience participation (i.e., Shouting out, chanting, raising hands etc.)

Speaker doesn't understand the question/dodges the question by feigning ignorance.	Majority cis-hetero-white-male speakers surrounded by stock images of diversity and inclusion	Horrific jazzed-up version of corporate mascot	No useful information for your actual job

Finally—questions about the new GPS-chipped ID cards. A nice, little surveillance for monitoring and recording every movement made in the office when we are not attached to a computer. To track our every move from workspace to toilet to kitchen and back. There's a rumour, whispered to me by Craig in the mailroom, that it will collect all our data like how quickly we can move round the office, a more efficient way to lay out the furniture, how we can shave milliseconds off making a cuppa and the like. There's also a counter-rumour saying that's all nonsense, so it would be really good if someone in a position of authority can dispel the myths and say some comforting words about the intention they have for this technology.

No one expects a direct answer from the panel… which is fortunate seeing as none is given.

I don't know what bright spark had the idea to follow our every movement round the office with a microchip to micromanage every toilet break, cigarette break and kettle natter, but someone clearly has too much faith in technology and in people not working out how to disarm or trick the hi-tech babysitter.

Maybe I have too much faith in my colleagues. Maybe there really is some diabolical theft of corporate time. Maybe people are going to the kitchen a dozen times a day to pick up their next fix, or are wandering around the office rather than sitting at their desks and working, like anyone with eyes can actually see them do.

Apparently, the CCTV isn't enough to keep a check on people, and a lanyard noose is needed instead.

I already have to demonstrate how I use my time. Once in a while they pull out the old, broken spreadsheet for us to fill in with every take we complete in an hour, noting the time it took and how valuable it was for Ieso Financial. Regardless of whether a piece of work was valuable or not it still had to be done. Could we be doing something to prevent that kind of work task? Email. Letter, phone call from coming into us again.

Short answer—no; because there will always be someone that loses their documents and needs a copy resent, or someone that doesn't understand the corporate jargon on an email they've received.

They could at least make a shared spreadsheet that doesn't break every time we are asked to do this. Poor spreadsheet can't cope when a hundred people try to update it at the same time.

I spend more time those days filling in the bloody spreadsheet than doing actual work.

The vice something-or-other describes the consultant-suggested new way of working as a Herculean task.

"Sisyphean," mouths Megan.

"Geek," I say under my breath.

"Nerd," she corrects me, grinning while scrunching up her nose.

She's told me this story before. After cheating death twice, Sisyphus was punished for cheating it by being forced to pointlessly roll a heavy boulder up a hill and watch it roll back down. Over and over and over. Doing the same task again and again. An endless cycle.

Relatable.

I've no idea what I'm being punished for, but I must have done something terrible in a previous life to deserve it.

Actually, scratch that! I *envy* Sisyphus. Sisyphus didn't have to work next to Carol. Carol with her six cats and no eyebrows. Carol who is constantly spraying herself with a sickly perfume that catches the back of my throat and who rubs this oily, scented lotion on her hands between each phone call and so her keyboard is permanently sticky and catches lint.

It's always worth checking who was last sitting at the desk you've reserved. Sticky keyboards is just the start of it. Beard clippings, chipped nail fragments, the lingering smell of tuna mayonnaise and the odd bit of rogue sweetcorn clinging to the chair. There are too many disgusting people in the office that it's worth checking before getting your pen from the box inside your locker and setting up for the day. Click sticky mouse, clack knackered keys. Swap out the mouldy, lop-sided chair for the one that doesn't change height, and pray as the clock rolls on to five, that no one has done something nasty in the toilets[4].

---

[4] Whatever you are imagining, please know that this is worse. So much worse. But for the sensitive readers I will not be describing the incident here.

This meeting is never going to end. I think we live here now. We live in the function room of a hotel above a railway station. I'm going to have to set up a cot in one of the smaller meeting rooms. We're going to be brought cheese and onion finger sandwiches, mini quiches and other miniaturised beige food. I'll never have Wi-Fi again. This is my life now.

End.

Please end.

I just want all this to be over.

I am out of luck. There are still messages to be given. There's an industry event they want volunteers for.

This but on steroids. Fuck off.

Every time I think we are in the last segment of the meeting-presentation they tack on another thought, another important note, another just-one-more-thing.

I zone out and think of lunch. My stomach angrily bubbling away. I was too tired to make anything last night, and I didn't have time this morning after snoozing three alarms. I sleep too much.

People are clapping. It's all over. I can finally stretch my legs, arch my back and roll my shoulders.

"Hungry?" Megan asks as she rises from the table. I nod without interrupting my stretch. "Yiorgos?"

She has said the magic word. My stomach leaps at the memory of it. Yiorgos is hands-down the best food vendor on the market. We don't usually have enough time to get from the office, queue up, eat and get back. The queue can be a mile long by the time you get there. But today, we are in the centre of town and I now have the taste memory of Yiorgos between my teeth. The man has—I swear to God—the BEST tzatziki. In the 3-month-long Greek street food drought of two years ago last March, I dreamt tzatziki in all its delicious, creamy goodness. There were literal celebrations when Yiorgos got his licence back.

Sure, he may have lost his original licence due to vermin being found in his preparation area, but that is a small price to pay for the damn tasty vegetable gyros and sweet, sweet loukoumades balls that Megan and I say we'll share before we 3D chess our way to eating the most.

It's not even midday and the queue for Yiorgos already stretches past several of the other stalls. I window shop the second-hand books and glass jewellery as we wait. The queue moves at a decent pace and it isn't long before we are sitting on the steps in front of the art gallery in the centre of town eating our lunch and waiting for the security guard to chase us off for blocking a fire escape.

It's sunny for once. Small tufts of brilliant, white, candyfloss clouds dot the sky, but the majority of the dome above us is blue. The sun bakes us on the concrete and I bathe in it, letting the sun soak into my skin and hair. I wish I could sit out here for the rest of the day—but the guard moves us on and it's time to go back to the office for the afternoon.

It's a fair trek up to the industrial estate our office sits on. The old building at the centre was a cotton mill way back when, but now the wide, cavernous great workroom houses a touchdown centre for local government employees. Local council, social services, and the overflow from the court buildings at the bottom of the hill that needed additional space for their workers.

Our office is one of the newer buildings on the east side of the estate. It has, in some ways, attempted to fit into its surroundings, using red bricks in its façade and leaning heavily on an industrial aesthetic, but the architect decided that floor to ceiling windows inserted at an angle would be the best way forward. Keep the lighting costs down and allow the employees to be seen from every angle. Half the time it's impossible to see out of the building, the light is so strong. But it's not about the employees. It's about the aesthetic.

Inside is no better. Someone saw 'open concept' and thought—hey! That's cheaper than walls!

I'm sure it was a good idea to begin with. Someone opened up a dark and dusky space—like the mill opposite—and filled it with natural light and space. To create a workspace that functioned perfectly for this one particular office. A concept that would have worked for many offices, given the right tweaks and insights.

But no, we have this: a bad copy of a bad copy. An idea that was probably lauded on its unveiling—or maybe it wasn't, not at first. Maybe there was a slow burning appreciation. But some businessman got a hold of the rights to the idea and commercialised it, took it out of context and mass produced a viable idea.

I'd make a terrible architect. I can't draw. Can't do physics. I can't even pretend I'd be good at it. I would question everything, every little thing, and doubt, always doubt it. I would have no confidence in my abilities and would worry that every building, every wall would fall down as quickly as it was put up.

23

I work in a building designed by a famous architect that literally cooks people working inside of it. He's one of the good architects—or at least he's one that gets work.

Maybe he was born with it. Maybe it's nepotism.

I am not ready for the onslaught of sound and movement when we enter the office. A mass of people who were all at the meeting this morning are returning from their lunches and making their way through electric turnstiles in front of a grand staircase. We're queueing for a terrible theme park ride. The whole layout of the atrium amplifies every slight sound and it resonates throughout the offices and workspaces on each floor. The close maze of desks force people to dance their way round everything.

When everyone arrives at once, the office furniture is unprepared for it.

The bank of desks I usually opt to sit out have been reserved for the dignitaries that are up for the day. I booked myself a seat last week in one of the far-flung corners, hidden behind a thick pillar, one that hopefully makes me invisible, but importantly, provably, there on any of the numerous electronic ways that my attendance can be checked. Natural light doesn't reach this nook of the office, but as I'm facing a window, that in itself is a blessing. No glare, no reflections. I can turn down the brightness of my screen and just get on with doing things without a constant stream of managerial interruptions insisting on checking in and catching up.

Megan tucks in beside me. She had booked a chair by the kitchen which restricted how many people could sit next to her, but after checking who had booked the chairs around her, she moved to the pillar chair. The half-desk. The space you have to sit at a crooked angle. I shimmy over so she can use my desk as well.

Over the low partition between our row and the row facing us, Hannah sits down, letting us know that Ben will be joining us in a moment. Hannah pulls her mousy brown relaxed hair back into a long plait that reaches her waist before she wakes her computer from its sleep. She's younger than the rest of us by almost a decade, and still has puppy fat in her cheeks and jaw. Her light-skin has caught the sun over the weekend and it is tinged pinker than usual. She finished school after her exams and came to work here.

An aunt or cousin had just got a job and recommended her. The family member hadn't survived probation which, given that the bar is practically lying on the ground, is genuinely impressive. Only in the past few months has she decided what she wants to do next in her life. She's going to evening school and is applying for university. She wants to be a teacher. She can still ask for a half on a bus, and has to prove to shocked doormen that she is indeed over 18, but somehow, she has taken some time away from education to decide what she actually wants to do.

Hannah has caught the attention of Lord Soanso, a blotchy middle-aged peer who attended this morning's update. He's on the board, or a board, or is friends with someone on a board. It never seems to be important. He is in the foreground of many company photos and speaks on our behalf at countless events and meetings—offering an introduction to our services.

He then keeps turning up at our office like the worst of bad pennies.

He has commented previously that he just really likes how friendly we are. That there is nothing so stuffy up here. That we are *real* people. I take offence to that. I haven't quite worked out why, but I do. Everything he says sounds like a compliment, but he says too many of them in a row to be believable, and always with the same smarmy grin plastered across his face. There are times it looks as though he taught himself how to smile in a mirror. His leering eyes are set close together, hovering over a potato nose, and his top front teeth jut out while the bottom set are so crooked, they seem to lie on top of each other. His cheeks and head are far broader and dwarf his eyes and lips. He always seems to be leering at one or more of us.

Happily, though at the same time worryingly, I seem to be beyond his taste.

"Hello ladies," he says. My legs clench together in discomfort as I force a smile. His words sour the air around us. I can smell the fish he had for lunch. "I don't think I've had the pleasure…?"

He has. He's met all of us. Repeatedly. At every business update, at every event. He's even sat with us before at these very desks. We remind him of our names.

"I'm just going to take this seat here," he says, taking the seat next to Hannah. She doesn't have the nerve to tell him it's taken. Megan does though. "Oh dear," he says, sinking into the fabric and setting his feet flat on the carpet. "Well, I'm sure they can sit somewhere else." He speaks slowly, carefully. Considering every clipped word that passes his lips. His tone and metre at odds and so foreign to our rounded vowels.

He slides his chair, somewhat surreptitiously so that he pushes into Hannah's space. His elbow nudging hers. She looks over to us pleadingly, but averts her eyes so he doesn't see her beg for our help. He's pushed his way into her space before. When he was here last Christmas, he'd spent almost an entire evening standing over her, head bent over to talk to her, marking every point he made by tapping on her arm.

Hannah had told us how uncomfortable this had made her, but hadn't gone into detail.

"I don't like it when they stand over you like that, when you can feel their breath on your neck," she told me. "His hand was all clammy and hot every time he touched me." We promised not to leave her alone with him again.

But here he was. At our desks, in her space.

Helen, a manager from another team has noticed and is already coming over. She has a daughter Hannah's age, and I think Helen is related to the aunt or cousin that got Hannah the job here. Maybe it's Hannah's Aunt and Helen's cousin. I don't think Hannah and Helen are related.

"Lord Soanso," she greets him loudly as she comes over. "We wondered where you'd gotten to! We've arranged a small get together for you and the other VIPs with drinks and nibbles on the terrace."

She's said the magic word; VIP. His face lights up and he chuckles to himself.

"Oh, how splendid!" He says. "Will these three charming ladies be joining us?"

"I'm afraid they should be getting on with their work and not distracting you," Helen says apologetically, then throws us an eye roll when he is getting up out of his chair.

"No, no," he insists. "They've done nothing of the sort. Good sports, these young girls are. Good sports."

Helen waits for him, smiling kindly. I'd love to know what's going on inside her head. She's so good at holding up that façade, I'd love to know the narration that goes on with it. "Please," she says, holding out an encouraging arm to direct him over to the stairs up to the terrace.

"If I must," he says.

He must.

Megan has dipped her head so she can't be seen over the screen, pretending to be scribbling on a piece of rough paper. Her tongue protruding like she's about to vomit. She snaps her head up in time to offer a courteous smile goodbye as the lord is whisked away.

Finally able to react, my arms erupt in goosebumps. I open up my email inbox to see what I've missed from this waste of a morning, but my manager, Jan, appears around the column, a large file in her arms. She has found me.

"I need to have a word with you," she says, masterfully indecipherable. "Now, please."

What have I done?

I last spoke with Jan on Monday, and I can't think of anything in the past few days that would be cause for complaint. No, I haven't been even remotely rude to anyone (not that I ever am), I last checked my stats on Wednesday—they all seemed fine. Have I offended someone in the office? Did I tread on someone's foot? My mind plays the past few days on fast-forward through my head as I try to locate any moment that would merit being pulled aside. We are heading towards one of the small, frosted glass, private rooms where people are taken for 1-2-1s or to be let go.

She dispenses with the niceties.

I say 'dispense', she never usually uses them anyway, and I would be far more worried if she used them.

"I've been asked to put together a team for a new project and I want you to be the lead on it."

"Oh," I say, and nothing more. This isn't a choice. I do sometimes enjoy the projects, and even if I don't, they never last very long so it's often no more than a jaunt to another floor of the office for a few weeks.

"I don't have a lot of details yet, but I've just spoken with Aji, he's one of the managers over in sales, he's got this high-priority account that needs some special attention. It's a large account that needs to be set up," Jan places the file she's been holding on the table between us. It doesn't appear to have anything to do with this news. "It's a lot of processing and we need someone that can do it speedily, though it may take a few weeks."

"Weeks?" I ask.

"Hmm," Jan hums. "Yes, we'll be taking on some temps to help you with it."

"Right," I say, and nothing more.

"You'll be on loan out to Darren Neal while it's being set up. He's one of the sales reps, do you know him?" Yes, I know Darren-fucking-Neal. I've not needed to work with him before to both know he's reputation and to have been in trouble with him over the phone for failing to deliver on a promise that he had given a client. A promise that was literally impossible for me to keep. A promise that the computer system had no way of honouring.

Anyone who has worked the late shift has spoken with him. He's the sales guy that will call through and conference in a client without prior warning and introduce you as the greatest senior admin that Iseo has. He will big you up, then talk for fifteen or twenty minutes, sometimes longer, way past your finishing time, before asking one solitary question on behalf of the client that's on the other end of the phone.

Darren-fucking-Neal forgets that he is the only one working on commission.

"There's a lot of paperwork," Jan tells me. "It's going to come to you directly instead of the mailroom…"

"Why would the mail come directly to the office?"

"I don't know, something about us not being allowed to hold the agency's files on our computers, but we have permission to manually scan them for information."

"They aren't sending us applications? Like our application?" I ask. "Shouldn't they be submitting the information online or in our paper format?"

"It's a large account," Jan wafts away my queries with a hand. Her voice tightens as she says, "Large accounts get perks like us doing their admin work."

I nod slowly. That's not really an answer, and it's not really what I asked. I mean, it sounds dodgy. "You said we're getting in some temps?"

"Yes, we're getting in some temps. They'll be able to fill in our online applications for the agency. You'll be in charge of making sure that the team gets the information in accurately, and keeping all the documents secure."

Whoop-de-fucking-do.

"If you have any questions about it, you'll need to get in touch with Darren Neal. When you come in tomorrow, you'll need to go to the third-floor conference room. They are setting up computers in there for you now. You'll be in there until it's sorted."

"I'm working from home tomorrow," I say. I was looking forward to working in my pyjamas and getting a running start at the weekend.

"No, you're not," Jan says.

Our conversation is over.

Chapter 2
An Exciting New Project

As I walk up through the industrial estate, I see Frances, the stout office manager, at the door balancing a stack of hefty cardboard boxes on her hip as she wrestles with the key in the lock.

I don't like getting the bus in on a Friday. It's always busier than usual and I've never understood why. Maybe there's a particular business in the city centre that has Friday as a mandatory office attendance day. They finish early and go to the pub for office drinks. God, that would suck. Whenever the word 'socialising' is muttered by someone in the office, it doesn't matter where I am in relation to the speaker, the word runs down my back like a really useless spidey-sense.

Or, maybe Nandos has an offer on that everyone wants to take advantage of. Now, that I can respect.

But there are only certain people in the office I would want to see outside the office. There are only so many times that Carol can tell me about her alopecic cat, or Pam's daughter's gap year photos which are so old they include Yugoslavia, or that inevitable long, slow chat with Brian about which steam train he saw at the weekend.

To be fair to Brian, he does have the occasional good story—like the time he saw the recreation of the Lancashire Witch inaugural runaway run through the Pennines and Brian had to matador the iron beast into a field. I imagine capes and the train having a Thomas-the-tank-engine face of a bull. But that's only one story of Brian's, and I've been subjected to a thousand.

Anyway, my point is; I prefer my colleagues in small doses.

Frances is still trying to get the door open when I reach it. I offer to take the boxes she is carrying so she can use both arms to turn the stubborn key.

"I think those boxes are for you," she tells me through gritted teeth and expletives. "That sales rep drove them over TO MY HOUSE last night so it would be here first thing in the morning."

"Why didn't he just drive them in this morning?"

"Apparently, he didn't think about that," she says, twisting her body to get enough purchase on the key and pulling the door towards her in case that's the issue. "Then he changed his mind and said it was because he had to take the kids to school this morning."

"He has kids?" I don't mean to sound incredulous, but I don't always have control over my tone.

Frances shrugs. "He never said they were his kids." She finally gets the key to turn and opens the door to punch in the security code to turn off the alarm. The shape of the punched numbers makes a pleasing shape on the keypad, criss-crossing over themselves down the pad and then ending with a naught.

"I've got a key for you," Frances says. Pushing open both inner doors.

"Oh?" I wasn't expecting that.

"Yes, I'm off on holiday in a month's time and one of your managers… Jan? Jan asked me to give you one," Frances is clearly irked by Jan's request, but says nothing more about it and walks over to the light switch and turns on the lights in the atrium.

The three storeys of the atrium fill with light. The reception desk sits as a lonely, round island between two banks of turnstiles. Behind the reception desk is a grand, sweeping, glass staircase, split into two, that helixes up a central column. To the right, there is a cramped office. To the left a bank of lifts and a staircase down to the mailrooms and the back fire exit.

Frances holds the wide turnstile open for me to carry the boxes through. "Wait here," she says over her shoulder, moving towards the door, "I'll get some of the others out of my car."

Others? How many more boxes are there?

As I wait, some of the early shift arrive. John, an old banker taking a step back from his previous stressful job after having a heart attack, is the receptionist who usually works in the mornings. He comments that I'm in early. I reply that I am. He nods and asks how I've been. I nod and ask him the same.

Frances dumps her handbag behind the desk next to John, throws up a hand to say hello and tells him she'll catch up with him later.

We take the lift to the third floor, and cross over the bridge at the top of the atrium past the top of the stairs, and into the office on the right-hand side of the building. I don't usually come up this far. Here be dragons… and the IT guys. We pass the kitchen and toilets and turn left to see the glass panelled room. An afterthought slotted in when the need arose for a mid-sized conference room.

One that needed no privacy and no air. There is literally a pipe out of the side of the box that is supposed to draw away carbon dioxide so we don't all asphyxiate. Like we're supposed to just trust it. I don't think there's any actual science to it—I think the pipe is just there to reassure people that they aren't *actively* trying to kill us. But there is no cooling system in the glass box. Nothing to stop the warm stuffy air building up and sending us all into a never-ending sleep.

A half dozen computers have been set up in the room. I place the box beside the one I am going to take—at least for today.

"You're the one running the project team, yeah?" Frances asks.

"Am I?" It's a genuine question. "I thought I was doing data entry because the client couldn't be arsed?"

Frances flashes a mischievous grin. "I was told you were," she says. "Here, before I forget," she hands me a key. "This key is for this glass monstrosity," I'm glad we agree on that point. "So, you can lock it and keep all this," she whirls her hands over the boxes, "safe." I smile and nod. "How many are there of you doing this?"

"I don't know," I say, honestly. "Apparently we're getting in temps."

"Oh, Christ," Frances says with a sigh. "They'll be wanting access cards. It's nice of someone to give me a heads up!"

"Heads up," I whisper cheekily. Frances chuckles. "It's just me for now."

"Just you for now," Frances echoes apologetically. "Me and John'll get the rest."

There's still more?

I push the glass door until it clicks fully open and will stay open, and nudge the boxes along the carpet out of the way so that more boxes can be piled inside the door.

There's nothing written on the outside of the box. Nothing to indicate what is inside each box. I open the box on top and find a mess of documents. Applications with the brands of other companies, residency documents that aren't attached to any personal documents, proof of occupation, bank statements—all single sheets of papers, nothing attached to each other, no order, no block of a single type of document. Some of the documents are too old to be of any use. Even the applications filled in for other companies are incomplete and have vital information missing. Presumably because the information is on a sheet in another box somewhere else.

Within an hour, still before I actually clock in, I am swamped in disparate documents. A literal swamp. Musty cardboard boxes smell like they've been sitting under a dripping drainpipe. There are watermarks, coffee stains, torn paper and grit. The quality of the paper itself varies from standard printer paper, to that brittle stuff that forms one long length of paper with holes on perforated seams that my old primary school was chucking out when I first arrived there.

One of the boxes, I discover, is still damp. I tip out its contents and at the bottom is a wad of mulch that I carefully peel and lay on the carpet to dry. I'm going to spend the day tiptoeing and pirouetting round paper like one of the ballerina hippos in Fantasia.

Frances brings up the last box. I can't even imagine how she managed to fit all of this in her car. I am surrounded by a literal ton of paper.

"The rest will be here on Monday," she says as she places her hands on her hips to signify she's done.

"The rest?"

She hums and leaves.

I'm going to need a cup of tea before I even attempt to sort out any of this.

Clambering over the paper, careful not to put my foot in it, I beeline for the kitchen.

That is a ridiculous amount of paper. Did Jan know how much work this would entail? Did Darren-fucking-Neal warn anyone when he picked up the boxes? It kind of explains why they aren't inputting the information online. There could be all sorts hidden in that amount of paperwork. A ton, an almost literal tonne of paper.

Imperial or metric?

Oh, shut up, back of my brain.

*

Imperial, surely?

I know we have this weird mix of sensible metric and emotional imperial; the tower is forty metres tall vs. I'm 5'9", miles to the gallon vs litre capacity, I'm sure there are other examples I can't think of right now—but paper feels like it should be measured imperially[5]. It's something that has been measured for centuries, and so should be measured the old way…

Stop dawdling. **Concentrate**. Pour your cup of tea and get back to it. The whole day today is going to be spent separating and sorting out documents so that on Monday, maybe, we'll be able to start moving the information onto the system. One thing I know, I'm not going to get anything onto the system today.

My shift starts. I sign into my desk on the app otherwise they'll think I'm not here.

I take my cuppa back to the glass room and sit at the one chair free from the drying paper.

Tea first. Log in, the work.

Are there tea tasting jobs? I could do that.

I could work on the tea terraces of assam. Quality control the leaves. The perfect job. Good tea, bad tea. Make my own blends. Earl Grey's got nothing on me. Work from home, business trips to sun-soaked tea country.

Bliss.

I open the app and click to advise that I am actually working in the office today. It asks me which desk I'm at.

Ah.

The room I'm in doesn't show up on the floor plan, why would it—there aren't usually computers in here. 24 hours ago, there weren't any here. I try to book a desk at the nearest block, but with no luck. Apparently the third floor is incredibly popular, who knew? If I book my usual seat—no one else can use it.

That said, it is Friday, so although the third floor may be a hub of activity, the first floor certainly isn't.

Can I book this room out? That would certainly be the most accurate and sensible. I search through the app. Nope, never mind. I can't. I need manager or team leader access.

I resign to booking my usual seat and then drop Jan a message through the app letting her know what I've done and why and then screenshot the evidence and click the red flag to let the system know that this is an important message and not to let her ignore it.

---

[5] I'm not sure that's a word, but I stand by it.

Maybe she'll give me some temporary authority to book the room. I doubt it, but you never know. Maybe she'll be able to book the room and assign me a seat in there. Does that make sense? Would the system let her do that?

I'm going to send her some photos of the state of these boxes as well. I don't think I'll be believed when I tell her. I wouldn't believe me. What professional company would send over documents in this manner? As far as I can see, there are no documents that detail what is in each box.

Knowing my luck, I will find some index at the bottom of the last box I open, glued to the cardboard base or wedged between the folded cardboard bottom.

Pick a box.

Pick any box.

Pick any box you like.

I don't even have space to lay the contents of a single box on the table. The computer cords haven't been tied up or routed away. The only clear surface was the floor and that is now covered in mildewy paper.

I need to split the papers in the boxes into types at least. That's a start. Take a box, divide its contents into small manageable chunks and put them in boxes with labels. I only have the edge of the desk. I could bookend the keyboards, that way I'd have some space in front of the computer screens.

Tiny space. No space. I need space to put the box I'm emptying and then other space to put the boxes with the sorted-out stuff.

Plastic boxes. I'm not going to risk any more damage to these papers.

The stock room next to the mailroom will probably have plastic boxes. I take the lift down to the subterranean levels. The bowels of the building, where there is no natural light. There's a guy ringing the bell for the mailroom. I recognise him from last year's Christmas do but can't for the life of me remember his name.

"Ay!" He chimes cheerfully as I walk past. Then bursts into song, "This is the rhythm of the night!"

I chuckle. Yes, I was drunk enough to dance at the 90s disco we found round the corner when the venue kicked us out at midnight. The door to the mailroom opens and the guy dances his way into the room.

I find a stack of plastic boxes and lids at the back of the stock room. On my way out, my hand hovers before hitting the light switch. I could do with a new pen while I'm here. Some post-it notes would be useful too. The temps will probably need some pens and notepads. Cardboard I can stick in the box with lists of what's in it. I wonder if there's any of the coloured stuff left. I might as well pick it all up while I'm down here.

With my stationery packed into the top box, I make my way back to the lifts and upstairs, across the bridge by the stairs, through the office space where the desks are now filling up with people awkwardly making small talk, and back into my little glass box.

There's no way I can work in that room. Even looking at it from the outside I feel cramped. I take a box and set it down on the floor outside the room. I sit cross-legged in front of it and place the plastic boxes around me.

Ok, application material in pile one. Bank evidence—pile two. Secondary evidence—pile three, what-the-fuck-is-this?—pile four, miscellaneous—pile five.

I'll start with that and see how it goes.

The miscellaneous pile grows much faster than any of the others. But the growing what-the-fuck-is-this? pile concerns me. I don't recognise these documents, half of them aren't even in a language I can read, let alone understand. Some of it is just pages of notes scrawled across lined paper. With random names on it. Ionut, Dana, Timur. No surnames. Clients probably. I make a note of their names on a post-it and stick it in my notebook.

Some of these are original documents. I groan. We shouldn't have been given these; we should have been given copies. I'm going to have to make copies of these and return the originals. **I don't even have an address to send them to**.

Pile six—originals that need copying and returning.

"Good morning," Jan pulls up a chair beside me.

"Morning, Jan," I say without getting up from the floor.

"Just wondered why you are sitting out here when you've got a whole room?" She asks while looking directly at me.

The walls are made of glass. There are boxes on the little table space there is and the boxes are stacked four high in the corner. There is paper covering the entire floor that is crinkling up at the corners as it dries.

I realise I've not said anything and I'm staring at her slaw-jawed. I have to say something.

"I needed some more space," I tell her.

"You have the whole room to yourself," she says motioning towards the glass room. Towards the room with no space to sit and breath, let alone work. "You're creating a bit of a hazard sitting out here."

Hazard to who? There is literally[6] no one sitting anywhere near me, there is nothing on this side of the office that people would need to get to, the only fire escape I'm obstructing is my own, and no offence to the paper, but I think I can beat it.

That's the kind of thing a rock would say.

I look through the glass wall into the room. Is she not seeing this? I point through the glass walls.

"The computers are taking up all the table space, one of the boxes was damaged so I'm drying out the paper on the floor in there so there is no space for me to sort out the documents which have been delivered without any description of what's in each box and without the pages being in any order," I realise that I'm speaking slowly. I would even go so far as to say I'm speaking patronisingly. But and I can't believe that I have to say this again, the walls are **made of glass**.

"Just try and keep things contained in the future," Jan instructs. me I nod my acquiescence. "You need to log into the computer. Darren Neal in sales is trying to contact you. You need to be available."

It's not even 9 o'clock and I have my first violent thought of the day.

*

I spend the dark, stuffy bus ride home fuming as I relive the conversation with Darren-fucking-Neal.

He wanted to express how excited he was with this new business. How important it was for us to go that extra mile for this case. How important it was to keep this client happy. How much business they had pledged to us. What a great opportunity this was to work with some of the big boy companies. It may be difficult at times for us, it may be a lot for us to take on, but we can do it.

That was a lot of 'we' and 'us' and as far as I can see it will be me doing the work.

He made the foolish error of asking how long I thought it would take to process all the applications. I advised him I hadn't found any applications yet, just reels of paper that I was trying to match up.

---

[6] I do mean *literally.*

36

He sounded disappointed with my efforts.

"You're welcome to come into the office and help me find the application information," I offer.

"Find them?" He asks, incredulous. "I dropped the boxes off with Frances on Thursday! What are you even looking for?"

Deep breath.

"I've gone through eight of the seventeen boxes and I..."

"I just think that the client is going to be a bit disappointed with the speed of things," Darren-fucking-Neal's taut voice cuts me off. "I just need to manage his expectations and make sure that we are doing everything we can at the best speed for him and his clients."

There you go again with that 'we'.

I bite my tongue and repeat, "I have gone through eight of the seventeen boxes, and I have not found a single complete application. I understand," I raise my voice when I hear him drawing a breath to interrupt me again. "That they haven't sent in full applications on our forms, so I am trying to piece them together..."

"Why haven't you gone through all the boxes yet?" He snorts.

Because there are seventeen of them and I'm on the phone with you, numb-nuts. Because I'm on my own. Because there are seventeen boxes. Because I only have two hands, and they are both currently busy restraining myself from throttling you.

Don't say that.

These phone calls are recorded for monitoring and training purposes.

"One last thing, before I let you go." Before you *let* me go, hmm. "I want you to join the weekly meeting I have with the3rd party business that submitted this."

"Ok," I reply. "When is it?"

"Five o'clock this afternoon," he says.

"I finish at four," I say.

"It'll only be for like half an hour, tops," he promises, his voice softening.

"I finish at four, I will have left for the day. I won't be in the office."

"Just this once?" He pleads. "Just so I can introduce you to him. It's good for the company. It's good for business." I sigh. "He gets to meet you and you can explain why it's taking so long." *I'm not sure you want me to answer that question honestly, mate.* "I'll send you through the invite, thanks," he hangs up before I can reply.

I send an email to Jan asking her if this will be paid as overtime.

She doesn't respond. She has the whole afternoon to reply and I can see her at her virtual desk. I know she's there; I can see that she's read the message.

Four o'clock strikes and I'm determined not to work for the hour between finishing and the meeting. If I have to stay late, I am going to play on my phone, text friends and family I've not spoken to in ages and see who's about I get into a chat with a cousin who used to stay with us when we were little and promise to meet up with him for a drink soon.

On the bus home, I make a note to remind myself that his birthday is coming up and I need to send him a card.

There's a shift in the office atmosphere at ten to five. People return cups and plates to the kitchen, locking things away in drawers and slyly slipping their phones into their bags or pockets. No different to when they were at school and were expertly preparing to run at the bell.

Waiting for the meeting, there grew an angry gnaw at the pit of my stomach. It's either hunger, or some sort of weird guilt or anxiety. I've never been able to tell the difference between those two. It's annoying that those two sensations seem to emanate from the same place so it just confuses me. I would usually be home by that point with a cup of tea and a biscuit, instead I was waiting for the call to come through.

But it might not have been hunger. I hadn't, and still haven't, received a response from Jan. I don't like doing things without the right person knowing and acknowledging it.

I grabbed a biscuit from the kitchen and set myself up at the computer, lazily flicking through the documents I'd managed to dry out.

Darren-fucking-Neal's face appeared centre screen with the ring tone blaring through my headset. I turned down the volume before I answered.

Apparently, we're honoured to be on a call with the CEO of III Holdings, Ivan Ivanovich.

Sounds fake.

Though, to be fair, I had two great-grandfathers called John Jones, so you never know. It might just be one of those quirks of naming systems.

Darren began hyping me up as the best administrator in the office, the most senior administrator, someone who has won awards for their discretion and efficiency, someone with commendations and positive client feedback.

I had no idea who he's talking about, but it was not me.

None of it was technically 'lies', but it does feel a little overkill, and just embarrassing to hear someone praise you over the phone. I know he was just trying to make it seem like he secured the best in the office for the case, but it still makes me feel uncomfortable.

After the call this morning, he can do one. I do my job; I do it well. There are plenty of others in the office that would do it just as well. Some of them would even be flattered. But Darren, you can't be a dick on one call and six hours later be the nicest guy in the world just because some third-party bigwig is listening in.

"How long do you think it will take to set up the account so we can start investing?" I was expecting a thick Soviet-Russian accent, from an old Bond film, but it sounds like Ivan Ivanovich studied in London.

Darren-fucking-Neal suggested that I take that question.

"It's difficult to give an exact timeframe at this point," I tactfully replied. "We're currently going through and sorting all the documents. There is a much bigger team being assigned as we speak to input all the data. We're still assessing the scale of it, but we should be able to advise you of timescales later next week."

Now I was being overly generous with the 'we'. A one-man-band drumming my way through an avalanche of shuffled paper.

Mixed metaphor.

At some point though, it's not just a mistake or just something being overlooked. Somebody from III Holdings packaged up those documents and sent them over. They might as well have shuffled the papers inside. How is it physically possible that not a single piece of paper is next to its neighbour? The bus is turning onto the main road out of town and it shouldn't be long before I am home. I wish I'd brought gloves in today. The tips of my fingers are going white.

"How much will be done before Monday?" Ivan Ivanovich asked.

"…None?" I reply cautiously. "Because it's the weekend?"

"Mr Neal, you said that Ieso would be willing to go the extra mile. I expected this to be round the clock."

"An oversight I'm sure," his tone is defensive. "I'm sure we'll be able to get someone on it…" he trailed off, and I realised that he expected me to rescue him.

"I don't have the authority to authorise overtime," I say. Darren-fucking-Neal makes an indignant grumble, unhappy at being let down. "I'm sure Darren," fucking, "Neal and I will speak with our managers on Monday and see what we can organise."

"I can assure you," Darren-fucking-Neal said, regaining his voice. "That we will be looking into all possibilities to ensure that your account is processed as quickly and efficiently as possible…" is he repeating himself? I'm sure he's already confirmed that. Ivan Ivanovich mumbled about the lack of urgency on the case (he might not have been mumbling, to be honest I started blocking out the sound of his voice).

Darren-fucking-Neal suggested that I contact my manager to ask. I hummed non-committedly. My manager didn't reply to me when I asked her a direct question in the middle of the work day, does he really think she would reply when she's already two glasses of chardonnay into the weekend?

Jog on.

But I am on the bus now. It's already dark and my hands are numb with cold. I follow my feet home from the bus stop not caring if I stand on the cracks in the pavement and paying no attention to whatever the argument outside the chippy is about. As I reach the front door of my flat, I swab the fob across the door sensor and make my way in.

Another argument.

Two neighbours, the woman from the ground floor easy-access flat in her pyjamas and a housecoat, and the bloke from the second floor wearing a t-shirt that smells of fags and lager, are at the bottom of stairwell surround by ripped open rubbish bags. The woman accuses the man of being at fault for using weak carrier bags that leach out the smell of the waste, and the man adamantly says it's not his fault and foxes will find rubbish anywhere.

Don't get involved. It's nothing to do with you. the binmen are due tomorrow, take your bins out later when things have settled down.

As the corridor is narrow, I do have to squeeze between the two of them. I duck under their conversation, bowing my head beneath their words, before trekking up eight flights of stairs to my flat on the fourth floor.

"You're late," my flatmate Holl says as they cross through the hall on their way from their bedroom to the bathroom in a stunning, short, glitzy dress. "How do I look?" They ask, turning face on to me for a split second before scrunching up their dark curly hair.

"Fabulous," I answer honestly. They always look fabulous—however they are presenting. I never look fabulous. I blame a genetic disinterest in fashion.

No. Stop. I'm in a bad mood. It's been a shitty day. I cut my thoughts off before they grow limbs. "There any food in?" I ask while taking my shoes off. There's always a couple of tins in the cupboard, but I never know what to make.

"No, I'm eating out," Holl's voice echoes from the bathroom.

"Oh, aye?" I ask suggestively. Holl pulls a disapproving face at me through the bathroom doorway. They've done a neat, swooping line on eyeliner flicking out into a crisp wing with a fine point. Bright, neutral toned eyeshadow. An orange-tinged lip stain that complements their skin tone. I don't know how to do that.

"Which heels, do you reckon?" They ask. I see the options lined up by their bedroom door. I would break every heel if I tried to wear any of them. Holl has been excited about the date for weeks, trying on every possible outfit—dresses, suits, more casual open-shirt ensemble, depending on the day. They are the only person I know who gets so excited they devastate their room like a tornado has just whipped through it and yet it will go back to its normal, organised self before the weekend is over.

It's their first anniversary. A whole year with the same person.

"Silver ones," I say. They won't pay attention to my choice anyway. Bad thoughts. Stop. Your opinion is valid. It's going to get ignored or overruled, but that doesn't make it any less valid. "With the little buckle at the ankle."

I'm not in the mood for inner monologue therapy, crack open a beer, get the delivery app open. I should have picked up a packet of chips on the way home.

"Jacket, no jacket?" Holl asks as I have my coat on a hook.

"It's going to rain tonight," I say.

"Good point," Holl smiles, putting on a skinny blazer with white piping around the lapels.

"That's not going to keep the water out," I throw my bag through my bedroom door onto the bed.

Holl smiles and shrugs, "but it looks good." Their face narrows, concerned, "How was your day?"

"Awful," I say quietly. "I'm just happy it's the weekend."

"Proper catch-up tomorrow? You can tell me all about it and I promise you my undivided attention."

"Yeah, of course. You have yourself a great night," they kiss me on the cheek as they leave.

The flat falls silent. It's always silent when I'm alone. If I want to listen to music, or watch tv or a film, I plug in my earphones so that I don't disturb the silence.

I stand in the hallway for a moment listening to the faint tap of Holl's shoes echo up the stairwell, until that too falls silent.

Lina and Ximena

Couriers

US-Mexico Border

Lina leant against the mesh metal fence that ran alongside the line of people waiting for the border guards to start waving them through. It was early. The sun only came up an hour ago, but even at night the temperatures hadn't fallen more than a few degrees from the blistering heat of the daytime and so, for the third week straight of that most recent heatwave, Lina soaked up her sweat with a rag and tried to stay under the corrugated tin roof, trying to keep herself out of direct sunlight

She was tired. The ground that day was too hot to sit on, especially for bare skin. She wore a pair of shorts that she loved. She thought of them as her lucky shorts, though there was no real reason to think they were. She had once tried to run away from the boys in her village while wearing them, though they caught her. She had been wearing them when her uncles and aunts came round to shout at her. To knock some sense into her.

They weren't going to be able to do that again.

Lina couldn't bring a coat or jacket, not in this heat, not even with the promise that the states had air-conditioning in every room. Lina's handbag, for the sake of optics, had only her passport, purse and phone. She hadn't crossed the border since she began growing her hair long and worried about what the border guards would say. She had been tempted to cut it short and wear her old clothes for the sake of matching more closely to her passport and preventing any kind of holdup at the border. But she decided against it. The guards had seen her before and she would enter as herself.

Ximena joined Lina in the queue. She wore a thin, wafting skirt and t-shirt with short sleeves rolled up into caps at her shoulders. Her thick, curly hair tied at her neck and covered with a wide-brim, sandy-coloured fedora that kept the sun off her face and neck. Ximena's bag was bigger than Lina's. Not only did she carry her passport, purse and phone, but also a couple of bottles of water, their lunch, a charger, and one of her father's old sweatshirts that, should they need to, they could both squeeze in to keep warm.

"Did you get the chance to say goodbye to your little sister?" Lina asked.

"No, she wasn't awake. I didn't want to wake her," Ximena turned away and looked out into the yard. She feels the insides of her cheeks prickle and her brow fall. "I'll send her a message later. If her sister was a couple of years older, or if Ximena herself had been a year or two older, or if her sister had a passport, if they weren't making a delivery. There were too many reasons not to bring her, too many reasons that trying to bring her would be difficult, or delay things, or make what they were doing more dangerous. Ximena hoped that one day, her sister would join her."

It was still getting warmer. The tin roof groaned and cracked above them.

"Did you say goodbye to anyone?"

"Who would I say goodbye to?" Lina snapped. The old woman in front of her in the queue is woken from her short doze at the loud noise. Lina smiled apologetically, before returning her attention to Ximena and saying quietly, "the boys at school?"

Ximena laughs, "Maybe not." She pulls the brim of her hat so the shade covers more of her back. "I heard Temo got a job down in Hermosillo."

"Good for him," Lina said sourly. "Have a good life." Ximena raised her eyebrows without looking at Lina. "He had really nice hair," Lina sighed, remembering the time he let her tussle it. It was longer than most boys in the village. He had a sweet nature, kind and gentle. No matter what the other boys said, Temo would be kind.

"As did his brothers," Ximena said.

Lina scrunched her nose at a sore memory of the time Temo's older brother, Gabriel, had broken her nose because she had been talking with Temo. Temo had also received a black eye. "I don't want to think about his brothers." They had said cruel things about Lina to Temo, but he had brushed it off. It didn't surprise her that he had already left for the city, if only to escape his brothers.

Lina ran the rag over her shoulders and the sweat ran down her arms. She exclaimed impatiently at the heat. Her hair was going to look awful by the time they got to the other side. "Are you going to miss Maricarmen?"

Ximena scoffed, turning away so that Lina couldn't see her lie. "There is nothing to miss."

"You know I have better legs than her," Lina said, turning her legs to emphasise how lean and slender they were.

"But you also have a flat arse," Ximena quipped with a grin.

"No me bufes!" Lina exclaimed, hand on heart, half feigning injury though also keenly aware that she did in fact have a very flat arse. "Bolleras are always so jealous!"

Ximena blew her a mock kiss.

The old woman in front of them shifted uneasily. She took a few steps away from the girls. Lina clocked her, but said nothing, leaving the small space between them, assuming that it was because they were being loud, and not because of who they are. Soon she would march in a parade and these buga-women wouldn't be able to make her feel small. The men that beat her in the day and catcall her at night wouldn't be able to find her, wouldn't be able to offer her money for service. Lina would stand proud and no one would ever knock her down again.

Lina was good with children. Everyone said so, even if they only left their children with her as a last resort. She would get a job in a school, or kindergarten, or teach children to read at the library. She and Ximena would find a tiny, one-bedroom apartment to begin with. They would decorate it with flags and pins and little trailing lights. Lina had already declared herself the designer-decorator. Ximena didn't care as long as the water was hot and the door had a lock.

The line moved forward. The border gates opened and the guards called the first person through… Lina held all her fear in her weighted stomach. She tried not to look worried or anxious, but she felt as though she might bring up her unusual breakfast.

They had to get through the checkpoint, make the delivery and then they had a few hours to get on their bus and go as far as they could.

Ximena had planned their movements for the day. Lina trusted that Ximena would get them far away before nightfall. Lina ran the plan over and over again in her head. She leant into Ximena and lowered her voice to a whisper, "The bus will be there?"

Ximena smiled and nodded. "It says so on the internet." Lina rested her forehead against Ximena's shoulder. She was tired. She hadn't slept in days. Worry and fear kept her from sleeping, but it was excitement that kept her head spinning in the middle of the night.

Women started coming out the far side of the border gate having passed their checks. The two girls watched them walk down the long road to the edge of town where buses and vans were lined up to take them to work in the factories and homes.

It was too hot to keep her head on Ximena's skin.

The line moved forwards. The two girls stepped forward. They had both done this crossing before and it had always been fine. The guards had seen them both several times. The guards didn't know that this would be the last time they would see Lina and Ximena.

While both had done this crossing before, and both had done the crossing carrying goods, they each worried that their plan might show on their face and with a little further inspection they might get caught. Caught on their last delivery. Caught when they had plans to leave. To run.

The line moved forward. The two of them were next. Wracked with nerves, Lina looked up to the sky and offered a short, determined prayer.

The line moved forward. Lina and Ximena were guided into separate rooms.

Chapter 3
Work-Life Balance

I lie down on the sofa, not bothering to turn on any lamps, letting the dark consume me. I close my eyes for a moment and when I reopen them it's gone 2am and I drag myself to bed. An hour or two later I hear Holl and Syd stumble in. Holl's unsubtle shushing as they fumble with the key in the lock, giggling as the two of them crash into Holl's bedroom. I roll over and fall back into a restless sleep. It's not long before I am woken by the sun.

Holl is already up, the smell of freshly ground coffee beans coming from the kitchen. I'm going to need some of that frothy goodness.

"Morning," they say, their cheerfulness piercing through my morning fog.

"Morning," I reply, rubbing crispy sleep from my eye and yawning as I open the fridge and try to construct a breakfast, but seeing nothing that interests me, I close the door and lean on it.

"How are you feeling today?" Holl asks, placing a cup onto the plastic grate at the foot of the machine. "Coffee?"

"Hmm," I accept their offer of coffee. "Shattered."

"I'm sorry, did I wake you?"

I shake my head as they hand me a warm mug. The slow roast aroma filling my nose. Silky. Smooth. For a moment I stand and inhale the caffeine, slowly rousing me from sleep. "Syd still here?" I ask.

Holl shakes their head. "Early shift." They place some bread in the toaster. "Breakfast?" I shake my head, I'm not in the mood.

"You sure?"

"I'm going to sit down," I take a sip from my mug, testing the heat before taking a longer drink. In the lounge, I ball up in my favourite corner of the couch, the large mug warming my hands, feet tucked under me. I pull a blanket across my lap and lean over the side of the sofa tilting my head round so that when I look out the window, I can see the sky instead of the block of flats opposite. The same drab cladding as our own block, apart from the occasional siren, it is pretty quiet, though Saturday mornings usually are.

Holl brushes some dust off the clear coffee table and places out a couple of coasters. "I'm here," they say. "What happened?"

"Just the usual," I say, tired of only ever talking and thinking about work. "It's just work."

"I thought you were supposed to be working from home yesterday?"

"I'm sorry," I say. Holl went into their office yesterday so I could have the workspace. There is technically space for the two of us to work from home, but it feels cramped. We did both work from home during lockdown and it got to the point we were looking for separate places. I ended up working in my room, which didn't help the situation. I spent almost every working hour sitting on my bed. The office furniture is actually a kitchen table we have in the lounge, one that barely sits the two of us to eat.

With two laptops and all the little extras around us, with both of us being on the phone, it was cramped and uncomfortable. "I was told on Thursday that I had to come in for a new account. I was going to tell you on Thursday, but then I didn't see you. I should have sent you a message."

I hate forgetting things like that. Forgetting things that have a tangible effect on someone else's life. Holl could have worked from home. They would have had more time to get ready for their big night out and not been in a rush when I got home last night.

"I am really sorry," I say.

For Holl it's already forgotten. "It's ok," they say. "How come you were home so late?"

"There's this new account. And then there was a meeting arranged at 5 with the CEO of the company that was opening it."

"I thought you were on an early yesterday?"

"I was," I can hear my own voice. I don't even sound annoyed about it, just tired. Maybe a bit bitter.

Holl scoffs and shakes their head.

"You better be getting overtime for that."

I shrug.

The union worker comes out of Holl. "That's not on," they are affronted for me, then instruct me, "make sure you claim those hours."

"They weren't authorised," I say.

"Did you have a choice to go to that meeting?"

Did I? How am I supposed to know? I was told to be available for Darren-fucking-Neal, but did that include after my shift had ended. I can see my manager arguing that the meeting should have been arranged for during my shift. However, this was a regular meeting between the client company and sales with a regular meeting time. It was a meeting for a VIP client. Would a meeting really be rearranged for someone at my level?—No. No, it wouldn't. I wasn't even needed for most of the meeting and honestly probably pissed off both sales and Ivan Ivanovich. Did it make the company look good? I guess so.

In the end, it is going to take more energy and effort to fight for some recognition when I could use what little energy I have elsewhere.

Holl doesn't interrupt my thoughts, they sit studying me over the rim of their mug.

"What is the new account?"

I take a deep breath in before I start answering, careful not to reveal any details that could breach data security and privacy regulations. "Er, a new company that wants to open an investment portfolio for their clients. It's a new company so there are checks to be done on them, which I have nothing to do with that's for Legal and Business Onboarding to deal with."

I take a sip from my mug, then place it on the coaster that Holl put out for me, then allow myself to sink. "It doesn't usually take too long. The company sends us the details of the clients they want to set up and I just put their details into the system so we have everything on file, but I swear this company is making it impossible to do anything quickly. Their documents are all over the place. and then on this meeting-call their CEO goes mental about how disappointing I am."

Holl raises an eyebrow.

"Ok," I backtrack. "How he expected me to be further along, and how I should be working on this all weekend. He literally wanted to know how much of it would be done before Monday and was annoyed when I told him none."

"But the applications are messed up?"

"No," I say. "They haven't filled out any applications. They've just sent over all their client's documents and I have to work it out."

"Is there anyone you can talk to about it?"

"The only person working on it is the sales guy and he's as bad as this CEO."

"Does the CEO of a company usually get involved like this?"

I shake my head and have a search through my brain. "Not that I've ever had," I reply. "At least, not unless they were a one-man band."

Holl's phone buzzes. Their face lights up when the message appears on screen, but they turn their phone over and look back up at me. "What's the plan for today?" They ask.

Life, I guess. I need to do at least two loads of washing, go food shopping, hoover, clean, dust—at least try to pull my weight in the flat. I need a to-do list. I should just use last week's list; write in on a whiteboard so I can erase the ticks ready to start again.

"Is the showerhead still broken?"

"Ah," says Holl, reminded. "Yeah, still broken."

"I'll pick up a new one at the shops," I mentally add it to my shopping list. Then pick up my phone and add it to my actual shopping list because there is no way I will actually remember the mental one.

"Let me know how much it is," they say. I nod—must remember to keep the receipt.

"How was your date?" I ask. Holl's face lights up and a smile radiates from them.

"He was so sweet and I had such a good time," Holl says, tilting their head. "We had a meal and then went dancing. Not at a club, like proper ballroom dancing. So romantic!" They swoon. Syd has stepped up to the mark after the two of them spoke about their relationship getting a little stale already. "Did that guy ever get back to you about a date?"

My heart sinks, I shake my head.

"Oh, no!" They say. "How come?"

"I dunno," I say. "Last weekend we were chatting and then just radio silence after I asked if he wanted to meet up. No, I just stopped reading my messages."

After he left me on unread for three messages, I didn't want to embarrass myself any further so I wrote nothing further.

Up until that point, it had been going so well. At least, I thought it had. We had likes and interests in common, similar political outlook, more or less the same activity level. We even liked the same bars and restaurants.

I'd love to just go out to one of those bars and meet someone. Just chat someone up, but I've no idea how people do it. Or even at a party. It probably says more about me to be honest; sending out the wrong vibes. At least on a dating app I know that the other person is interested and I don't humiliate myself asking if they are single.

Holl's phone buzzes again, and I can see the physical restraint as they force themselves not to look at it.

"Do you want to answer it…?"

Holl shakes their head. Her smile strains and again I can feel the resistance, the utmost control they have over their actions.

"Do you want to go out today?" They ask.

Fresh air, a bit of green—sounds really nice, but as I check in with the rest of my body, it slumps further down into the sofa. It doesn't look like I'm leaving this spot today. "I think I'd like to just veg out today."

"Watch telly?"

"Sounds good," I say.

"Maybe go to the café on the high street a little later?"

I smile. Without Holl I think I'd spend every waking moment with my eyes half-closed in bed. "Sure," I say.

"Mind if I join you to watch TV?" They ask, handing me the remote. I shake my head; I'd be happy for the company. "Can I see those dating apps?"

I scoff, but unlock my phone and hand it over. "Be my guest." They snuggle down with their coffee on their side of the sofa about to start swiping when they hand my phone back.

A dick pic. How novel.

Has anyone ever done a study into what makes people send phallic images to someone they've never met? And may never meet! The study would be called something like *exploring the psychology of 'dick pics'* or *how phallic imagery pervades in modern courtship*. Then some academic somewhere (though probably in the US) would argue that this is a part of the male psyche and it is the militant feminists blah blah blah.

Mores to the point; do dick pics get dates?

Surely the more sent, the less likely someone is to say—oh, yeah—he seems nice—wanna date?

Much like my attitude to ridiculous curveball questions in interviews, I would love to know: is this purely since the digital age? Or have people always been looking for ways of delivering cock pictures to unsuspecting acquaintances? Etches done hurriedly by candlelight, or whittled into wood, or weaved into a tapestry. Cave paintings hastily covered over with hands in case

51

their mother wondered in while you were waiting for someone to join them. Wicker figures lost to the bogs of time, dry grass bent and shaped. Awkward stone rubbings made with an erection and charcoal. Was the Cerne Abbas Giant made by someone saying—hey, want some of this?

(Actually, I think I've seen some mediaeval paintings and bible artwork with naked people sticking flowers in their bums… so, probably?)

I screenshot the dick pic that I've been sent and go into edit. A pair of googly eyes. A hat of some description. The pubes are setting off major ragged pirate vibes—I place a parrot on its ball-shoulder, an eye patch, a boat in the distance. In mere moments, I have Captain Penis and his parrot companion ready to message back to the owner, or at least the operator, of the prick.

Knowing my luck, he'll be flattered.

Holl laughs approvingly and jumps up off the couch to go to the kitchen to boil the kettle.

I delete the pictures from my phone.

I should keep them. I should keep all of them. Format them into a novelty Christmas gift. I could have tableaux of festive scenes. Wise men and wonky cattle around a manager with a winged angel Gabriel. Outside of Christendom—Daddy Christmas[7] and his reindeer all trussed up in BDSM gear—still all style on penile photography. Hanging up their stockings. Christmas trees covered in baubles. Bright, white, micropenis snowmen with their own little snow-penises (Peni? Penese?). Christmas movies with the dick in place of the main character (well that's going to ruin some childhood memories). A feather boa wrapped around a flaccid member lolling to one side. Ballsack dreidel.

I'm going to hell. I have thought 'penis' far too much in the past minute to be allowed any peace in the afterlife. I'm going to hell and I'll be surrounded by jubilant cock.

That's not actually that much different from the present.

I exhale a long and full breath.

Back to swiping. Left. Right. Left. Left. Left. Right. Match. Banter. Weaksauce banter. Swipe, swipe, swipe.

I back out of the app. It drains the life out of me. sucking out any desire I might once have had.

Holl is still in the kitchen. Their phone is not on the coffee table.

---

[7] Sorry, not sorry.

I open twitter and brace for the emotional whiplash. Trawling through the newsfeeds of articles I have to care about, at least for this week. Dead celebrity, war, cat. Bombing, terror, cat, meme mocking foreign president, riot, protest, feline palette cleanser. Another injustice. Another reason to be angry and hateful. I am too small, too insignificant and too far away to do anything. I'm sorry. I send a like. A small thumbs up that says *I am with you, even if not in person.*

The MPs are debating again about a protest limit bill, one that puts restrictions on being able to protest the police. Syd was talking about it the last time I saw him

I try to follow a thread about it, but the constant back and forth between content and comment wears me down. An advert for mental health pops up and advises I shut down my app and step away from the digital world. Like the digital world is somehow imaginary.

I sit on the sofa in silence. Staring at the blank TV screen on the wall opposite, waiting for tea but not wanting to interrupt Holl after they were kind enough to sit and talk about my work—a subject I know they find thoroughly boring.

I'm bored.

I re-open the app.

Chapter 4
Performative Morality

Saturday disappears in a marathon binge of the latest fad series. Sunday disappears in chores. The weekend is gone and Monday rolls around as fast as ever. Even though the workday seems to extend and grow ever longer, as soon as I arrive back home time speeds up and the evenings disappear in a snap.

I work my way through the card boxes and rehouse the paper in the plastic ones. I manage to start dividing the piles into sub piles, with even smaller piles that I wrap a folded piece of A4 paper around them and note their sub-pile name on them.

The temps that were promised haven't arrived. Darren-fucking-Neal calls twice daily for updates, even though he is fully appraised of the situation. I can't even ignore his calls because someone has told him that I have an entire room to myself and therefore will always be available for him.

As the week goes on, the sun begins to shine ever more brightly—which is nice. The stuffy heat grows but the forecast promises a break; that there will be storms going into next week.

While the walks from the bus stop into the office are more than pleasant enough, I am trapped, back at a desk in the brutal, glass box, sweating as though my life depended on it, and reminded why the architect had to come back in after finishing this building to address the convex-concave issue that threatened to cook the people inside the office.

Clearly not enough people have spent enough time in this particular box to realise that the issue is not completely resolved. My skin is damp. It's not like the sweat is running off me; it's like my pores are waterlogged and my skin is a swamp. My clothes have soaked up as much of the excess as they could in the first half-hour of my working day.

I am disgusting. There's only a couple of seats not yet sat in on this floor, but they are all showing up as reserved on the booking app. If no one is sitting there by 11, I am packing up and moving with a boxful of papers that I've managed to fit together into some form of application. Manager be damned if she wanders up to this floor. I'll lock her in the airless glass tank and she can say that it's an appropriate workspace.

I go to the loo and spray myself with the complimentary deodorant that is kept in the little basket by the sink. As I leave the toilet, I am followed by a plume of smelly mist that now hangs around me, thick and hazy. For a split second I worry I might set off the fire alarm, but fortunately, I don't.

Taking a box from the heated death chamber, I sit myself at the end of a row of desks. The app says the chair should have been occupied since 9 this morning.

There were a group of portly, middle-aged IT guys sitting here earlier that went off for a meeting. I think it was a meeting, but I did see one of them retrieve a lighter from the gap between the underside of the desk and the top of the free-moving cabinet stored beneath it. They might just all be out on a smoking break. I keep the storage place in mind in case I ever take up smoking. They aren't the forward face of the IT department—they don't take calls and fix your computer over the phone. They usually sit in a quiet murmur writing or fixing programs.

Being that there are six of them and they never speak to anyone else, you would think that the computer programs work perfectly. They don't.

Barely a moment after I have sat down and sent an email to Jan, she slithers over and pops up at my desk like a terrifying Muppet crouched beside me, hovering so that no one else on the floor can see her.

I think she's embarrassed to be seen up here. The third floor is usually reserved for support teams and contractors, rather than those that the company has graciously employed.

"As long as the desk is free, it doesn't matter," she says in response to my email. I turn to face her. I don't tell her the desk isn't free on the app, there's a can of worms down that road. "The temps are coming in tomorrow morning," she tells me. "They all know our systems—they came in when we were handling complaints on the ReFloat account a few months ago. I don't know if you remember any of them."

I nod and hum. I remember the complaints. I don't really remember anything else. I got reprimanded for typing out the complaints verbatim, swearwords and all. It was the one time I pushed back against a reprimand, using the defence that the complaints I was logging were a true representation of the calls and the anger and vitriol our end-customers had for the massive fuckup we weren't owning. To remove the offensive language would be disingenuous and would sanitise one of the biggest 'incidents' the company has come up against.

It's the first and only time I won.

Mark it on my gravestone *defended the use of the word 'cunts' on a complaints form.*

My mother is so proud.

"Now, before I go, is there anything else, while I'm here," she asks, letting it slip that she knows I've sent her other emails, but she hasn't bothered to read them.

"Yeah, there was a meeting on Friday with sales and the account owner. I had to go after my shift had ended."

"You shouldn't have gone without confirming it with me. You need to send an email."

"I did," I say, opening my sent mail in the outbox to show her. "Friday morning."

"And you didn't wait for a response?"

"I waited five hours for a response," I say quietly.

"You need to flag these kinds of emails," Jan replies curtly, her tone acidic. She's not happy that I answered back.

"I clicked the little flag to show that it was urgent in your inbox," I push as cautiously and gently as I can. She's warned people against using those inbox extras before.

Jan releases a slow, disappointed sigh, that I'm not entirely sure it directed towards me. "I'll see what I can do," she says. "No more meetings unless prior approval."

I nod. I may be filled with wishful thinking, but I'm fairly sure I won't be invited back to any more meetings.

"Submit an overtime pay request and I'll try and authorise it." She's not going to like that it went on for over two hours. But I've got receipts. I've got a message from the end of the call that shows its length, I'll attach that to the request.

"Remember to pick up your new card today. It'll be waiting at reception."

Joy of joys. The corporate ankle monitors have arrived.

After lunch, I am joined at the bank of desks by several middle-aged men in shirts pulled taut across their bellies who aren't wearing ties. They barely acknowledge me beyond a grunt of recognition that there is someone new in their space. An intruder.

I begin to mash the keyboard, and realise just how much information is missing for each investor. Most have names and dates of birth, but beyond that there is a hodgepodge of missing information. Half the addresses are empty. Occupations, incomes and wealth are completely empty. I can't even save half the applications I manage to type up because there is so much information needed.

I fill in the blanks with obviously inaccurate details (01.01.1900, email@email, 1 address, etc.) and make a note in my notebook of what is missing for each person.

Taking a break from the screen, my eyes list over to the screen of the guy next to me and I am transported into the matrix. He's typing lists of commands into a DOS-like screen. I slowly become aware of their conversation as I resurface in the land of the living.

"We're British," one says, in a brisk baritone. His red face pulled to the nose like a pitbull. "We live in Britain. We should take care of the people here first."

I immediately regret sitting here. I try to zone back out and bury my head in the paper, but it's too late.

"I pay my taxes, I have been paying my taxes since I was fifteen," he says.

"Exactly, it's our tax money," another chimes in. the corners of his mouth pulled down into a permanent sour expression "they can't come over here…"

"I don't want my money going somewhere else," the pitbull butts back in. "My tax money should only go to things in this country. For things that *real* British people need."

"Exactly," sour puss agrees. "They can't come over here and expect to get everything handed to them on a silver plate."

"And they do expect that," pitbull approves of his co-worker's assessment.

Bite. That. Tongue.

Bite it!

Did I bring my earphones today? Are they in my handbag so I can drown these fellas out with some angry heavy metal?

"It's not just the good ones coming over here," sour puss informs the table, as though no one else has ever tried this line of so-called reasoning. "All sorts come over here."

"There are so many people here already, and we don't know who they're loyal to!" The pitbull turns and looks at me, "you know what I mean."

You know what I mean. It isn't a question. He expects me to agree. He has taken one look at me and decided that because I look like him, I must therefore be on his side. Think like he thinks. He sees me as one of his people.

"I don't," I say, without engaging. No eye contact.

"You think you can trust those types!"

You think I can trust you! It's people that look like you that make comments in the street about the way I look. It's people that look like you that walk closely behind me late at night because you're *one of the good ones*. It's when people like you get in the lift at my block of flats that I will get off at the wrong floor so you don't know where I live. It's people like you who still believe that they are *not all men*.

You think I trust you?

I stare into my computer with what I hope appears to be a judging glare. He doesn't care for my opinion; he just wants me to back him up and agree with him. I won't do that.

I've had this argument before. It doesn't matter what I say. It doesn't matter what facts I give, what opinions I have cultivated over a lifetime. His lifetime is longer, so he knows more. He has thought about this longer, so he knows more. He reads the tabloids, so he knows more—he's informed. He doesn't want to know my opinions or thoughts. He doesn't even care about the thoughts of the sour puss that agrees with him, he just wants it to be known that he is right.

I won't do that.

I know that what I say will be thrown back at me as 'wokeness' and 'not seeing the whole picture'. I know he will cherry pick incidents, and when I cherry pick a dozen examples of my own, he'll say that it was a one-off that happened a couple of times. He doesn't care about the big picture, or the small, intimate one. He only wants me to speak to validate his own world view.

I stay firm at my computer turning a little away from him so I am no longer available for comment, and drop a message through to Darren-fucking-Neal about the lack of information in the documents I've received, and can he go to

Ivan Ivanovich, or whoever he needs to go to, to get this information for me to be able to do my actual job.

Not my *actual* job.

Just the job I'm doing right now.

You know what I mean.

I'M ON IT

Bounces back on the messenger in a sudden ball of energy. But that's it; that's his entire message.

It doesn't fill me with confidence.

Pitbull turns to sour puss and throws a few offhand comments about 'the youth'—I'm in my thirties, pal. I don't think there is any stretch of the imagination where I can be considered 'the youth'. He launches into a prepared statement, influenced by all his favourite bigots, about how all the months have a focus on a particular group of people, none of which are him[8] and after a slew of offensive terms he glibly demands, "I mean, who's next!"

In a low and menacing voice that resonates inside the screens in front of us, I reply, "the gays." The tone of my voice is shocking enough to throw him off his conversation-balance and he silently stutters for a second.

I'm not wrong. It's Pride next week. We'll be marching through the city and I am going to roller skate backwards past this fucker shoving fingers up at him as the parade goes past his dingey, gammon pub.

I'm going to have to learn to roller skate.

"I've nothing against the gays," he splutters as he finds his voice. "Did you see that email that head office sent round. *We have Pride in our staff.* They are just kowtowing to political correctness." He forgets to remind me that political correctness has 'gone mad.' Sour puss nods in agreement. "They are sponsoring Pride and want people to tell them what they feel pride in. Did you see some of the responses?"

"I don't read that nonsense," sour puss says.

"Don't bother," pitbull advises. "Nothing of interest to people like you and me." I can feel him looking at me. "Now it's got nothing to do with me what people do in their own bedrooms. Man's home is his castle—do what you want, I say. But when they have tr******s teaching little kiddies in libraries, that's just

---

[8] Poor baby

59

flat out wrong. Why do they want to do that, eh? It's because they're grooming them. It's because they're all perverts!"

I get up, swing my bag over my shoulders, and walk away. My fists in tightening balls at the end of my arms. my face flushing red as I walk through the office, unblinking and full of rage.

Fuck him. Fuck his tiny little mind. Fuck him as he throws the word *snowflake* at my back like it's supposed to wound me. I grit and grind my teeth, sucking in my lips and stomp my way down the staircase down to the atrium, hitting every step with a thud that I can hear echo round the grand room and reverb through the next step as I stomp on that one too. At the bottom of the staircase, I stand to the side for a moment in the shadow cast under the steps.

What a horrid, little man trying to force me to live in his horrid, little world. I close my eyes and try to push out the conversation of the past few minutes.

A bumbling crowd of people are gathered in the atrium, forming a long line that leads out from the reception island in the middle. The queue meanders round the open space and dissipates just before it reaches the door to the ground floor's work space. It is in constant flux as people coming back into the office from their lunch are given gaps to pass through on their way to the lift or the stairs, the gaps then fuse back together again to prevent anyone trying to skip in.

Frances is going through the boxes, pulling out new cards and lanyards and striking off the person's name from a long list secured to a clipboard. Some people working this thankless task might look flustered, but Frances has a calmness and matter-of-factness about the procedure.

It will get done.

People will get their new cards and lanyards.

It will take as long as it takes.

There is a low, complaining mutter from somewhere in the queue. I can't hear the exact words, but I can tell from the tone that someone was expecting this to be sorted by now.

Frances throws the guy a withering look, like when your mother would glare at you across a busy gathering when you are being a little bit close to rude or loud or impertinent. Are there better ways to arrange this? Sure. Would it be better for several people to be giving out the new ID cards? Yes, of course it would. Is that Frances' fault? No. So wait your bloody turn.

I wait for the anger to subside a little, even though sparks of the conversation keep setting me off again and I am ready to tip over the edge, go back up and tea them a new one. But I suppress that urge. It won't do any good. Three more deep breaths, and I will join the queue. A legitimate reason to be away from my desk. I will be able to stand in their queue and take my time to recompose myself before going back up to that bank of desks.

I join at the back of the queue, behind a group of lads from the mailroom chatting nonsense about the latest celebrity dance competition that they are only watching because their girlfriends or mothers have it on in the evening.

"Hey!" A voice behind greets me cheerfully with a tap on my shoulder. A shudder runs from the spot she taps across my shoulders. I turn to see Megan, wrapped up in a thick, woollen cardigan.

"Hi!" I say, relieved. "Fancy seeing you here."

"I saw you through the glass as you went past the door," she says, standing beside me in the queue as we take a step forward. "How's it going?"

"Nightmare," I say, without going into any more detail. "How are you cold?"

"Air-conditioning on the first floor is stuck on 'arctic blast'," she replies. "It's fecking freezing in there."

"At least you can put on a jumper," I tell her. "I'm being cooked in that glass box."

Megan smiles sympathetically before asking, "did you see the email from Lord Soanso?"

"No," I reply, sounding miffed. "What does he want?"

"He's invited some of us to a charity event at the Modern Art Gallery," she says. I'm about to ask 'why us?' but Megan sees the confused expression on my face and replies before I have the chance to ask. "The email was also sent to Hannah, Lexi in auditing, Rachel and Cathy in sales, and a few others. We've been picked at random to represent the company at the event."

"Who picked us at random?" I wonder aloud sardonically.

"Who do you think?" Megan counters.

My top lip curls up in disgust. I can feel the air-conditioning hit my top teeth. "Do we have to go?"

"Apart from it being Soanso, it is a good charity. And it could be fun," she smiles. "Put on nice dresses, eat fancy food. Smuggle Ben in."

I chuckle, "Was he not invited?"

"Funnily enough, those selected at random were all women," Megan says in a comically accusatory way. "But Lexi will be on her honeymoon in the Maldives, so we're going to sneak Ben in on a typo."

My smile grows broader. "Or we could put him in a dress?"

"I'll run it by him," Megan grins wickedly. "He might be up for it."

We step forward in the queue. "How's things in the team?"

Megan's eyes widen and her lips flatten in contempt. "Your queue is piling up."

"What do you mean by *my* queue?"

"Well," Megan starts, speaking so quietly that we're in conspiratorial mode, heads tucked in close together. "No one so far has thought about divvying out your normal work."

"Of course, they haven't," I reply in the same hushed tone. "Why would they?"

"I sent Jan a message about it on Tuesday, but she hasn't got back to me yet."

Fuck's sake.

"I brought it up in the team meeting this morning," Megan continues. My eyebrows shoot up waiting for her to finish. "But I was shot down for bringing it up unnecessarily and causing the meeting to go over."

Brilliant.

Just brilliant.

We step forward and are within arm's reach of the reception island.

"When do you reckon Jan'll work it out?" I ask.

"What makes you think Jan cares or knows how to check your queue?"

Touché.

We reach the front of the line.

"Hello, girls," Frances says warmly. "Surnames?" We give her our surnames.

"And I need to pick up Hannah Campbell's," Megan adds.

"Ok," says Frances distractedly, flipping through the cards at high speed.

"Where's Hannah at?" I ask Megan as we wait.

"She's got that meeting with Yetunde from the office in Leeds. They go out and have coffee and talk about stuff."

I didn't realise Hannah still did those meetings with her mentor, not after deciding that she was going to leave. "Does Yetunde know...?" I trail off realising that not everyone in the office knows about Hannah's plan's yet and I have no right to invoke speculation or gossip.

Megan lowers her voice and turns as she speaks. "I think she's letting her know today." I make small, imperceptible nods.

"Here, we are," says Frances, handing over the three new passes with their high-tech leash. The same terrible photo that they use for all my pictures in this place. the one where I'm staring off into the mid-distance like some crazed lunatic fresh out of Arkham, frizzy hair sticking out one side and a wattle like a bloated toad about to drop a croak.

I hope this isn't what people see when I'm moving.

They do. They see this picture in motion.

Megan has gone back to the counter. "There's been a mistake," I hear her say to Frances. "This isn't Hannah."

I turn back and go to stand beside her while this is sorted—it gives me a few more minutes before I have to head upstairs.

"It has her name on it," says Frances, taking a look at the card that Megan has handed back to her.

"Yes, but the picture is of Patience Ibeh in finance," Megan tells her.

"Oh, I thought she'd just done her hair differently," says Frances.

I should point out that Hannah, 19 years old, with Jamaican and Polish ancestry, looks nothing like Patience, a middle-aged Nigerian woman with three grown-up children.

"I'll message the card-manufacturers," says Frances. "Can she not use it until we get the right one back?"

I hesitate for a moment, not wanting to cause a fuss, but knowing that a fuss should be caused and Hannah shouldn't have to be the one to cause it.

I'm guessing they managed to get the identical twins in the mailroom the right way round, so two women on different floors, different ages, different ethnicities… I mean you'd think, but no.

"No," I say, as lightly as I can, knowing that Frances probably didn't mess up the cards. That said, they are ID and we can be confronted with them on the way in, so it would be weird if they didn't match up if Hannah or Patience were challenged on them… "No, she can't." I say nothing further and Megan and I begin to walk away from the desk.

"I'll let Jan know," Megan says. "She should deal with it."

I arch my eyebrows. "Good luck with that," I say. Pointing to the stairs I continue, "I better head back up."

I take the earphones from my bag as I start towards the staircase, then, thinking better of it, change direction and head to the lifts. I'm not even sure what I want to listen to and so go into my most played and start there.

"Oh, she's back," I hear one of the men at the bank of IT desks say contemptuously as I retake my seat.

Fuck him. fuck his tiny, little world.

I see a new email pop up on my screen from Darren.

Spoke with Ivan: all the information has been provided in the boxes that were sent over.

*

We begin to gather at the west gate of the park, near the punk brewery built inside an old mill. The doors are already open and there is a lax attitude to those carrying their pints across the road and sitting with them in the park to enjoy the sun and festival atmosphere. I sip my own drink, enjoying the naughtiness of a cheeky pint at 10am in the park, and looking out over the groups of people attending, sitting in their small groupings, but knowing we are all there for the same reason.

Over to the right, basking under an old oak tree, a gender-bending outfit that glitters and sparkles when the sun hits it, shines shards of light all over the park. The sun hides behind a cloud, and briefly peaks out at the costumes.

No rain yet, no rain forecast, but of course, the sky openly threatens us with the possibility of a downpour.

Over to the left of our group are a group of excitable pups, ready for their first pride, running round each other, getting tangled in a mess before falling, giggling onto the ground. Painting rainbows on each others' cheeks and already dancing.

While I don't have the urge to wear sequins, I do harbour an ounce of jealousy towards those who willingly, and proudly, include them in their wardrobes. I always feel like a small child performing on the stage when I have them on. I love the home-made outfits—people with the talent to create what was previously only in their head. Long, flowing, gossamer capes, dyed all shades of the rainbow, finely stitched together. Hand stamped t-shirts and slogans and quotes honouring those who came before us, insulting those that stand against us, and expressing all the love and loyalty to the people who stand with us.

And I, with my pint, on a small patch of dry grass put on my sunglasses, fold my arms behind my head and begin nodding off to the sounds of my friends talking above me.

I left Holl at the flat. They were taking so long to get ready that I was in fear that we'd miss the whole thing before they'd chosen an outfit. After weeks of planning, they woke up in a different mind space and decided to scrap the whole thing and begin again. I suggested that I leave early and see them there.

A few friends had already arrived, and as well as the core of the group that I knew, others arrived from the long, spiralling tendrils—friends/partners of friends/partners of friends/partners, some I once met at a house party and may (or may not) have had a conversation with. We begin sprawling out over the patch of grass we have commandeered until there is a lump of us, soaking in the meagre sun.

Jenni introduces her new girlfriend Sara, who I recognise from the time Jenni asked me to go visit the Yuen Family's Acupuncture Clinic for her IBS. I'm not sure if she had ulterior motives for that visit (in which case, I'm not sure IBS was her best option), but it seems to have worked out well. The two of them fawn over each other, and I can't help but smile at their new found happiness.

Jenni and Sara begin chatting with the other couples, Laura and Claire, Tom and Danny, and they start arranging to meet up for a fancy couple's dinner.

I drink it all in, and as I do so, I pray to the sassiest of gods: good weather.

It took me a while last night to find my flag, pink and blue stripes overlapping in the middle. It's not as long as it once was, having been pulled and torn at various points over the past few years—partly through wear of use, partly from a scuffle—but today I proudly pull it through a belt loop on my trousers, and let it hang there.

Someone starts blasting anthems through some pretty powerful portable speakers, an on-duty officer goes over to talk to them but doesn't ask them to turn it down. Instead, they join in with the dancing.

Holl eventually joins us, having thrown together a long pair of black satin trousers, peep-toe, bejewelled platforms, and a white shirt with billowing sleeves. Hair from a long silky wig runs down their back. Of course, they look spectacular, but this is also much more mature that I was expecting—possibly Syd's influence. Syd appears beside them in earthy, easy-going chinos, loafers and an eco-cotton shirt.

An official wearing a rainbow lanyard and high-vis vest appears at the edge of our group. "Hi, everyone! I'm Ross (he/him). How's everyone doing today? Enjoying the sun?" We nod in agreement that we are enjoying ourselves. "Great! I just wanted to see if you will be marching with us today?"

We chorus that yes; we are here to march.

"Fantastic!" Ross says, with a wide-beaming smile. "We'll be starting in the next fifteen minutes or so. There are a few groups that will be in front of you. If you look over there," he says pointing towards a fleet of floats near the north gate of the park, covered in corporate recoloured corporate logos. "Those are some of our corporate sponsors. Their floats will be nearer the beginning, with some of the charities marching between them."

I can see the Ieso float surrounded by some of my colleagues.

It must be the LGBT+ Network. They meet at lunch sometimes. I went once and they were talking about any issues that needed bringing up to the managers, or Frances for the building, or even corporate about what they could do to make things better for us.

It was then I realised, admittedly cynically, that they were letting us use our own time to give them a free consultancy.

If you want my ideas, pay for them like you would from a consultant. If not, you don't get them.

There is a part of me that would like to believe that something positive would have come from those lunchtime meetings, but I'm yet to see an article on the news blast with a success story.

They have, however, paid for a float, and I wonder how many Parades this will be going on.

The floats are lined up on the tarmacked area just inside the gate along with a pink car and then two long chunky lines of groups dressed in uniforms, or banded together with matching signs and banners, splaying out from the tarmac onto the grass.

"Hella Fyne is opening the parade this year so she and her entourage will be leading in the hot pink Rolls Royce, the one that looks like Miss Penclope's from the Thunderbirds," he turns to point out the next group. "After the sponsors and Ms Fyne, there will be the local LGBTQ+ charities that we are raising money for this Pride. This year's focus is on supporting the elders in our community, so there are representatives from the health organisations, and from the Queer Care Home that opened recently in Southside."

Ross turns to the other side of the main gate. "Then there are the dancers from the local dance schools who have been putting together a show for us, the Queer Brass Band is playing for us as we march—they still have a connection to the pits which is awesome, and then all that purple and pink you can see, that's the Queer Women Choral Society—whose name I have completely forgotten— They are going to kill me for that," He chuckles. "I heard them warming up earlier. They are amazing! Great harmonies and they sing all the greats. You're going to love them."

He turns back to face us properly. "After them, it's people like yourselves. And of course, bringing up the rear we have the anarchist and anti-pride groups." Ross points over to some men wearing dark military style clothing, but flicks quickly back to his bright and shiny persona. "The march is about a mile long. There is a slight incline as we march up Lancaster Road, but there are no steps or any narrowing of the path. If anyone has any mobility issues, or accessibility concerns, just let me know. We have got a hearing loop system in place and there will be people along the route if anyone has any visual loss or impairment or would like any assistance." His work done, a chipper Ross, smiles and waves as he makes his way over to the next group to introduce himself. "If you get lost," he calls back over his shoulder. "Follow the music! Have a happy Pride!"

The cynical side of me now thoroughly cleansed, I finish my drink and pass the empty glass to Syd who offers to walk the empties back over to the pub.

Holl watches him go. "You joining us on the ground?" I ask them.

"God, no," they reply. "Absolutely ruin my trousers."

We set off, and apart from being condemned to hell by a self-appointed group of self-righteous, religious zealots, it becomes a fairly comfortable and enjoyable walk around town.

"Yet the police face us, and not the bigots," says Syd, leaning over.

I know Syd works for an NGO about corruption in the police or something, but I do sometimes wish he wouldn't bring it up all the time.

An elderly gentleman, looking a little lost, has the widest and most beautiful grin on his face. He ambles slowly, though confidently, alongside the march. He looks old enough to be shuffling, but in his Sunday best and with his lacquered, wooden cane, he stands tall and takes his time to march the mile.

"Hello," I say as our group saddles up next to him, speaking a little loudly to reach him over the noise of the crowd and the music blasting from the band ahead of us.

He turns to face me and my group of friends, grinning. "I've never done this before," he says. His smile is infectious, bringing out an even wider smile than I had before. "I've always wanted to." His eyes fill with tears and I can't help but mirror him. "I've *always* wanted to," he says again.

"Do you want to walk with us?" I ask him. Jenni and Holl smile warmly at him.

"Oh, I'm a little slow," he says, shyly, regretfully. "And I wouldn't want to intrude on your nice day."

"Nonsense," Holl tells him. "You can't intrude when you've been invited." He grins, though doesn't make eye contact with Holl. We slow our steps to walk with him. Sara and the others also slow down.

"Marvellous," he says, as he looks at the crowded streets. "It's all so marvellous."

"Would you like a badge?" Jenni asks, taking a small enamel flag out of her shirt and offering it to him.

"I couldn't," he says, like the way my own grandfather would reject the offer of the last biscuit.

"Of course, you can," she says. "I make these. I have loads with me and even more at home."

Jenni helps him affix it to his suit jacket. The boys in our group have slowed down too, and we now have him marching in the middle of the group. Introductions fly round, and if I were him, I wouldn't have caught any of our names.

"I'm Joseph," he says. "My name is Joseph. I'm now 85 years old and this is my first time marching." Other groups pass us by, waving their flags and singing, as we walk with our new friend. "I've watched the parade before. I would try and be in town to see it, but I never walked in it. I never marched."

"Why today?" I ask.

He tucks his chin down and scrunches up his face. "Because I've always wanted to. And I was always ashamed. And you young 'uns. You young 'uns— no shame. No fear."

No fear—I wish that were true.

He brings his head back up. Lips crimped together, holding back tears. "I wanted to feel young," he says. "Young like I've never felt young before."

"I'm not sure if we count as young," I laugh.

"You are though," he counsels tenderly. "With so much more to go. And with no shame." He sighs as he steps and mumbles to himself, "I should have done this years ago."

We enter Elizabeth Park at the tail end of the march. The Queer Women Choral Society are already set up under the bandstand singing us into the park with rousing a cappella renditions of the queer anthems. As I breathe in the songs, I feel my chest expand with joy. The words speaking directly to me. For the first time in a long time, I am at peace. I exist only in this moment, with these people. There is a clear boundary between the here and now and the rest of my life.

Hella Fyne strolls out onto stage in an outrageous runway garment, "Queer people," she calls to the crowd in a low, sultry tone.

"Oh," says Joseph, startled. "I wasn't expecting that!"

"My friends: the fabulous people who make up this fine city, I would like to welcome you to the opening of this years' Pride!" Hella steps back from the microphone and claps above it. as the crowd cheers and applauds. "But first," she says, holding up a gloved hand to silence the crowd. "First I would like to welcome today's sponsor, Arnold Little of Meadow Weir Shopping Centre."

Scattered applause.

"Thank you, Ms Fyne," he says as he replaces her at the microphone. "And thank you all for allowing me to join you here today. We at Meadow Weir Shopping Centre are glad to have the opportunity to sponsor an event like the one today. We are working to ensure that our Centre is a welcoming environment to all who wish to visit…"

Wait—did anyone think it wasn't? Is there a surprise uber-religious bookshop that sells homophobic literature I'm unaware of? Is one of the cleaners making bitchy comments at the queers as we walk through? Does the manager of the bubble tea place refuse to serve mixed drinks as a form of bi-erasure? Does LGB headquarter there?

Seriously though, I am concerned now.

He's already finished his speech. Short, sweet and I have already managed to dream up a drama.

Joseph starts shifting his weight back and forth, grunting a little in discomfort. He frowns as he straightens his back.

"Do you need a chair or something?" I ask.

"No, thank you," Joseph says. "I think that's me for today. I need to go home and put my feet up."

"Do you need a taxi?" Holl asks.

He smiles directly at Holl and nods, "please." Holl struts off down the road beside the park to hail one down.

Syd, being the only proper adult among us, hands Joseph his business card. "If you want to go for a drink or meal with us, you can get me on this number."

Joseph takes the card and studies it deeply. "Thank you," he says, shaking Syd's hand. "Thank you."

We wave our goodbyes and promise to meet him if he calls.

Hella Fyne is back welcoming the first musical act of the day, a local band with a fan base in the front row.

The afternoon is long, but Syd remembered to book us a table at the nearby restaurant so we can regain our strength before heading out to sing for the rest of the evening, then dance till the sun comes up.

I am with my people.

Life is good.

Gene Boone

Patient-Inmate

Revelation Rehabilitation Centre

(Part of Daniel Pit Correctional Facility, USA)

"Amen, pastor," one of the inmates cried out, ecstasy washing over them, trembling in the wake of the pastor's words. He held up his arms to welcome in the message. The 'amen' reverberated through the sullen grey walls, competing with the squeaks of red, plastic chairs. The pastor rained down his blessings over the sinner who dared to cry out.

"This man," the pastor bellowed. "This man—this sinner!—cries out to the Lord and he will be heard. Some of you sinners will sin and sin again and again and again and again. But some, like this man—who dares to cry out in front of the Lord, can be saved, will be saved, from the devil's fire."

This was the Thursday sermon, the long rambling declaration that Pastor Abner would give. Gene Boone had heard it many times before. He was usually sentenced to the correctional facility, rather than this, the rehabilitation side of the business. This time, the judge had been kind enough to direct Gene to rehabilitation rather than prison, but the difference was minimal. Both the centre and the facility had the same spartan rooms with the same square footage, the same whitewashed walls, same food, same staff—none of which was surprising seeing as both the rehabilitation centre and correctional facility are in fact located on the same premises between the two rivers south of the city. The two entities may have had separate gates to enter by, but both backed onto a workshop that the inmates and patients shared for prison industries and recreational time. The canteen served food to both sides of the site. The guards patrolled both gates. Even the grounds themselves were only mutedly distinct due to being re-grassed at different times and by different companies using different seed.

The difference between 'inmate' and 'patient' was even less distinct.

The rehabilitation side of the complex, Revelation, had its own particular brand of therapy: one that focused on the corruption of the soul—the judgement of which lay at the mercy of Pastor Abner, the owner of the private prison and the medical facilities.

There was, supposedly, criteria for release; completing certain courses, getting certain treatments, but the patients were rarely, if ever, offered anything outside of the weekly sermons. There were rumours that these supposed courses were recorded in the patients' files.

Pastor Abner, a greying man with many years of unchallenged preaching, came to minister both patients and inmates in two sessions—one in the morning, one in the afternoon—and were it not for the time of day, he would have had trouble discerning who was who.

Gene Boone sat and took the hellfire. He quietly sat through that venom and judgement. Gene was fortunate in that he had only come across the pastor when part of an enormous congregation within the prison. He was certain that Abner would not recognise him in the slightly more intimate setting of rehab.

Gene was wrong.

Whether by righteous memory or access to records, the pastor knew him.

Gene stared down at the linoleum and concentrated on his breathing. He was careful not to make eye contact with anyone, and tried to resist the painful urge to scratch the burning sensation in his arm.

Pastor Abner held his microphone so close to his mouth as he raised his voice that sound would blow out. There was no need to use a microphone, the room was small enough that even a weak voice would carry back. But Pastor Abner insisted that a microphone was needed for him at his sessions.

"Addicts," spat Pastor Abner. "Degenerate addicts. Sinners. What are you?"

"Sinners," the men half-heartedly chorused.

"Say it again!"

"Sinners," they said, making the smallest attempt to raise their voice.

"There are some that say, God loves the sinner, but hates the sin. Well, how can that be?" Abner asked. "Do you think that God loves you? After everything that you've done?" Abner shook his head and stormed across to the other side of the stage. "Do you think God loves you when all you do is sin? Well, do you?" He left the briefest of pauses where only his faithful acolyte called out. "Do you treat your body as a temple? When you fill it full of these disgusting drugs? Do you?"

Gene felt a sharp stab of pain in his gut. One that pulsed through his entire stomach and he tried to shift in his chair to relieve the pressure building inside of him.

"You do not," Pastor Abner shook his head, dropped his microphone holding hand to the side and looked across the congregation in disappointment.

Some in Abner's position would be merciful. Some would have shown kindness to the lost sheep, to the prodigal sons, but Abner saw only the failure within his captive audience and was willing to shame them for his own gratification.

Sin.

Wickedness.

Pastor Abner cycled through sermons, taking hours to get to a point, while Gene writhed in silent agony. Eventually, the pastor's words would fade out of recognition as the familiar hurt returned to Gene's body. He found it uncomfortable to breathe—each breath grating one organ against another, too deep a breath and he risked pushing beyond his tolerance and would need to cry out for help, unsure if any help would come.

He's tired. He had been tired since the day officer Hendry picked him up from his room at the Shield Hotel, the cheapest room on the edge of town, the only thing he could afford after losing yet another job due to downsizing and streamlining. He had a week until the next payment was due and he didn't have enough even for this one room. Officer Hendry was also aware that it was coming to the end of the month and he had quotas to fill.

Gene Boone was as easy a target as Hendry would ever find. He had followed the dealer coming into town, but waited until all the deals were done, and took in every person the dealer had sold to. The drugs were still in their system, their minds still elsewhere.

Yes, officer Hendry had done his job that night.

Gene was still waiting to hear if he would get any of his possessions back. His hotel room had been emptied by the owner, there's no doubt of that. His worldly possessions thrown in some trash can. Officer Hendry had already seized the last of the cash that Gene had had and put it in his own back pocket.

Gene's thoughts got caught on the fear that he might fall asleep. Dreams, or no dreams—either was terrifying. A horror-filled, nightmare landscape, or the absence of existence; Gene wasn't sure which scared him more.

Pastor Abner, who had moved on from his talk about the sinner and the man, delighted in lecturing the patients about his good friends; the governor, the warden, and the judge. How their faith, guided by his, were the cornerstone of this community. How they invested their time, their political will and their money in making this community a better place for all. How the four of them had conceived of this place. How even the weak-willed, bleeding-heart, woke liberals loved this place because it had the word 'rehabilitation' in it.

Gene felt a cold sweat building on his face. He wanted to vomit. The pain in his belly was overwhelming. His whole body shook as he tried to focus on pushing the bile down. He gasped as the pain overcame him.

Pastor Abner heard him.

"You see this man?" Pastor Abner asked while pointing at Gene. "The addict? He has the sin of gluttony and greed and those sins lead to lust because men like this one here have no control over themselves. They sin against God! This addict, with his own body, sins against God! And you know what," the pastor paused for a moment, rubbing his finger and thumb across his lip and chin. "He sins against us. That's right, I said he sins against us."

Gene was now only dimly aware of the room. The men around him had turned to face him as he scrunched his eyes from the pain and tried to restrict the tremor that reverberated along his hand and arm. His breathing was no more than a light pant. Hyperventilating, his mind crashed and struggled to focus on any one thing. He fought against the chills that rose to violent shaking that started in his back. He gripped his muscles tightly to keep him sitting in his chair.

"Did I hear an 'amen'?" Pastor Abner demanded.

His congregation whispered, "Amen."

Chapter 5
Telephony

I discover, a moment or two before it is about to begin, that a new meeting has been added to my calendar today. More specifically, some training that I wasn't aware of. Three hours of training, to be exact. Three hours of learning how to talk on a phone.

I talk on the phone every day.

Obviously not when I'm working on a project like this one, but generally speaking I have spent the past decade making, answering and enduring phone calls. There isn't a situation that this trainer can throw at me that I haven't dealt with a dozen times before. Difficult callers, legitimately upset callers, unreasonably hostile callers, I have had them all and in multitudes.

But there is one thing I can't get over: why have I only just found out about this, five minutes before the session starts?

One of the trainers from business support sits in the one swivel chair at one end of the long conference table. He introduced himself the last time he came over to train us on 'emails; how to write professionally'[9] like we are all children, but I never caught his name then, and I haven't caught it now. I'm sure his name must be on my calendar or on any of the numerous emails he has sent, but without checking, I have no idea what it is. He is completely forgettable.

And punchable.

But most importantly, forgettable.

I checked with Jan before coming into the room, to see if I should even be doing this when I'm supposed to be on loan for a 'special project', but she assured me that as this is a part of my usual job, I would need to participate in these annual refresher courses.

---

[9] fml

Christ. Annual refreshers.

After a quick fumble over getting the presentation to show on the large screen behind the swivel chair and not just on the laptop in front of him, the trainer smiles, says hello to us all and welcomes us all to this telephony course.

"What is telephony?" He asks rhetorically. I want to die. He launches into a prepared definition. I open my notebook and lay it on my lap rather than the table so I can doodle unnoticed.

He taps the mouse and the presentation slide screen wipes from right to left.

Preparing for Phone Calls

Oh, dear Lord! I don't think I'm going to survive this. If we are going to the depths of having a clear workspace for a clear mind in order to be in the right headspace to take the call—I am not going to survive this.

Three hours, I remind myself. This is a three-hour course. There's going to be *shudder* *role play*.

The last time I *role-played* anything in the office I managed to make one of the temps cry and walk out on her job. Not one of my proudest moments. The poor thing said that no job was worth the stress. In many ways I agree with her.

He asks us what sort of information we should be recording during the call. How can we make sure that our notes are clear and precise and don't contain any sensitive information?

In the business update down at the Station Hotel, I could hide in the anonymity of a crowd. But here, here I can't hide. Here, squashed around this table with only a dozen of my contemporaries, I can't disappear behind a column or a colleague's head.

Megan is taking notes as always. I fold over my notebook and write out the key phrases the trainer is pointing out in his presentation, then I decorate them with plants, birds, and swooping lines. Embellishing any capitals, heads of small flowers instead of bullet points, circles with circles.

"Ok," he says, trying to engage us like a supply teacher in a silent classroom. "How do you answer the phone usually?"

No one offers an answer, so picks on Hannah.

"Hi, you're through to Hannah. How can I help?"

"And do you think that's good enough?" He leans into the table as he asks.

Hannah falters for a second, unsure, but puts forward a brave, if questioning, "yes?"

He hums. "Can anyone think of a way to improve Hannah's... Hannah's?" He checks he's got her name right. She nods and smiles. "Hannah's introduction? Is there anything missing from it? Anything she can add to really make it pop?"

Make it pop? No. Nothing. There is nothing missing. It's a perfectly sensible, reasonable, professional way to answer the phone.

"She could say the company name," Carol suggests.

Fuck you, Carol.

"The automated message tells them the company name every 45 seconds," I say. If they haven't been paying attention to that, why would us saying it make it any clearer?

"It's nice though, don't you think? For a real person to say it?" He smiles and nods to himself, waiting for me to nod back in agreement. It takes all my strength to maintain a neutral expression and not give into his manipulation. I think he's overthinking this. I think he's an idiot treating our callers like idiots. He's not entirely wrong there, many of them are, but even if the hold music on our line was a jingle made purely of the company name, they would still come through and want to book a dog grooming appointment with us.

I wish that wasn't an actual example from my memory bank of ridiculous calls... but it is.

"How about saying 'good morning' or 'good afternoon'? Using that positive word 'good' to just draw in the caller a little more, making them feel a little more inclined to like you."

Ffs.

"We're going to talk about positive language later, but let's start with," he clicks the mouse and the next slide swishes onto the screen.

Assessing the Needs of Callers

"How do you know what a caller needs when you answer the phone?"

"They ask us for something," says Carol confidently.

Oh, sweet naïve, Carol. No. Pay attention: the caller is an imbecile who doesn't even know who they are calling—you think these hypothetical callers *know* what they want?

"That is one way," the trainer says. Smiling wickedly. "But you know. They might be calling for one thing—something that they know they need," the *known knowns, the unknown unknowns,* "but we hold more information, more knowledge about their account with us. We can advise them…"

Buzzword.

Nope, nope.

"We can't advise them," I blurt out before my brain actually processes what it's doing. I don't even realise I'm talking. It's such a knee jerk reaction that has been drilled into me.

"I'm sorry?" The trainer looks at me intently, frustrated that I have interrupted a second time.

"We can't give advice," I say sheepishly, though not without authority. "We're not trained to. We're not financial advisers. We can't give people that call in financial advice."

"Well, obviously, what I meant to say…" he says, stung. "Obviously you know your jobs best. What I am saying is that there are things the caller might not know about their account that they might need to know, and as you can see their account and know what's happening and what has been happening, you will be able to inform them of that."

Like we do already. Because we know how to do our job.

Megan's still scribbling down notes.

Attitude

Fuck.

Don't say anything. Don't put that foot in your own mouth. I can hear the air being sucked through my teeth, a tiny scream, I swear I'm not doing it on purpose.

"Did you know," he begins slowly. Whatever he's about to say—I want proof. I want to see the peer-reviewed studies on it. I want to see if it can be replicated in the office setting, because we all know whatever he's about to say has been pulled out the arse of some sensationalised, pseudo-science report in the back of some industry magazine. "That people can tell when you're smiling on the phone!"

Bullshit.

He smiles and nods as if it were the most profound thing anyone has ever said in the history of these training sessions. Carol lets out a little excited gasp.

"It's true!" He says. "The caller can always tell!"

No, they can't. And you know how I know that they can't? Because the caller can't even tell when I'm miming obscenities down the phone at them. They can't tell when, exasperated, I throw my arms in the air or turn to a colleague and scream, 'what the fuck?' when I've put myself on mute. They can't tell when I am staring up at the ceiling in desperation for the world to swallow me whole just so I don't have to talk to them for another moment.

So, one—I doubt the caller knows when I'm smiling. And two—I doubt whether they actually care.

I'm told I'll need to practise. He doesn't specifically say my name, nor does he look directly at me or point his finger or anything like that, but I know that he is speaking directly to me.

For the rest of this part of the session, until the break, I sit with this ridiculous smile on my face, that burns into my cheeks and makes my jaw shake after too long. Callers should know better. We who take your calls have sold our time to the company and this is how they chose to use our time, not how we chose to use it.

Short break. Quick trip to the toilet and grab a cuppa on the way back.

Positive Language

"Let's have a quick round of getting all that positive vocabulary on the board. All those happy words that we can use to brighten up phone calls. Words that can put the caller in a great mood and show that we are willing and able to help them!"

Great. Fantastic. Absolutely. Perfect.

He has us draw up our own individual bingo sheets with a different positive word in each box.

"See if by the end of the day you can get your positive language bingo!" He says. Far too cheerfully. "But first, let's practise. I have scenarios here. How about you pair up and you can take it in turns to be the caller and the call taker?" He passes a wad of paper round the room.

I grab hold of Hannah as a partner. At least the two of us can have a little fun with it.

"These scenarios all get wrapped up at the end," Hannah says, looking through the options. "That's not realistic."

"Ah, but the customers can sense our smiles down the phone and that may change everything," I say, grinning painfully.

Hannah, unconvinced, points at the first, "Hi, you're through to Hannah…"

I interrupt her, "Good morning, you're through to Hannah at the fantastic Ieso Financial, what do you think you need from this excellent phone call today?"

Yes, I'm being facetious. The trainer is facetious. This whole exercise is facetious. I'm supposed to take it seriously?

You know what would actually be a good use of time at school? You know those PSHE lessons—we had it maybe once a fortnight and depending on who your teacher was you either had a lesson on personal hygiene or you had an extra hour to do your homework. Take one of those hours and teach people how to speak on the damn phone. Not from the job POV but from the customer POV. How to call for information. How to make a complaint. How to request something.

Here's what they'd learn: shouting gets you nowhere—you're going to be put on hold for an extended time so that we have a moment to collect ourselves. We have to deal with our shitty systems already, reading through a colleague's notes—and depending on whether it was someone competent or someone *bearly abel 2 right in Inglish*, it might take a second. Customers screaming in our ear while we do that is not helpful.

What works, what really works, is being nice and sounding a little disappointed. I would go well above and beyond for that person. I feel genuinely bad and a little bit guilty for someone who doesn't understand what's happening on the account and is unsure what their accountant or financial adviser is doing. I can even summon up some form of empathy for a financial adviser or sales person who desperately needs some information on an account. Get what you want from a call, say 'thank you', say 'have a nice day'. It's not hard not to be a dick.

Also, have your shit ready: I get it, some people don't have their reference numbers, that's fine, but they should expect to answer some questions so we can find them.

I don't even mind when someone has no idea what's going on. That's fine, I can help. What I don't appreciate is some old fucker coming on the line and demanding to know 'what's this all about' then refusing to tell me his name because he doesn't know who I am and then getting angry that I'm not being more helpful. Helpful with what? I don't know your name; I don't know what you have with us. I don't know how, who or why you got signed up with us.

That's the problem with these examples at the phone call practising seminar—no authenticity.

Training people at school age probably wouldn't work, none of the people who call us have been to school in decades.

Some kind of public service announcement might work instead.

"No volunteers?" The trainer asks, humming. I hadn't noticed that we have finished our role plays.

Pick me, I dare you.

I double dare you.

Ah, clever sod. He doesn't pick me. He picks Carol. There is a delightful little sketch, completely independent of reality, in which an angry person is calmed through the use of positive language and smiling. Of all the years I've taken phone calls, of all the phone calls I've listened to for *training and monitoring* purposes, this has never happened.

Competency and charm—sure. But not positive language and smiling.

"Ok, one last thing for the session this morning," the trainer says as we are about to pack up. "We should never use the word *can't*. *Can't* is no longer in our vocabulary."

There is a murmur around the room, until someone lifts their volume to voice their opinion and asks, "what if the caller asks us to do something we can't do. Like something that is impossible."

"Or illegal," I add in a whisper. It wouldn't be the first time.

"Well, you would need to find a way to express that without using negative words."

Linguistic gymnastics. Got it. while at the same time making sure we remain clear and precise…

What exactly is wrong with using negative words when something can't be done? Why can't we just tell the caller it is what it is. This is why we get calls back from people who expected one thing and got another and when we go back and check the original call it's because the person taking the call had to say it in such a roundabout way to make sure that they weren't marked down by the *recorded for monitoring*'s sake.

"Right," he says, handing out copies of the presentation slides and bringing the session to an end, and giving us no further direction on this 'don't say can't'. "We'll be listening to calls over the next few days and sending you all some feedback. Have a great day everyone."

Great. Fantastic. Absolutely. Perfect.

I go back out to my usual space down by my team, checking with Jan to see if I should make and take a few calls for this feedback from the trainer because if I go back up to the third floor I won't be making or taking calls for the rest of the week (and that would be a terrible shame).

But when I log on and open up my telephony system I find, to my genuine surprise, that for once not a single call is waiting to be taken. Not a single call is queued up waiting to be answered. For a second I'm not sure what to do with myself.

I open up the emails and letters that have been sent in in the past few days, looking for an outbound call I can make. There is an invoice that seems to be missing the amount payable. That'll do. A nice, quick phone call just to get the total amount, I can send it off to finance and that is a call done, a debt paid and a piece of work complete.

Yes, I know. I jinxed it.

I set up a line to record the outgoing call to this third-party company and spend just shy of twenty minutes on hold listening to a jazzy rendition of Pachelbel's Canon through my headset. My eyes glaze over, but the length of time it takes to answer is not the fault of the person that picks up, I remind myself, and sit practising my smile while staring off into the mid distance.

The woman that answers says 'Hi' and asks for a reference number that I find at the top of the invoice, and then some security questions, which I answer while still smiling in case she can hear it in my voice. After passing security, she says 'hi' again.

"Hi," I say. "I've just got this invoice and I need to check the total amount so I can get a cheque sent out to you today." I speak at a nice even cadence, upbeat but not too fast. "And if I can check on the status of our request, that would be awesome!"

Polite. Direct. Positive. Perfect telephony. Probably not personable enough—they can send me feedback for that.

"Ok," The voice has clearly brought up all the information on her screen. "Have you received proof that your request has been received with us?"

"I've received an invoice," I tell her, remembering to smile.

"So, what!"

"So, what?" I repeat back to her with a tinge of confusion but still smiling.

"That isn't proof we have your request."

"Right," I stammer. "But you sent us an invoice with this client's details on it."

"That's not proof."

My mouth hovers open for a moment before I camp it shut in a deranged Joker grin.

Are you in the habit of sending out random invoices with a long series of letters and numbers attached to random names, dates of birth, and addresses to a random company in hope that one of them magically matches up with something on their system? I want to ask. Infinite monkeys flinging shit and seeing what sticks? I think this, but I don't say it. I remain calm and polite, like the training presentation slides beside me demand.

"Ok," I start slowly, "I've received an invoice here, which I can only have received from your company after you received our request."

#Logic.

"An invoice isn't proof of receipt," she says haughtily. "We have a specific letter for informing people that we have received their request."

"Ok, but I have an invoice from you—"

"An invoice isn't confirmation of receipt," she cuts me off.

"But it does prove you have our request."

"No, it doesn't."

My eyes narrow. All the muscles in my face hover between two expressions—a smile and utter confusion. "Can you let me know when the confirmation letter will be sent out to us for this case?" I try.

"Yes," she says. I hear rapid typing. "It was sent out yesterday."

OH, FOR THE LOVE OF ACTUAL FUCK

83

I check the date on the invoice which was also sent yesterday. The confirmation letter is probably the next item in my queue—unless the mailroom didn't bother to scan it onto the system because WHAT FUCKING COMPANY deep breaths deep breaths

"Ah yes," I say unconvincingly. "Here it is. I have the confirmation letter here."

She gives me the information I need and I pick up the phone purely to throw it back into the receiver.

Funnily enough, that wasn't in the role play exercises now, was it?

A call comes through before I am able to blink. I shouldn't pick it up. The absolute shock of a call that was, but the call is already in my phone and I can't reject it without gaining the ire of whichever manager is currently monitoring the incoming calls.

I smile ready to introduce myself.

"Finally!" An infuriated voice comes through the line at me before I am able to speak. "You sent me an email and there's something on it I can't open."

Don't say can't.

"Could I have your details and I'll be able to hel..."

"You just sent it me!" The rough, hoarse voice of a bitter old man rumbles through.

"I'm sorry, sir, I haven't sent any emails," I say kindly but firmly. "If I can have your details, I can look up any emails that have been sent to you from our company."

"Aren't you Stephen?"

"No," I say, raising the pitch in my voice a little. "I am not."

"I called Stephen's number," he bellows.

"Stephen," whoever he is, "isn't available to take a call at the moment, and so I'm taking the call on his behalf."

"Eugh, fine," the old man huffs and spits. "So, are you going to help me?"

I ask for his email address, but find nothing on our system. He gets more and more enraged the more I request from him. Eventually I ask for the full email address that the email he received came from.

It's not even our company.

"So, you're not going to help me?" He challenges.

"I have no visual of the email you've been sent, because it's been sent by a different company. I am unable to see what the attachment is and so I am unable to help you in this instance[10]."

"You're all the same, you big business people!"

I sigh. Replaster my smile across my face. "What does the attachment say?" I ask.

"It says *name of client and date of birth*[11] and then 'dot word'. What does Stephen mean 'dot word'?"

"It's a word document," I say cautiously.

"And I'm just supposed to know what that is? I've been in this business almost 30 years and I have never had to open a 'word document'."

"Really?" The word escapes me before I can block it. But seriously, *really*? You've worked in an office for 30 years and have never once used a word processor. Are you kidding me?

Stephen, whoever and wherever you are, I'm so sorry. No wonder you gave this caller our number instead of your own. He must be driving you up the wall!

"Have you tried double clicking on the attachment?" I ask tentatively, holding my bottom lip in my teeth for a second. "Like click on it twice."

"I know how to double click," he rages. "I'm not an idiot!"

Aren't you?

I caught that one before I said it.

Patience.

Patience.

Patience.

Lean back, stare up at the ceiling. Does this count as resting my eyes— staring up at the fluorescents rather than my screen?

"It opens a bloody box that says I can't open it," he screams. "What is this nonsense?"

"Do you have a word processor on your computer?"

"DO I hAVe a WOrD pRoCEssOR oN mY ComPuTEr?"

Ladies, gentleman, and all others, I introduce to you; peak idiot. Words come running out of his mouth like an erupting volcano, spitting out noxious gases. He screams in my ear, his voice breaking as it hits the higher notes. *How dare you? How very dare you?* I push the headphones forward so that the sound is hitting

---

[10] Didn't say 'can't'

[11] He *really* shouldn't have told me that.

bone rather than the air in my ear canal. I can still hear every word in his ear-splitting rant.

Swear.

Come on, swear at me.

"Bitch!"

Got it. disconnect the call.

I am excited at the prospect of receiving feedback on that call.

To anyone who has ever muttered that feeble cliché—fuck off: the customer is never right. The customer seldom has a grip on reality.

Chapter 6
Temps and OT

The temps that were promised are finally set up with their own passwords on the system and are (at least in theory) ready to go. After weeks of promises of 'tomorrow', I arrive one morning to find a gaggle round my door. They are finally ready to be settled into the glass box for me to delegate out the work from the plastic boxes.

I introduce myself. I give them a quick rundown of what sort of data we will be inputting.

It takes a while to collect all of their names. I don't know if they are being evasive on purpose, or whether they are the sort of temps that just turn up to do work and have no interest in the social side of work—which is fine, I totally get it. When I'm surrounded by random people, I don't want to talk to them half the time either.

I do actually recognise two of them from the ReFloat incident. Sean—a career temp who kept going on about the joys of temping—nothing tying you down, nothing you had to get too attached to. He did make it sound good, take breaks whenever you wanted, moving on if you didn't like a job, having fingers in all the right pies if you ever did want to settle down. He has met pretty much every manager in town and had half of their phone numbers, not that he intended to leave the #TempLife. He wore shiny suits even when the rest of the office was in dress-down Friday mode four days out of five, and he put so much product in his hair that it didn't move even in high gales.

From what I remember, he does have good banter. Funny office stories from the other places he worked at, and he was also careful not to reveal what office which happened in. That was especially comforting after Carol managed to set fire to her own hair with a candle in the toilets. That story has come back to me in so many ways, but no one has ever been able to pinpoint the origin.

Next to him, is Rachael, who had her second or third child a couple of years ago and is now building her CV back up after a decade raising kids. On ReFloat she was only doing part time, but it looks like she is working almost full-time hours on this, or at least no one has told me any different.

Not that I expect they would even if she were.

During ReFloat, which I suspect was her first outing back into the world of the employed, she talked about everything to everyone, she had maybe been starved of adult interaction a little too long, and revelled at not having to discuss kids. I don't think she ever once told us their names. Or that of her husband. I remember her saying she was looking for something permanent, but it looks like she is still looking for that.

The older man, Paul, I don't recognise.

"It's my first gig," he tells me. "Never thought I'd stoop to this." He huffs and heaves his belly over the chair backs as he makes his way to the opposite end of the table. I can tell he's going to be *fun*.

Never mind, never mind. Brush off the negative vibes. The last is Carlie, a recent graduate looking for a gapless CV while she looks for her first job in finance, which is why, I suspect, that she got a job with this particular temp agency. We, and half a dozen other financial institutes in the city, use this agency because every time there is a redundancy drive, people mostly end up there until there is another great employment drive, when everyone gets hired back for less pay and fewer benefits.

Or, at least, that's my experience.

I hated temping. With no back up, no one to share the bills and pull up the slack, I found waiting for possible employment torturous.

I know Jenny likes it though, so *shrugs*.

Carlie is a little quiet, though, bless her, she has brought in a printed off CV with her in case I need to see it.

No, sweetie.

I place an inch high pile of papers on the desks beside each computer and let them know I don't expect them to finish the whole thing, just to get through what they can and let me know if they need more.

She raises her hand to ask a question.

"You don't need to…" I start. "How can I help, Carlie?"

"What do we do if there is missing information?" She asks, holding up her first paper to show me an almost empty page. "Like this one, where all I've got is a name."

"Ah," I say. "If you leave that particular one with me." They are all looking at me now. I pick up a board marker and write on the board. "If there is like only one or two missing fields, fill them in with these codes," I say. "Email addresses are email@email.com, phone numbers are 01234567890, address…" I continue. At least we'll be able to get all the information. "I'm going to make a spreadsheet to collect all the missing information, so, if you use one of these on the board, could you drop me an email," I hastily write that on the board too. "And when I have the spreadsheet ready, I'll share it with you and everyone will be able to update their own."

Humph, I hear from Paul as he releases either an unconvinced sigh, or a really quiet fart.

"I'll then be able to go back to III Holdings, who are opening the account, and I'll be able to get this information for us."[12]

The room becomes eerily silent as the four of them study the top page of paper. Sean and Rachael jump in to some ferocious typing, Paul takes his time before he begins prodding the keyboard with his two index fingers, tucking the rest of his fingers in his palm and holding them in with his thumbs, which is a technique I've not seen in a long time. He isn't particularly slow, but it does change the sound of his typing to a low steady thump, rather than the hands skipping over the keys like the other three.

Carlie passes me the almost blank piece of paper and I use that as a guide to create the spreadsheet. I email the example spreadsheet to Darren Neal so he can see what I'm dealing with. If he comes back at me. I'm going to invite him in to see the glass room that is now stuffed with people and paper.

I look like a hoarder. I look like someone with a fascination for financial documents and personal and private information. Either that, or a really creepy Santa, who's not only made a list and checked it twice, but also saved information not necessary for his business and is in clear violation of privacy.

I might wear my red top tomorrow. The one with the white stitching. It could come off as festive, but it is just a pretty top.

It takes a while to make the spreadsheet after I receive an email from Jan asking how the temps are settling in. I stretch out the word 'fine' to a paragraph.

---

[12] Not that I have any sincere hope that that will happen.

There is only so long I can sit and stare at a computer screen before I start going cross eyed. Apart from the occasional stretch to crack out my spine (which gets a shiver and recoil from Rachael), I am glued to my desk. I'm sure there was an online lesson that insisted we take ten minutes away from our screen for every hour of work. I've never been able to work out how or when to do this. Everything is done at the computer and everything is time sensitive (at least according to the statistics that are collated on us). I have physical paperwork and yet I still have to sit at a computer.

I can't see my manager willing to give me a ten-minute break for every hour, she gets miffed if I go for more than one cuppa in an afternoon. Am I supposed to get up and go speak to a colleague at the other end of the office instead of emailing them? I know from experience that when I get back to the desk there will be a little email icon waiting for me asking why I'm not available and I need to waste a few minutes begging managerial leave for my shocking behaviour, and justifying the necessity to go speak rather than send my query electronically.

Somehow, it's worse now. I get offered a brew every hour by one of the temps who needs to stretch and rest their eyes. How dare they steal my time away from me.

Of course, I say please and thank you for the tea. I'm not a monster, but they are stealing my away-from-desk time.

"Would anyone like a tea or coffee?" Carlie asks as it reaches three o'clock and no one has offered to make one in at least half an hour.

A chorus of 'oh, yes', and 'yes, please', and I offer to go too so we can carry all the mugs in one trip.

I'm not going to tell them about the trays on the top shelf of the cupboard yet. They can discover that for themselves.

"How long have you worked here," Carlie asks as we cross the office, past the gITs, and reach the zip taps with the hot water for tea and the coffee machine.

"About 5 years," I engage in her small talk, before confiding. "It feels both longer and shorter than that." She smiles and takes the coffee mugs off the mug tree and starts selecting the coffee for Paul, who was oddly specific about his choice. "Are you looking for something permanent or are you like Sean and are happy to temp?"

"I like temping," she says, unconvincingly. "I mean, it's good money. Not sure I want to do it for long. I had a gap of almost a month between the last two gigs. Nearly sent me crazy."

"What sort of things do you get up to between 'gigs'?" I ask.

"Mostly send out applications for permanent jobs," she sighs. "I just want to come in at 9 and finish a 5 and know that that's how it will be for a few years at least."

"Nothing's as permanent as that," I say under my breath. "It would be nice if it were."

"Hmm?" She hums questioningly. I shake my head, pretending not to have said anything. She starts on the second coffee as I pour the teas.

Carlie seems nice enough and I make a mental note to let her know if we are ever hiring. Not sure she'd want anything this low-level, I get the impression her degree is specific, but I can at least keep an eye out.

There is an email waiting for me from Jan letting me know that a comfort break should take less than 7 minutes.

I'd love to know where she got that number from.

I'll remember it the next time she has waterwork issues.

I let go of a stretch hand bring my arms down behind my back, teasing out that last tense neck muscle that didn't shift when we were walking, pushing it just a little further, hoping that it cracks before it releases lactic acid[13].

The stretch turns into a yawn.

I rest my hands back on the keyboard and re-read the last bit of data I typed in—a bank sort code for an investor. The number looks familiar. I've seen the shape of it on my screen before.

I don't have a head for numbers, I doubt I could balance a cheque book (if that was still a thing), but shapes—shapes I can do. The sixes and eights and zeros make a round infinite shape of my screen.

Have I put the wrong number in? The scraps of paper with all the different information, maybe I've put the information in twice for different people.

I can't search for people via their bank codes (tbf: what would be the point?), so I rustle back through the papers for the people whose bank details I've already entered and find the exact number on someone I input last week.

Different account, same sort code.

Maybe that's not unusual. Lots of people use the same bank. Maybe they are family members, or the adviser at III Holdings has a large group of people investing from the same area. Maybe that group all opened new bank accounts for the purpose of investment.

---

[13] If that's how that works?

91

I read over the rest of the details for both men. Both Romanian, or at least Eastern European, both live at the same address. Ok, maybe they are a couple. That would make sense. Live together, go to the same financial adviser, the same bank. They are both marked as single—but that could be a typo, or the adviser doesn't know or care that they are in a relationship, that happens.

I put the papers down and go on with the new application.

No, stop. That postcode, I've seen that before too. Not just these two men. And if there's five of us plugging this data into the server, then maybe other people have been assigned this address too.

Now, a postcode, I can search by.

Twelve names flick up onto my screen. All living at the same postcode. It could be a postcode that covers a huge area with lots of houses, I've seen that before.

Nope. Same house number.

I'm back to being suspicious. I pick up a pencil and scribble their names into my notebook

I google their house. It must either be some sort of timeshare situation which everyone is just using to set up their bank accounts, or they are lying and the bank account checks are going to come back messed up, or it's a house that belongs to the agent—but that cannot be legal. One of the investors might own it and the others are his friends that are using it as a UK mailing address. That makes more sense.

It's probably some nice, detached country cottage with a large garden. They spend summers there and it's near a beach, or a hill, or some pretty woodland.

It isn't.

It's a red-brick, mid-terrace on an estate down in Bath.

*

Maybe one of them rents it out?

I am being a bit generous with my trust, there. It's weird. And it's weird enough to no longer be my decision on whether it is weird or suspicious. It is at this point that I should report it as suspicious activity. Legal can work out what is going on.

I type up an email with a list of the investor ID numbers and details of the address and matching sort codes and send it through to legal to check out.

An email pops up on my screen which at first, I close, thinking it's an automatic reply from Legal.

OT tonight—pizza

Ah yes. The most exciting and enticing overtime: overtime with pizza.

Way back when (but actually, probably not that long ago), we were paid time and a half for OT. Not me personally, but the company used to pay extra. The generation before us got double time. Now? Now we get a pizza to share, usually just cheese. Never from the good pizzeria. The pizzas are picked up by a manager and placed down on the cabinets in the middle of the office between two banks of desks. Help yourself; but more than two slices and you're a greedy monster who hates their colleagues. They never buy a second round of pizzas no matter how long you pledge to stay.

Pledge—like I'm joining some sort of fraternity or declaring an allegiance. Semantically, I don't like the word. It is full of this creepy, dare I say *American* attitude to work. To promise or vow, on your word of honour, to commit yourself to the cause of overtime, knowing full well that the reason it's needed is because we are not at the required headcount, no matter how often they tell us we are. Sure, you can reduce the number of hours you plan to do after you've pledged, but then you are no longer trustworthy and they are no longer able to count on your hours next OT sesh.

I open the email to see which team is falling behind and needs assistance.

Ah. My team. The one I'm not in because I'm dealing with this nonsense.

I forward the email to Megan.

Is this cos of me?

Yes, she replies immediately. A second email comes through from her, *they were surprised that you actually did work and so never bothered to allocate it.*

I scoff and resist replying with an obscenity that would be rejected or quarantined by the server.

Brilliant.

I email back without any punctuation, knowing that Megan will pick up on my sarcasm. *You going to stay?*

Not tonight, she responds. *I'm off out with Jack—anniversary.*

So, not only would I be at the world's most depressing pizza party, filled with no one I actually want to talk to, eating a greasy cheese ball from Giovanni's (who should be shot for his offensive cuisine), while doing my own work that should have been resourced away to someone else.

I see messages replying to all from the newest recruits in the department, eager to show willingness[14]. They are going to touch my work, send emails to my contacts, and mess everything up. Piss people off, piss me off. Overwhelming dread crawls up my spine and over my shoulders into my cheeks.

I don't want them touching my stuff.

Shit.

Pizza it is.

I can do a couple of hours. I email the manager in charge of OT. *Do you want me to focus on the stuff that has been left in my queue while I'm away with projects.* **Hint, hint.** I'm not responsible for this clusterfuck

I message Holl and let them know I'll be late.

At five o'clock, after saying my goodbyes to the temps, I wander down to the desks on the first floor, still a hub of activity. A constant stream of incoming calls. Ferocious typing at stiff keyboards, knowing looks over the short desk dividers, soft, hurried explanations between colleagues, tapping of spoons on the rims of mugs. Desk drawers opening and closing, perns scrawled with notes, the microwaves in the far corner whirring and chirping—even at this hour, and the air-conditioning humming, pouring pools of cold air onto certain desks and ignoring others altogether.

I don't have a jumper. I'll just have to sit in the heat.

The noise rises and falls like an accordion breathing in. Every voice rising to a crescendo, then brought back down to the rustle of clothing on skin.

I see Hannah at one of the desks by the window. "Hiya," I say as I approach. "Is this one taken?"

Hannah shakes her head, "Are you here for overtime?"

"Yeah," I say, deadpan. "The pizza was too enticing."

Hannah smiles sadly, "I just don't want to go home."

"What's up?" I ask as I log in.

---

[14] That'll get beaten out of them in a couple of months

"Just not in the mood for an argument," she says.

"You want to talk about it?" I offer as I log in.

Hannah shakes her head. "Not really," she says apologising for bringing it up. "There's just a lot going on."

"You still live with your mum and dad?" I ask.

"Stepdad," she corrects me. Her hands rest on the keyboard for a second. She takes a long drawn in breath before she starts typing again. "They're just arguing all the time. It'll start off as some disagreement over the dishes and then all of a sudden one of them's accusing the other of having an affair."

"Drama," I whisper sympathetically.

"They've both been having affairs," she informs me.

"You don't have to talk about it." I say, realising that this is now the topic of conversation for the evening and Hannah shouldn't feel pressured into talking about it so openly in the office.

"I don't understand why they don't just pack it in," Hannah sighs. "It's not like either of them has had problems with divorce in the past, but now they are putting each other through misery saying they want to make it work."

"They getting counselling or owt like that?"

Hannah scoffs. "Don't be ridiculous. Neither of them believes in talking their problems through; it's one of the few things they still have in common." Her bottom lip pushes up and squeezes the top one. I smile sympathetically. "It's not like it even gets loud or violent. They'll just disagree at the table, put down their knives and forks and leave through different doors. She watches TV in the lounge with one of those huge wine glasses that fits a bottle in it, and he'll spend all night in his office messaging his 'online friends'."

"Dare I ask?"

"Porn," Hannah nods.

I might be imagining the wrong place, I've only been over to Hannah's place once when we were getting ready for a leaving do at one of the posher bars in town, but if memory serves, it's a tiny flat down on the quay. "I didn't know your flat was big enough for an office?" Maybe I'm thinking of the wrong place.

"It's in the second bedroom."

"Oh. But then, where do you sleep?"

"In the second bedroom."

Oh. Ew!

Apparently, I don't have my poker face on today. Hannah can read exactly what I'm thinking on my face.

"Overtime = deposit," she says.

"To... buy?" I ask incredulously.

She laughs at me (rightly so), "No. The flats I've been looking at need two months' deposit and first month's rent, and the month's rent is like almost everything I take home in a month." She shakes her head and grimaces, "there's no way I can afford that while paying rent at their place."

"Withhold rent," I suggest. Hannah gives me a doubtful look, to which I shrug and continue. "Your landlord is watching porn in your bedroom, surely that's... wrong?"

Hannah laments, "I just want to be out of there, and I don't want to kick up a fuss doing it."

"No one you know looking for a flatmate? Or, anyone online?"

"There was one place online that looked nice. One flatmate. Free room, just needed to pay half the bills and share the one bedroom."

"Oh, God no!" I exclaim a little loudly.

"It was the only one I could afford," she says, feigning innocence. Eyes wide open, nodding slightly. She's teasing me and I'm relieved. "He actually put a photo up of himself."

"I'm going to need to see that," I grin.

She brings up the offer on her phone. Yep. He's exactly what I thought he'd look like. It's either a photo from the passport photo booth, or he's cropped his mugshot. He stares through the camera lens and straight into the back of my retinas. The corners of his mouth turn upward and come to a stop at his cheeks. There are, fortunately, some faces that scream DON'T TRUST ME and his is one of them.

"How's the new project going?" Hannah asks as she puts her phone face down on the desk.

"Well," I say at the end of a long and drawn-out breath.

"Oh dear," Hannah says as she begins typing again. "That bad, huh?"

"I think this is possibly the most frustrating thing I've ever worked on," I say, opening up my old queue of work and seeing how bloody long it is. Nothing has been done since I last touched it. "They haven't uploaded any of it so I have gone through I don't know how many boxes of paper. They've not completed our applications, so I'm wading through single sheets of other applications that aren't even complete or in order. The evidence is all over the place and non-existent for most things. It's incredibly frustrating. I think he's given us the wrong bank details—so that's being looked into now. Who even does their paperwork on *actual* paper?"

"Sounds rough," Hannah agrees. "Are the temps any good?"

"You remember Banter-Sean and Rachael-with-two-As?" I ask. Hannah nods and mouths 'Raachel'. "They seem alright. I spoke with Carlie, she seems nice. And then there's this fella—he didn't really say much, so I've no idea." I can see Helen making a beeline for us with her OT notebook. "I need to audit today's work, tomorrow. I'll let you know then if they're any good."

Helen pulls up at our desk, "Hi," she says. "You're on overtime, right?" We both nod. "Ok, there's a massive queue on the phones at the moment so we need everyone on them."

I smile and nod and sign into the telephony system.

This is not what I want. This is not what the OT is for. This is… bullshit. There's no sugar coating it. They (the folks that sit in corner offices) have realised that there's a problem that needs focus and attention, so they rustle up overtime—getting permission from some higher authority to grant it. Any yet. Here we are. A second problem has arisen and will be dealt with first.

None of that's Helen's fault.

At least I don't think it is.

I open up the call centre portal to see a queue of a dozen calls waiting. I open my line.

"Good afternoon, you're through to…" I am cut off.

"Are you the right person to speak to?" A clipped query comes through the headset. A man of a certain generation whose voice indicates that he has no time to be doing this.

"It depends what you're looking for, sir?" I say politely. The 'sir' can go either way. They either like that you are addressing them so politely… Or they think you are patronising them. To be honest, sometimes I am mocking them. Depending on the call, depending on the caller, either or both is possible.

"I have called in three times today, and each time I am told that I am speaking to the wrong department. I call back and I'm told the same. So, are you going to help me?"

"Did no one offer to transfer your call through?" I ask.

"Oh, they offered!" He says, somehow offended at the concept. Then repeats, "Are you going to help me?"

"I will certainly try to help, but I need to know what you are wanting?" I ask. My body has already begun to tense up.

"I. Want. My. Commission," he says, stating each word as separate entities. Christ, he's an actual financial adviser and not a client. It should surprise me that someone who does business with us is being so rude. It doesn't.

"That's fine," I chirp. "You need to speak with the commissions department."

"That's what the last person said!"

"DID THEY? I WONDER WHY THEY SAID THAT!" He raises his voice, "I don't want to be transferred or put on hold or whatever you're about to do. I want you to fix this!"

"Ok, what's the problem with your commission?" I offer. You never know, I may be able to help. Sure, the person who works in the commissions department may be able to help better; because it's their job and that's probable who the other call takes were helpfully trying to put you through to you absolute bellend.

"It hasn't been paid yet," he says. "Your company is trying to keep the money in your account past the first of the month. I know how you work."

You know that saying about revealing more and more about yourself depending on how you expect or anticipate others to behave? Well, *you're revealing a little but much about his own business practices there, mate.*

"I'm sure that's not the case," whatever piddling amount of commission you're waiting on is probably tuppence compared to what we've clawed back from you on miss-sells. "Can I have the reference number for your account with us?"

He gives it me. I look it up. The plan has started, but he's right; the commission isn't showing as having been paid yet.

"Right," I say. "So, I can see the plan here. It shows that it started last Tuesday, is that right?"

"It's on your screen!" He says, wanting a punch down the phone.

I look through the other tabs—the most recent notes, phone calls, and letters. All show at today's date. Even the email confirming that the plan started only went out today. I relay this information to the caller.

"Yes," he says indignantly. "I called in this morning and backdated the policy to a week ago. So where is my commission?"

"Your commission would go in their week's commission run…"

"No, I backdated the policy, so the commission should have been paid last week."

I'm not sure what to say to that.

I'm not sure what I can say to that.

Trying to mask my disbelief, I try to lay it out a little simpler for him. "You expected this to be paid last week, even though you only started it today?" I ask.

A loud, angry burst of air comes down the phone and I can feel the hot sickly breath in my ear. "It started last week, so it should have been paid last week."

"But you only called in to start the policy today?"

"I don't see what that's got to do with it?" Don't you?

I look up his agency. "Your commission last week was paid on Friday."

"Yes."

"You then started this plan today."

"Yes," his voice growing ever louder.

"And you want us to pay the commission last week."

"Yes! What's so hard about that?" He demands to know.

I stare at my screen, mouth gaping. I lose track of thoughts and words and my mind blanks. I don't know how to respond politely and professionally to someone so insistent, so adamant that they are in the right. I thought I had experienced the length and breadth of stupidity, and yet here we are in new depths. I have had people demand the impossible. I have had people demand the downright illegal. I have never had someone demand that I **travel through time.**

"So, when it comes to commission, it gets paid the week that the plan begins…"

"Which was last week!"

"Which was today," I say, a little slower, hoping beyond hope that the penny finally drops and knocks him out. "The plan started this morning when you called in to start it. We artificially moved the start date back at your request, because… well there are many reasons—if a product's price has gone up, or the client missed the day it was supposed to start. What I'm saying is," slow it right down. "The plan started today, it was the date that was moved back."

"No," he says defiantly. "The commission should be paid when the plan starts. It shouldn't matter when I call in to the office, the commission should have been paid already."

"You're saying that we should have paid the commission to you before the plan started? Before we knew you wanted the plan to start?" What the fuck? What the actual fuck? The arrow of time falls forward, you massive cock womble. If I had any control over the passage of time, whether to stop it, nudge it, or otherwise move it, I would not be sitting here having this ridiculous conversation with you—a man with no concept of reality who doesn't understand the basic principle of time—sure it's relative but we perceive it in one fucking direction—you gigantic fuck trumpet. If I could control time, I would be ground-hogging my weekend to become the perfect version of myself so I could track you down and jujitsu you through your French bloody windows.

"No, you're not listening! It should be paid when the plan's start date is!" He screams down the phone. "You're just trying to get out of paying commission when you should!"

I push my chair an inch or two away from my desk and lift my tense hands off the keyboard in defeat, brush my hair out of my face and drag my lower eyelids into my cheeks.

This is happening.

This is actually happening.

I have nightmares about people like this, and here he is.

I must remain polite and positive and not say can't and grrrrrruh!

And I must remember to smile because they know when we are smiling.

Hannah catches my eye and tries to smother her smile.

"Right, what I can do is raise this with our commission's team and it'll be paid to you by Friday[15]. Would you like me to log a complaint on your behalf?"

"Fine," he spits. "If that's all you can do!"

"Is there anything else I can help you with today," I smile sweetly, forcing my jaw to relax and hold back the sarcasm in my voice.

Go on, say 'yes'. I dare you. I double dare you.

You say 'yes' and I will do absolutely nothing because I have rent to pay. But mark my words, I *will* bitch about you ferociously to my friends over a box of half-price wine, a large bag of crisps and a tub of hummus.

He abruptly hangs up.

I mark myself as unavailable for calls.

"What was that?" Hannah asks with a giggle.

---

[15] Like it would have been already, you fucking…

"He's unhappy with the service we have provided," I say while typing up my notes for the call. "And the space-time continuum. He believes it's all a bit wibbly-wobbly-timey-whimey."

Hannah smiles but doesn't get the reference. Oh, to be that young.

I register the complaint with the customer relations team and attach the phone call recording. I pity the poor soul who has to process that complaint. How could they possibly assess and decide if we were in the wrong when this… gentleman… doesn't grasp the very foundation of time or reality.

I explain it in great detail, I know that team doesn't handle a lot of complaints from us and therefore don't really know our processes and systems, but there is no way that I can write this without sounding sarcastic and patronising—but really, what other way is there to tell this weird little anecdote of a poor, little man who just wanted me to travel back in time.

I might use that wording. It pretty much sums this whole thing up.

Shortly after the last person on the day shift finishes, the pizza finally arrives for those doing overtime. Helen places it at a bank of empty desks. I'm not sure how Giovanni does it. The pizza is so greasy you expect it to be soggy all the way through, and yet the snap of the base is almost brittle. Eating it sounds like a glow stick being popped.

I imagine the taste is not dissimilar.

I take two slices and sit back at my desk. The phone lines are finally closed and I can finally get on with some actual work. I start responding to emails and realise how little has been done in my absence. I had hoped that at least calls were being returned and things marked urgent would have been picked up… but no. sadly not.

Jan comes round to check on us. It's odd seeing her in the personable role; clearly none of the other managers were available at short notice.

I work my way through my own queue of work, somewhat comforted by the familiarity of it all, being able to switch off a part of my brain and just get on with it.

Lady Soto Arias

Environmental Activist
Memorial Service, Peru

Celestina Arias Hernandez had been alone for over a year now. Her daughter's room remained untouched aside from the few moments each week that she came in to dust the surfaces and clean the floor. Shock had overwhelmed her, and so, for a time, she had left her daughter's possessions as they were. Now the shock was gone, and she maintained the room to serve as a shrine, a testament to her daughter.

In those long winter evenings, when the temperatures barely rose above freezing, Celestina would wrap herself in her grandmother's quilt and sit staring at the framed photograph of her family in the living room. Her gifted daughter, her brilliant son, and her wonderful husband who she blamed for all of this.

Not that he could help it. He died before the birth of his son, and Lady could barely remember him. He had disappeared many years ago, and had never been found. Celestina had maybe encouraged her children to see their father as a saint. His life, and death, was something to aspire to. Something good and noble and honourable.

The glass of wine she held in her hand was from the same vineyard they had at their wedding. The taste was not how she remembered it. it was drier, and bitter—she remembered it being full bodied and almost thick at the wedding, but perhaps that was just a fond memory.

They had had five wonderful years together, two beautiful children. At one point Celestina could not imagine a world without him. Maybe she still can't. She would still talk to him as she walked through the garden, commenting on the changes she made to him, made sure she cooked his favourite meal on his birthday, ensured that his side of the bed had the right number of pillows.

He had always been very serious about the last part. It still made her smile to think of it.

Her daughter, Lady, had been found and that should have made all the difference. But where Celestina had hoped to find answers through the local police, she was shown only indifference.

A year had passed and she waited for her guests to arrive so they could walk the short distance to the graves, one empty—one full, and lay the flowers she had collected from her garden.

In many ways, she still felt fortunate to have all her friends and family close by. Her son would visit often, though his work often took him far away. He stayed with her often, even though he had his own life in the city. She still remembered the moment he came in to tell her his sister had died. His friend worked for the coroner, the little boy with glasses that used to hang around outside waiting for him when they were younger. He stayed with her. He must have missed so much work, but he never complained. Celestina was so grateful that it happened to have happened one weekend that he had been staying. Alone, she might not have made it.

Celestina had kept the belongings that her daughter had on her that day in a box separate to the young woman's bedroom. Somehow it felt like returning these to the bedroom would finish the journey that Lady had set out on that day. Completing it. Finishing that last day. But a month ago, Celestina had built up the courage to open the box and go through her daughter's belongings. The shirt she had been wearing, the belt, the rucksack with the half-full bottle of water, and the camera.

The camera had been found destroyed not far from the body of her murdered daughter and had been beyond repair. She hoped, beyond hope, that maybe a few of the images might still exist in the camera's memory. Maybe a photo or two had been spared the destruction. The fact that Lady had taken her digital camera that day and not her preferred 35mm gave a glimmer of hope that some images survived.

Celestina kept the camera safe, never letting it out of her sight. She even kept it in her handbag whenever she left the house. She knew the fate that befell her daughter—and many years ago, her husband—would eventually take her as well, but she would fight to the last to keep that one last part of Lady safe. Even if there was nothing on it to protect.

Down a narrow side street two towns over, she had found an IT guy who promised he would do his best to retrieve the images, if indeed any still existed in the memory of the camera. Celestina had wrestled with the idea of handing over something so precious to a perfect stranger. She couldn't be sure that he wouldn't destroy the pictures—that someone would pay him to destroy the pictures.

She eventually handed the camera over to him, a few days ago, after almost a month of silence, he had called her and let her know that he had managed to pull a couple of images, some badly corrupted, from the camera's memory. He wasn't sure what they were pictures of, but he packaged them onto a thumb drive.

As the day of the memorial drew nearer, she borrowed a projector from her schoolteacher friend and set it up in her living room, facing a stark white wall from which she had removed the paintings.

Celestina gave her son a loving embrace when he arrived with two bouquets of flowers, one for his mother and one for his sister.

Celestina took a look at his shirt and remembered it as one of the many that she had mended for him over the years. He had a terrible habit of working too hard and his shirts would pull at the seam. He always bought good quality shirts and it seemed such a waste to her that he would throw them out, so every time he visited, he would bring her a shirt or two to mend.

Although Celestina chided him for tearing yet another shirt, she nevertheless fixed them and gave them back to her son before he left.

"No shirts today?" Celestina asked.

"Here," her son said as he shook his head and offered his mother the crook in his arm. "Let's go, mama. People are waiting outside."

Celestina took his arm gladly, and arm-in-arm the two of them began their long walk up to the cemetery. Both her and Lady's friends join the procession. Women who she had known her entire life. The young girls Lady played with. Well, they weren't young girls anymore. Some were married with children of their own. Her own doctor had been a classmate of Lady's. Even some of Lady's colleagues had made the journey out to the memorial. Celestine took pride in her daughter's ease at making good friends.

Just like her father, Celestina thought glumly.

Perhaps she had done wrong telling her children stories about their father. If she had said nothing, maybe Lady would have grown up to be a doctor or a solicitor or maybe she would have been married with children.

But that was not meant to be.

They lay flowers at the grave, a blessing is received from the priest, and the journey back downhill to Celestina's house is much easier.

"I have a surprise for all of you," Celestina said with a smile as she uncovered the food that was already laid out on the table, helped by a colleague of Lady's who was always so happy to help. "I found a man who could retrieve some photos from Lady's camera. He said he wasn't able to save them all and some of them were so damaged he wasn't sure what they were of. But I would like to share them with everyone."

"Maybe we can help?" The colleague said thoughtfully. "Maybe we will recognise what is in the images. And maybe we can understand what she was doing that day?"

It hurt that Lady hadn't even told her closest friends or workmates what she was doing that day. The whole thing had been a mystery to them. Celestina had found it hard to accept at first, and thought of them all as liars, but maybe they would be able to see something in the photos that she was unable to see.

Friends and family gush over the food, how tasty it all was. Celestina had picked the best from her garden to feed them, she had even spoken with her late husband and daughter about each vegetable that was going into the dish.

Her son was in the kitchen with some of the boys he went to school with (no longer boys) and the others gathered in the living room. Each holding their glass of wine, waiting for a toast to the deceased.

"Thank you, everyone," Celestina said to those gathered. "Thank you for coming great distances to remember my daughter." She opens the laptop and turns on the projector. "I would like to share with you now some of the last photos that my daughter took."

It's not much of a toast, but Celestina isn't known for words, and her food has already said more than enough. The gathered take a small sip of their wine and look up at the photograph blown up against the wall.

The first picture to appear on the screen was that of the village, taken from high up on the mountain side on a clear, bright day.

There are photos of Maria Jesus in her garden, studying the leaves of her plants, Irené waving her son as he headed off to school, Carmen taking a plastic bag full of bread down to her sick mother-in-law for breakfast. A series of snapshots of an ordinary day. At least it was at that point, a day in which nothing special happened, until it did.

Then there were photos taken from the window of a moving taxi. A sticker with blurred notices stuck to the dashboard and another smaller sticker on the inside of the car door. Then photos taken from the back of a motorbike.

105

"Where is this?" One of Lady's colleagues asked.

"It looks like the road south, the one that ends where she was found," Celestina said as she sipped her wine. "When she was very small, we used to drive down that way to a river in the forest. Her father would throw her into the river, and I would chastise him for being so careless." She smiles at the memory.

Off the motorbike and into the woods; pixelated photographs with missing data obscuring swaths of the image. The green of the rainforest disappears and a clay-brown takes up most of the screen.

Celestina stops to study the image in more detail. "What is this, do you think?" She asked, pointing at the hazy outline of a machine.

"Equipment for mining," a colleague said, standing up to point out the finer details that could be made out. "Here," he said. "Look here, where the spout is. They put sludge into this pipe and it gets spat out here. You can just see the edge of this large mesh square. The water goes through, but anything solid will hit this and go down here," he pointed to the small box jutting out the back of the larger one. "This looks like a generator. See, you can see the smoke."

"Do you think she found an illegal mine?"

"Yes," nodded the colleague.

Celestina clicked through to the next photo. The same image, but the focus is different. She clicked again and a whole series of photographs showed Lady trying to get a good clear image from a distance.

"Yes," the colleague said. Celestina took her hand from the laptop and stood to view the image close up. "This is an illegal mine. This carpet is from underneath the mesh square, it catches all the tiny flecks of gold, it is emptied into a tub and mercury is added so the gold binds together."

"Isn't mercury dangerous?"

"Very," said another colleague leaning forward on the very edge of her chair to get a good look. "It ruins eyesight, memory, internal organs. It gets in the water as well, into the fish. It poisons everything."

"Don't they know it's dangerous?"

"They know," nodded a third. "But either its dangers have been downplayed by the foreman, or the men have families to support now. They see the potential problems as a problem for their future selves to deal with."

Celestina tapped through to the next photo. The group of men are moving the barrel filled with gold tainted water. In the distance another man is arriving.

"Probably a foreman," someone said.

"Or a transporter, he takes the gold to the city to sell," The first colleague said. "Or perhaps even someone from organised crime, there to collect 'tax'."

Celestina was glad there was someone to talk her through the photos. She would have missed half of this without them.

In the next photo, the faces have all pricked up and turned to face the camera, alerted somehow to its presence. The crack of a branch. The generator may have stopped and Lady, not aware of how quiet the area had become had made a noise too loud to be hidden under the noise of the forest.

The next photo shows the group of men with the tax collector facing her, coming towards her. Still taking photos over her shoulder of the men behind her, as she ran back through the trees.

"This is the last one," Celestina said as she tried to click past it and found nothing more. "The last photo."

The last photo was shot from the ground, pointing up at Lady's attacker. His face was not in shot, nor were his hands. Most of the image was made up of a royal blue shirt and jeans.

Celestina stood to examine the image more closely and raised her hand to touch the wall where a tear had pulled in the fabric of the shirt. Her mouth became dry, and her forehead hot. Her eyes stopped blinking. She knew this shirt. She had been the one to repair it. She drew in a ragged breath as the shock realisation finally began to sink in.

Chapter 7
Charity

I like going to art galleries. I don't get to go nearly as often as I'd like. There are four galleries within walking distance of the office, but all close by five and I can't get round a single room during a lunch hour. Same with the museums in town. The library used to stay open late on a Tuesday, but government cut-backs means that hasn't been the case for almost a decade. There are now half a dozen coffee shops on every street, interspersed with chain pubs, both open late, some even have pretty decent artwork on the wall, but it's not the same.

It's late evening and I arrive shortly after the doors were closed to day traffic. My name is on a list, my ticket is on my phone; both are checked before I am allowed in.

It is dark outside and I feel half-thief, half-liar. I'm wearing the fanciest clothes I own—I last wore them to a wedding two summers ago, but I'm surrounded by people dressed in actual fancy clothes. Materials I've not seen before, where the patterns match on the seams. Nothing off the rack—except me. tailored suits, runway dresses, branded watches and rare gemstones. I, on the other hand, have on a small gold-plated pendant my parents gave me when I graduated, and a small silver bracelet I found at a car boot sale in a bucket listed 'costume jewellery'.

I don't quite belong.

I'm undercover. Sneaked my way in through wit and guile to... do something? Hmm. Steal something, perhaps. Yes, I could be an international art thief... though if I were I would be wearing much nicer clothes. But I'm in costume, hiding in plain sight. OR, I'm down on my luck after being tricked by an associate. Betrayed by the only person I thought could trust. I'm here to restore myself. restore my wealth and... anonymity.

Ok, it only kind of works—but I feel much better about being here.

I look surreptitiously up at the CCTV, then, taking a glass of champagne from a waiter and thanking him, I glance across the gathering crowd.

Small clusters of people are commenting on the artwork, or the charity. I don't feel comfortable enough to insert myself into someone else's conversation—I'm not even sure how to do that.

Thief: Me! How do I do that?

Side step up and then make a crisp turn?

I'm not sure if I have any anecdotes suitable for the occasion. I would much rather be serving the drinks. I worked as a temp down at the racecourse on race days serving champagne to the fancy people there. Paid an absolute pittance. I did get to watch the race for free and sneak a couple of sips of the good stuff. Not, like, the really good stuff—they kept an eagle on that—but not all sparkling whites are made the same.

I don't recognise anyone yet, except for Lord Soanso, and God knows I'm not going over there. He stands, hands clasped and tucked behind his back, leaning forward a little as though at any moment he could choose to topple over and crush the short woman standing next to him. In his cluster, there is a young woman wearing a party dress that I'm fairly sure was on a runway not too long ago; parts of the delicate bodice look to have been hand stitched[16].

I recognise the young woman from a photo that is plastered across a high street clothes shop—though I couldn't tell you which one; I don't go shopping for clothes all that often. She stands at one edge of the photo facing out, and then her blonde hair trails away behind her, over the doorway of the shop.

It's killing me that I can't remember the name of the place.

It's clear though, in this context and by her teeth, that she is closely related to Soanso. I imagine they guffaw in the same way.

I don't belong here.

But, here I am. A paying guest at a charity cocktail event in an art gallery.

I wish he'd mentioned that it was a paying event. Soanso's email was an invite and said nothing about expense. Half my month's rent. I was livid. And I doubt we get this back on expenses.

It's a good charity. It's a good charity. It's a nice event.

Charity work, night out, and gallery visits wrapped up into one. Get your money back on high end drinks.

---

[16] I presume. I have no idea. I've never watched a fashion show before. Maybe I should. I like clothes. I could design and make them. I'll put a pin in that for now.

It is at this point I see people handing money over at the bar.

I'm going to have to make some of that money back on champagne, vol-au-vents and crime.

Before I'm able to start making my way around the exhibits, Lord Soanso steps up onto a small raised platform at one end of the grand hall. Following in the footsteps of his ancestors who did the same thing while giving out verdicts and declarations.

"Thank you all for joining us today amongst this fine art to donate to a worthy cause," he says in his slow, considered manner. "As you all know, I am not an artistic fellow. No artistic bone in this body." Scattered, polite laughter at his self-depreciation. His own belly shakes as he leans back from the microphone.

"But I can appreciate the glorious work of these fine artists who spend their lives dedicated to a calling that is beyond most of us." He shakes his head and his wisps of hair stay shockingly still. "Well, at least some of it. Some of it is bloody awful," he guffaws, pointing out the modern sculpture exhibition. "I am fortunate enough to be accompanied this evening by my goddaughter, Pru," he wafts an arm in her general direction.

"Pru has been kind enough to take time out of her day-job running a rather successful fashion em-pire, an em-pire that believes in treating all its workers with the very highest of dignities, focusing on their safety and wellbeing—I can say it, Pru. It's all true. She runs this magnificent business—It's a shame to call it a 'business' really, it does so much good for the community and the, the, the people that are touched by the kind and thoughtful way that she attends to, er, to things. She has taken time away from that, taken time out of her busy schedule to organise this event. So, thank you, Pru," he starts off a round of applause.

"We have been fortunate enough to be joined by charitable people from all over the world tonight. People with a deep and abiding interest in changing the world. Remaking it in our image, to work in a way that is sustainable and improved for all men," he moves to the side of the stage to pick up another glass of champagne. "These donations will be put to work for Saint Peter's Children's Charitable Hospital Fund, ensuring comfort in times of need. So, I'd like to thank all of you, from the bottom of my heart. Thank you for coming to this event and being so generous," He nods and drinks as people begin to applaud. "Enjoy the art!"

He stumbles off the plinth, almost taking a nosedive into a waitress, but is caught and greeted by the charity workers all thanking him for arranging such an event. He takes their thanks and shuffles through them back to his own party; unwilling to get bogged down in chat.

"Pasha!" He bellows, welcoming his friend above the humdrum of the dissipating crowd wandering off to view the art. "Pasha, my friend, I'm so glad you could make it!"

Standing beside one of the charity's event boards, Darren-fucking-Neal, is hovering. Jittering back and forth over a small space as he builds up the nerve (or courage) to infiltrate Lord Soanso's group. He looks to be vibrating, unable to remain in one space long enough to make a decision to strike. It's kind of fascinating to watch. At first glance, he looks like a cheetah ready to pounce on some unexpecting prey. But, on further inspection, he looks like a silly lost boy who is failing to introduce himself to a new teacher after being caught doing something naughty.

Pru, the goddaughter, has split off from the herd and is graciously bending her head to speak with one of the head honchos from the charity. The man she came with splits off from the group and goes off to explore the artwork. The others stay closely knit discussing something at a surprisingly low volume.

Darren-fucking-Neal, finding his in, goes off to stalk the man, presumable the weakest in the herd.

He should have waited a moment though. Lord Soanso has a target in sight and is making a beeline across the hall. I move slightly so I can see past a statue in a hazmat suit and see who he is aiming for.

Hannah.

He approaches her while picking up a second glass, and hands it to her. The hall is almost empty now, apart from his circle of friends and the charity folk. There are maybe half a dozen people like Hannah and me left in the hall and none of them seem interested in what the old man is doing.

Lord Soanso places his open hand on Hannah's back as he gently pushes her towards a painting he is pointing at with the hand holding his glass. I recoil at the hand, feeling the same hot, claggy hand on my own back. I place the glass I'm holding on to the nearest surface—hoping that it isn't a piece of art, though not caring enough to check—and march over to them.

"Hannah," I call out in a hushed tone, increasingly aware of how quiet it is on this side of the gallery "Sorry I'm late. Thanks for waiting." She doesn't say anything and I continue with my charade only half caring if it is fooling anyone.

"I got a message from the others; they are waiting for us up on the next floor." I take her hand and pull her away.

"Thank you," Hannah whispers, shrinking inside herself as we reach the top of the stairs. She looks even younger than usual, pulling her dress at the sleeves and up at the breast. I let her rearrange herself for a moment. No one's in the staircase, the nearest people I can see are in the renaissance room.

"Let's go find the others," I say, looking down at my phone. Megan has just posted a picture next to some minimalist artwork. I show it to Hannah. "Modern art?" I ask. She smiles and nods cautiously. We find the others in the centre of a dark room looking at some Rothko. Ben has been smuggled in, but not in a dress (we can't have everything).

I like the Rothko room. Dark and hidden. The others have been in here a while and are ready to move on.

"I'll catch up," I say.

There is no glare in this room. No competing lights. I wonder what the colours look like under daylight? It's weird to think that a painting could belong in the dark, but here we are.

I step out of the room and take in the small cards of information beside each artwork before looking up at them.

Bold black lines and blotches of deep red—like Kandinsky painting a minimalist cherry tree.

I look back at the info tab. "Challenges of Solitude". I look back at the painting trying to match this title with the shape of the work.

Nope, still cherries. Two cherries.

Are cherries particularly lonely? They usually come in pairs or bunches. Is this what the artist is saying? The cherry is trying to be alone but can't because it has siblings?

I'm reading too much into this—they probably aren't cherries.

I take a few steps at a jaunty angle to the next painting. A vertical line of shapes. Circle on top of circle on top of oblong. I take immediate offence to the oblong. It is out of place, and while the top circle is a light blue swirling round like Venus, and the central one is this dark red with wooden knots like Jupiter, the oblong is a stamp of a single colour. The artist clearly ran out of planets they liked, or maybe space, or time before a commission was expected and potato printed the bottom oblong beneath the other two carefully constructed shapes.

I have every intention of hating the next painting. They have hung it pride-of-place in the centre of this wall. During the day, it will be lit up by all the natural light from windows above and across the hall, but at this time of night it is lit by a single, strong white light suspended ten feet away.

It is a white canvas. If I were to stretch my arms out to the sides, I wouldn't be able to reach the edges. The bottom lip is barely 6 inches off the floor and it stretches all the way to the ceiling. Standing in front of it I can feel the weight of it lording over me, ready to dislodge and crush me.

I take a step back.

It's not 'pure' white (whatever that is), in the broad brushstrokes, under a layer of white, a washed-out peach stroke lies trapped. It's not the only colour that's trapped. As I pace the length of the canvas inspecting it closer, I find every colour hidden beneath the white—struggling to be seen.

The longer I look, the more colours I can see and as I step back further, I start to see all the colours swim to the surface. The white angers me. The way it restrains the other colours, overpowers everything else, and from a distance is all I can see until I get closer, work harder, and can finally see what makes the painting interesting.

In spite of myself, I really like this painting. But my appreciation is hampered by my spidey-sense ticking the back of my neck. Someone is approaching.

"Hello," he says. The fair-haired gentleman that was standing next to Soanso when I entered, the one I assume is here with the goddaughter. He stands beside me, a little too closely, and looks at the painting with me. For some reason, I now find it impossible to leave this white painting.

Damn you, social convention!

Why do I care about offending this guy? Why is it even me offending him? It's an art gallery, so it is completely natural for me to get up and move around the artwork.

"Let me guess." Oh, God, he's talking! He turns to face me. His head cocked to one side, a wide, fixed smile, attempting charm but dripping with this uncomfortable unctuous grease. "You don't know art, but you know what you like?"

"I have a degree in Art History," I say, without turning from the canvas. I'm going to have to bluff this out with half-read articles and YouTube videos that I play in the background of my boredom.

That isn't too different from my actual university experience... hmm.

I catch him smiling wickedly out of the corner of my eye. "What can you tell me about this painting?"

Like every boy at every gig I have ever been to, he's demanding proof: Have you ever listened to them before? Can you name five albums? Who was the original drummer? Who co-wrote their third most famous single? What is the name of the tour that your t-shirt comes from? Were you even a fan before they came to this city? He's testing me in what will become a never-ending slew of questions.

"The white is confronting and places itself between the true art and the viewer, refusing to let the art be seen, or the viewer to see it," I say, taking a sip of my bubbly. "It's a portrait of you." I tell him.

Fucking social mores, I leave. Partly because I don't want to get trapped in a conversation, and partly because this is my fourth glass of the evening and I need a piss.

I walk past my friends and the refreshments and down a shallow corridor to the toilets.

I was enjoying the artwork, that's it. I was just enjoying some time by myself to look at pretty colours. And he might not have been a total dickweasel, but... no... no. I didn't want to talk to him. I don't have to talk to people I don't like. *You weren't rude, you walked away.* Stop nit-picking at everything.

As I turn into the toilets, I am interrupted by a woman standing with one leg up on the sinks, tweezers in hand. Carol. With no knickers.

Don't look down. Don't look down. Don't look down.

Bollocks.

My mouth drops open in surprise and I forget to breathe in. I didn't expect to see a bottomless woman, clam-spreading at the sinks, taming her intimate region. But it's Carol, and it's my fault; I should have expected this.

I hesitate hovering on the spot in two minds. Left into a stall or right into the gallery and find another bathroom.

I really do need the toilet and I'm on the verge of wetting myself.

This is getting awkward. Carol's not moving. She's just standing there holding the tweezers. Then I realise I haven't moved either. We're in a weird standoff. She's completely expressionless. Not embarrassed to be caught or...

Move.

I go into the stall.

Any other woman—oh who am I kidding? Any other woman wouldn't be standing bold as brass, flaps out in a public bathroom plucking her bloody... I mean... I... I... I have nothing for this. Literally nothing. It's beyond the weirdest thing I have experienced. I have no idea how to even... **over the sinks?** Who does that? Who actually does that?

I need to start peeing. All of a sudden, I am bladder shy. Pee, damn it!

I'm going to have to wash my hands! FFS. Do I have any hand sanitiser? I know I had some at my cousin's wedding, but did I leave it in the bag, or did I tip the whole thing out? I can't go rustling around in my bag, she'll hear. Why should I care if she hears?

Oh, for everything holy, please piss. I can hear the gentle tap of metal on metal—she's tweezing again.

There are going to be long, scraggly hairs left on the side. She's not going to clean up after herself.

I feel some relief as my bladder unclenches and I begin to pee.

Why did she look at me? Why didn't she just pull up her underwear, smooth out her dress and walk away?

Deep breath. Not too loud.

Thank, fuck. I do have sanitiser. I make sure I'm squeezing the bottle all over my hands as I leave. How I can be more concerned over Carol's opinion of me not washing my hands at the sink, than my opinion of her at the moment, probably says more about me than anything else would.

I find Megan, Hannah and Ben huddling round the buffet, trying to piece together a meal.

"Ben's going to dash to the Vietnamese street food place down the street if you're interested?"

I pick up a cracker with a small dollop of grey stuff on it, "I spent the last of my money donating to get into this place."

"On me?" Hannah offers.

I shake my head. Ben skips off out of the room. "I'm not sure I could eat that much at the moment. Remind me to tell you about my trip to the bathroom when you're not eating."

"Ew?"

"Whatever you are thinking... it is worse than that. Worse than anything. I'm never going to be able to look at Carol in the same way again."

Megan crumples her face, but shakes her head. "Did you go onto the hub today?" She asks as we step away from the bite-sized disappointments.

"No, why?" I ask.

"You're going to love it," Megan grins as she stirs the pot.

"What am I going to love?" I'm in an odd mood already and whatever has been put up on the portal is going to make me blow, I know it.

"They are just giving us some advice," she tells me. I'm going to have to drag this out of her.

"Advice on what?" I ask, suspicion heightened.

"Cost of living," she says, grimacing.

"Fuck off," I say.

"Just some friendly, corporate advice."

"You got the app on your phone?" I ask, holding my hand out. I know she has the app. She downloads everything they tell us to. She hands me her phone, open at the article. I scan over it. quickly at first, but the more enraged I am at it, the slower I become. "Are you kidding me?" The words escape my mouth before I realise I've said them. "Are you fucking kidding me?"

"Not too loud," Megan warns, checking round the room to make sure I haven't disturbed anyone.

I scoff. It's ridiculous. The whole fucking night is ridiculous. But this? This takes the biscuit.

I scroll back to the top of the page because I want to get this straight. You (my employer) are giving me (your employee) advice on money matters during a time of unprecedented financial burden. You (my employer) within the fecking financial industry, that last year—a good year—gave me a raise of 0.75% at a time when inflation was topping 2% and the company was making millions in profit, and this year with inflation topping out at nearly 10% and probably won't even bother to give me a raise even though you continue to make millions in profits—you are seriously going to give me advise on how to tighten my belt LITERALLY TIGHTEN MY BELT—with cheap recipes and A LIST OF LOCAL FOOD BANKS.

You—**my employer**—who made 100s of millions of pounds net profit year after year—probably not even paying your fucking taxes—have the audacity to turn around and give me tips on how to whittle away excesses like 'a weekly chippy' and turning the lights off when I have LED lights and gas and leckie bills

116

4 times higher than last year. You have the audacity to say we're all in it together? Even those earning[17] six figures are feeling the stretch to their budget.

Fuck off.

Then fuck off a bit further.

Keeeeep fucking off.

If you can't do a household budget on six figures, I don't feel bad for you. It explains the state of our sector that people supposedly so good with money can't even balance it out and live within their means like the rest of us are supposed to. Take the kids out of public school for a year. Don't go skiing. This tone-deaf article does not make me feel bad for you. It doesn't make me feel sorry for you, or that you are one of us; it makes me angry. Really fucking angry.

It angers me that you put in your Tory donations and laud them whenever something's passed in your favour that fucks over your employees. It angers me that you have right wing speakers at your big events that smack you on the back at how well you are doing when you literally acknowledge that you no longer pay us enough to buy food. That your trickle-down trickles up. I'm living with less money in my pocket than last year. I have bills and rent that have gone up.

I think twice about everything I spend, so much so that the first time I go out in ages, I am fucked over by a charity that isn't even offering food. The pathetic yearly increases I have to look forward to in my salary for all the shit and offensive things I have to take on a daily basis does not nearly match up to it.

I'm not even in a position that's particularly important. I understand that you could hire someone to replace me in a second—not that you would ever actually hire enough people to do the work. You keep telling me how replaceable I am.

There are nurses and teachers going to foodbanks. There are old people taking buses to keep warm. I am angry and I am done with this charade of an event. I am going home. Home to my shitty, rented flat that's covered in mould, where I pay the mortgage for my landlord while he ignores my emails on the water damage in the kitchen. I'm going home on a bus filled with old people in their thickest winter coats.

I'm going home to where I can scream into the void and no one will care because it will blend in with all the other screams. I am going home to seethe in peace.

---

[17] Why are they 'earning' whilst we are 'being paid'—I am genuinely curious

Chapter 8
Legal

Monday comes around far too quickly again. The weekend disappeared in a bundle of bedsheets as I had neither the will nor inclination to get out. Instead, I watched some 90s sitcoms to see if they lived up to my memory of them. Most didn't. The laugh-track in of itself was enough to annoy me, and I had forgotten how many of the jokes punched down. But it's Monday again, and I rose with the crows and met Frances at the front door as she punched in the alarm code. I am back in the office; trapped between four glass walls, circling around myself and wondering if I will ever be allowed back out.

"I'm off on my holibags next week," Frances grins as she dances on the spot, unable to contain her excitement.

"Where are you going?" I ask.

"Tenerife!" She replies. "I've got a full package deal. Two weeks by a pool, open bar. I cannot wait!" She squeals as she opens the inner doors. "It's been so long since I was last on holiday! Our Jackson was only seven, he's almost fifteen now." The door is stuck. Frances pushes her shoulder against it until it finally budges. "Last time, I had to drag him away from the pool. This time I'll be dragging him away from the bar!"

I chuckle. I've seen a picture of her son. He may be fourteen but he looks twelve. There's no way in hell he's going to get served at a bar.

"Here's the key for the main door," Frances says. "That's your copy for now. I've got a printout of the instructions for the alarm for you." She strides over to the reception desk in the centre of the atrium and unlocks the top drawer. A single piece of paper with instructions, photos and screenshots of how to work the alarm. "You'll not be locking up, will you?"

"I hope not," I say, shaking my head.

"Right," Frances says, taking her seat at reception and beaming in anticipation of her holidays. "I won't keep you. I've got to put up this display on the community board of the charity event you all went to."

My heart sinks at the idea of being caught in one of the photos. I always look terrible. Half-drowned and third-day constipated, unable to remember how to smile. And I'm wearing a dress. And it's tight and I hate to think what I actually look like in it. Wearing it, I couldn't care less what I look like, but when evidence is not only captured but displayed for the office to see. I wonder if I can pre-approve the photos that go on the wall, remove and destroy any of me before they are seen.

"You have a lovely time while I am away," Frances says before I am able to voice my protest.

"You have a lovely time on your holidays!" I say and head towards the stairs. I'll come by later and rip off any photos I disapprove of.

I know I won't. Just, let me have this. Let me have this belief that I would actually destroy a charity event's celebration on the community board. I won't. I know I won't. You know I won't. Just let me dream I would stick up for myself in this minor way.

I could just avoid it all together and not even look at it. But the photos would be there. On the wall. For everyone to see.

There are already three emails in my inbox from Darren-fucking-Neal that were sent in the very early hours with subject lines that read: *we need to talk* and *call me as soon as your* [sic] *in.* He does seem to be under the impression that I don't sleep at all, and I live solely to be at his beck and call.

Shortly before nine, once all the temps are in and settled with their work for the day, I pop on my headset and call him.

"Hi Darren…" he cuts me off.

"Did you get my email?"

No. I just randomly thought I'd call you first thing on a Monday morning.

"I'm just going through my emails now," I say.

"Ivan is not happy. Not happy at all!" He over-emphasises his consonants until they are crisp with a fine point that sticks in my ears.

What possible reason could Ivan have… "How come?" I ask.

"He thinks we are investigating him! He thinks we think he's dodgy."

He is proper dodgy.

Bite that tongue.

My heart sinks, this cannot be happening. There is no way that Ivan can know that his company is being investigated. There is no way that someone here has leaked it to him…

I am saved by the bell.

More specifically, the fire alarm.

I, like everyone else that is currently sitting in the office, perch up to look over the computers and look around to see if anyone is leaving. They usually do their fire alarm check on a Thursday, but occasionally the alarm goes off for no reason and shuts down like a moment late. I'm not sure whether this is one of those days. I'm not willing to be the first to get up—it would be too embarrassing to get up, half leave and then the alarm shuts off and I have to make my way back to my seat. I'd rather burn.

People are slowly, begrudgingly, getting up from their seats, and I, like them, grab my bag before heading out. My life is in that bag, there is no way I'm risking leaving it in an open office that is only potentially on fire. Somebody might hold back and rifle through it. That happened to one of my old primary school teachers.

The temps are all on high alert, meerkating in their seats waiting to see what to do. I wave my hand to usher them out of the room.

"Sorry, Darren," I say above the sound of the alarm. "Fire alarm's going off and we have to evacuate."

Darren, unimpressed, sighs and demands I call him back "the moment you get back inside."

"Yes, I will," I promise.

I walk down the winding back staircase, now filled with people from all floors shuffling down to the lower ground level to exit out onto the street round the back of the office. Looking over the handrail at the centre, I can see down a clear five stories of people marching round in circles, descending down into the bowels of the office building.

Actually, I'm pissed off. Pissed off with Darren Neal. That sigh at the end of the call. That sigh that says *you're using this fire alarm as an excuse to get out of this conversation*. That lack of understanding that actually this is an important thing to do—to leave the building. Sure, I can joke about being too embarrassed to leave first and would rather burn, but how fucking dare he assume that I should put myself in danger to take his fucking call.

When Dante crossed the eighth circle of hell—the one filled with panderers, hypocrites, falsifiers and fraudulent counsellors, he forgot to mention by name financial advisers and, by extension, anyone who works on commission.

While not necessarily fraudulent in nature (through my own experience tells me it's not an insignificant number that are), it is the way they manage to weasel into the small nooks of legal loopholes, sticking their heads through red tape nooses (niece?). A modern Dante would have Virgil pointing out the red tape that was stretched and warped beyond recognition.

Those that chase commission into dark alleys and force you to shield them from any potential dangers (both real and legal) should be forced to spend their waking eternity wandering through the deep caverns and concentric ditches of their circle, contributing nothing and demanding the impossible, dragging behind them a large anvil monogrammed with the initials *USP*.

If you want me to go above and beyond, share with me your commission.

I finally reach the bottom of the stairs and we spill out of the fire doors onto the street.

"Did someone set fire to the place?" I ask as I wander over to my old team on the corner of the street a block down from the office. Jan scowls at me disapprovingly.

Hannah shakes her head. "Jack and Sal had their high-vis on the backs of their chairs."

Ah, so the emergency team knew about it. They are pretty bad at hiding these planned events, and I'm not sure if I would ever trust them in a surprise emergency.

Actually, that's not fair. Jack was pretty good that time John Parker had a heart attack. Or a stroke. I'm not sure we ever did get to the bottom of that.

The wind whips through the tall buildings and freezes our cores. While many brought out their bags, few picked up their coats or cardigans, and so we stand freezing. We naturally begin to huddle around Hannah. The tips of her fingers go blue and purple when she gets cold—it's scary and I don't like it. So we gather around her like an awkward mass of penguins. The temps accidentally join in. I realise I should probably count them and make sure they are here in case someone asks, or we need to send someone back into the building.

Fortunately, they have all satisfactorily exited the building.

Nobody asks—but I did my bit.

I introduce everyone to everyone. Ben and Megan recognise Sean and Rachel and begin to chat. I stand in the cold with my eyes closed listening to the sound of the alarm in the distance.

The alarm goes silent, and the front doors are reopened for us all to get back into the building by swiping through the security gates.

It always takes considerably longer to get back into the building. As well as the people who left the building, there are also those on the half nine tile half five shift that are trying to get into the building. I am stuck in a slow-moving body of people and it is going to take a good long while to get back into the office.

The IT guys are in no rush. They are standing a further block away, all murmuring away about perceived evils of the world with lit cigarettes jutting out their mouth.

It is a long, slow haul back up to my desk, though the last set of stairs is almost empty as I skip up them.

I can hear a phone ringing. How is anyone calling in? The phone lines close when we leave the building and the calls are diverted to another office, so how the hell is one of the phones on this floor ringing…

I should have known.

It's my phone.

An internal call from Darren-fucking-Neal that bypasses the closed external line.

I let it ring. I'm in no rush to speak with him again. There are several hundred people trying to log back on at the moment and that is going to overload the system. The usually slow set up times double or triple in these situations.

I take a moment to adjust my chair; raising the seat and realigning the back support.

The phone keeps ringing.

I open up the settings on my screen as the small circle of doom rotates in the centre. Dimming and tinting. Making the screen appear a little warmer with a slight orange undertone to the white. A little more soothing on the eyes.

The phone keeps ringing.

I pick up my headset and set us over my ears, the microphone at my mouth. I take a sip of water and clear my throat.

"Good morning…"

"It's me again," says Darren. "I thought you said you would call me back as soon as you got back to your seat."

122

"I've just got back. You were already calling," I say.

"That's ridiculous! How long does it take to do a fire drill?"

"We have to go back single-file through security. And there are a fair few hundred people. Then the lifts are full and the stairs are busy…"

He cuts me off. "I can't even tell if you're being serious right now?"

I don't care if he believes me. "I am being serious. I just got back to my chair and the phone was ringing. I am trying to log back into the system."

"Well, are you going to help?" He demands.

"You're going to have to give me a minute to get my computer reconnected to the network. We all had to sign out before we left the building. So, everyone is logging back in now. It might take some time."

And this, matey, is why when I say I will call you back; *I* will call you back.

He huffs and puffs down the phone, even though he knows it will speed up nothing.

I really wish I could slap him down the phone—it would do so much to make me feel better about… life.

In order to do nothing more than shut him up, I ask "What is it you want to know?"

"Ivan has been told that we are investigating him," he says and my heart stops.

"He's 'been told'?" I ask, wanting to clarify this before going any further.

"So, are we?" Darren keeps going. "Is there an investigation into his business with us?" He demands an answer.

The whole of my core freezes tight and for the briefest of moments, I forget to breathe.

"What do you mean he's 'been told'?" I ask again.

"I have just had a call with him, and he is furious that we are suspicious, or whatever, of his account," Darren's voice gets stronger and louder the longer he talks. "He knows that Legal or somebody is investigating him, and I need to get in front of this before it spirals out of control."

"Spirals?" I repeat. Come on, brain. You need to snap out and catch up. Because this—this whole conversation—cannot be happening right now. This whole phone call is not real. There is no way that Darren-fucking-Neal is this stupid. So, I need you to snap out of it and give him what for.

"You know that I can't tell you if there's an investigation, right?"

"No, you need to tell me…" he goes on, and I begin to speak over the top of him.

"No, no. No, listen," my feathers ruffled as he bleats on about how unprofessional it is to investigate his client without telling him "You, by asking me for this information, are committing a crime." I tell him, and for a moment he hesitates. I can hear an awful squeak in my pitch as I continue. "If I were to answer you, I would be committing a crime." Keep going. "I cannot answer that question. And you cannot ask it. Do you understand?"

"You're being a bit unreasonable!" He replies, stubbornly.

"Oh, no," I start. "See, you are asking for confidential information about the possibility of a potential crime and you have told me that someone at this company has told someone at a company that may or may not be being investigated that they could be being investigated." Verbal gymnastics aside, I think I expressed that well. "You see, if there were an investigation, and someone here told someone there about it, they would be committing a crime."

"Look," he spits. "I just need to know if this is happening. You need to just tell me."

This call isn't recorded. Internal calls aren't. Did he do that on purpose? Is this why he called me instead of waiting? I honestly can't tell at this point if he is an idiot or somewhat clever.

"I can't tell you if there is or isn't an investigation."

"You're being ridiculous," he says. "We both work for the same company."

"Ok," I say. "Alright, put the information you want to know in writing and email it to me. CC in your manager and mine. And while you're at it, CC in someone from legal, because they will want to speak with you about one or two things when they see your request."

They'll want to know how the fuck you work for this company WHEN ARE YOU A COMPLETE AN UTTER MORON WHO IS A FUCKING LIABILITY.

Silence. He knows. At this point, his silence tells me that he knows. He knows he isn't allowed to ask. He knows that I can't tell him. He knows he can't tell Ivan.

"One last thing," I say, striking him with a hot iron[18], "If you have been made aware by a client or adviser that they have been informed by someone in this office that they are under suspicion of… anything —you should be making Legal aware. Because, if someone in this office has told a client or adviser that they

---

[18] That's the saying, right?

have been reported or are being investigated, then that person in this office has committed a crime."

Darren's silence is now deafening. I can hear both a pin drop and the penny drop, along with Darren's worried and hitched breath.

"You have to report that your client believes he is under investigation by Legal to Legal, because if you don't, you are committing a crime. And as we have had this conversation—I have to report this to Legal, or I am committing a crime." I realise my voice has lowered since the high-pitched frenzy at the beginning of the call, and I now have it almost entirely under my control. "If you've not got any other crimes, you want me to participate in today, I need to send an email."

I hang up on him. I can feel my heartbeat thud in my ears. My skin is buzzing, and my thoughts are stuffed with an excitable static.

I realise that the temps are all back in the office nervously peeking over their computer screens at me. Bless them, out of everyone in this office, I suspect them the least. They don't know what they are doing, and don't have phone access.

My home screen appears, finally alive after so many people tried to log in at the same time, and the hub pops up in front of everything with a new article highlighted on its first page.

Are you struggling with negative thoughts?

Struggling? Not right now, sweetheart. Right now, I'm not struggling; I am embracing all my negative thoughts. I am letting the little devils run riot. And you know what? After taking Darren-fucking-Neal down a peg or two about his grandiose self-importance in this company, and knowing that Ivan's company is all worried about the possibility of us investigating them for their clearly dodgy practices after all the shit that I've dealt with from them over the last month or so, all my little devil thoughts are having a great time. They deserve it. I'm throwing them a party.

I feel great.

Today is going to be a great day.

Chrissie

The two blues met at a perfectly still horizon. The cloudless sky and the waveless ocean. A calm beauty that dispelled all the horrors of the world and allowed Chrissie one moment for escape.

She leant over the railing, folding herself almost in half, her long auburn hair reaching towards the water. She hoped to see a sea turtle—her favourite animal. She wore a small silver bracelet with a hanging turtle charm that her brother had bought her from a pawn shop many years ago for her birthday. It stood out from the jewellery worn by others on the boat. It couldn't be cleaned to shine, but she loved it nonetheless.

In her room growing up, she had posters of sea life covering her walls. They reached the ceiling and covered the mould at the top of her wall where the rainwater came in. Framed in the centre of the wall—as far away from the mould at the top and the rats at the bottom, hung an A4 poster of a sea turtle. She loved to imagine swimming beside it, though she had never actually seen the sea and her only experience of swimming was in a community pool that would open for a few weeks each summer.

When she was around eight, on a walk around the neighbourhood during one of her mother's intensive diet and exercise periods, Chrissie had seen a small porcelain turtle in the yard sale of an elderly neighbour who had passed away. She had run home to her father to beg him for the money while her mother waited and protected the precious trinket from other would-be buyers, fighting off one woman who wanted it for her collection of model animals. The porcelain turtle was both her birthday and Christmas present that year and she loved it. It resided, pride of place, on her bedside table next to a sea-themed lamp from a previous birthday.

The porcelain figure was still there, back in her bedroom, with all the other tchotchke she had picked up.

Chrissie was determined to see at least one sea turtle in the wild, to see it swim by coral or crawl up onto the beach. As a child, she had poured over every book about turtles and the sea left in the town library. When that library was closed for lack of funds, she snuck in with her brother to claim those books for herself. Her mother had been appalled by the theft. Her father said nothing. She always adored his silent approval.

There were fish beneath the boat, most of which she could name, but no turtles. The other day when they had been a little further out, she had seen reef sharks beneath the boat, but still, no turtles.

"Hey," John calls over. Chrissie stood and rested her hands on the rail as he came over to her, his hands stuffed into his board short pockets. Although wearing loose and open clothes, his body is tense and knotted. He needs this to go well.

A few nights ago, he had broken down in front of her. He hadn't explained anything in detail, he was too drunk to string a sentence together, and Chrissie was unclear if he remembered telling her about how much money was in this boat and how he needed to get back on top or back on track or something. She didn't know John from Adam and the only thing she was sure of, was that he was in trouble and needed to flash some cash to get out of a hole he had dug himself.

He didn't know his guests. They weren't his friends. The day before, he had had trouble remembering their names.

Chrissie smiled at John, having convinced herself that her words would be no good. John stood beside her, his forearms on the rail.

"How are you doing?" John asked.

"Good," she replied. "How are you today?"

"Just ran a meeting while rocking a hangover," he admitted, staring out across the sea and sighing.

"Is there anything I can do?" Chrissie asked, but John was already lost in thought, muttering under his breath.

"I just need to get in with one of these guys," he said to himself. "Just one of them." He dragged a deep breath up through his nostrils and turned to rest his back on the railing. "The hot tub has been turned on, and the guys have gone to get changed. If we can just lighten the mood a little, make them happy, I know I can get them on board." He tucked his chin into his chest. "Can you just go up and make sure everything is ready?"

"Sure," Chrissie smiled and nodded.

She took the nearest flight of stairs up two floors. She had only been on the boat three days, but knew the whole thing pretty well. The steps were steep and almost ladder-like at this point, and it felt as though she were climbing a mountain rather than a yacht. She felt the warmth and bustle of the kitchen preparing the evening meal as she climbed past them.

Chrissie had never eaten so well. The portions were tiny, but the meals themselves were micro-explosions in her mouth. One of the guests had commented on the amount that she was eating. She wanted to make a comment comparing the guest's weight to a beached whale but knew that John would not like that. She began picking at the food during meals, and would then visit the kitchen later under the pretence of powdering her nose and would nibble at the leftovers.

On the upper deck there was a sweeping bar and lounge area. The pianist, Luca, absentmindedly twiddled his fingers over the keys. With only him, the barman and Chrissie in the open room—there was no one to impress, but he was paid to keep the music going at certain times throughout the day without any sheet music, and so, when there were no guests around, he would play over the same tunes he had played in his youth. He even composed a few ditties when no one was listening.

As a younger man, searching for any opportunity to play in public, he had worked on cruise ships. Now, a few years further into his career, he played on a slightly more expensive boat, with a more refined invitation-only crowd.

The trouble was, he wasn't a fan of the motion of the ocean, or indeed the small waves that carried the mega-yacht. It made him sick. This would be his last venture off-land. Though he had said that several times before.

Chrissie waved at Luca and sat herself down at the bar in view of the hot tub, ready for the men to appear. Fermin, the barman, placed a drink for her on the bar. He noticed that she only drank alcohol when with guests, and preferred some fruit juice dressed up as a cocktail between times.

"Eskerrik asko!" She said, carefully pronouncing each part as rehearsed.

Fermin chuckled to himself. He should have let her continue practising her Spanish on him. "You are improving," he said. She pulled a face. "Ez horrigatik."

Amber, a Russian woman with bleached blonde hair and long limbs that reached well beyond the footrest of the bar stools, joined Chrissie at the bar. She had on a long, opaque, silk kaftan. She leant over the bar and picked a bottle of white wine out of an ice bucket. Fermin exclaimed but said nothing.

"How are you, Chrissie?" Amber asked, pouring a tall glass of wine from the bottle before returning the bottle to the ice.

"Khorosho, spasiba," Chriss replied.

"Did you find your turtles today?" Amber asked, looking out towards the hot tub, ignoring the Russian.

"Not today," Chrissie said a little sadly. "But the water is very clear, so maybe tomorrow."

Amber sipped her wine, then leant backwards and draped her arms dramatically over the bar. When she sat back up, she turned to Chrissie and said, "I need a photo for my feed today. Will you take it for me?" Amber handed Chrissie her phone. Fermin grinned, but said nothing.

"Of course," said Chrissie, only too happy to oblige.

Amber strode across to the hot tub, lifting the kaftan off above her head and placing it over the back of a deck chair. She kicked off her heels and then stepped backwards into the tub. "Hold the phone portrait. Put me in the bottom, left corner. I want people to see me, and see what I am seeing."

It takes a few attempts to get a photo that Amber is content with, one without an unpleasant cloud in the sky, or a ghastly wave in the water. One with the sun low enough to cast a glow throughout the rest of the picture, but without throwing flares across the image. "I can work with this one," she said, reclaiming her phone and opening up the editing suite. "Do you need a photo?"

Chrissie shook her head.

"Have you thought about what you will do after this is gone?" Amber asked, waving her arms to imply everything around them.

"I'll go home, I guess."

"That is too defeatist," Amber said, lying back on one of the deckchairs while she played about with the image and taking a short sip of wine. "Even if he leaves me on a runway in a distant and hostile land, I will have a bag full of gold and diamonds." She never has anything nice to say about the man she came with. The one time Chrissie spoke with Ivan, she didn't like him either.

"He won't care, because they are small and uninteresting pieces. He can take all the cash off me. He can cut up my credit cards. But I will have my bag,"

Amber finished editing her photo and posted it. She turned to face Chrissie and spoke more solemnly, tenderly and almost affectionately, "Take what they give you, because they are very generous when they are happy."

Amber's face ages as she speaks earnestly, but the wry smile suddenly warms up into an open and welcoming one. "Here they are!" She waves over to the group of men ascending the grand, sweeping staircase. Both Amber and Chrissie waved to them. "Come," said Amber. "Let's get in the water."

The men got their drinks from Fermin.

The other women showed up and headed straight for the water.

Chrissie stepped down into the hot tub, and sat with a jet hitting her centre back for a moment before moving to the side and letting the jets run past her. Within moments, she was joined by the guests. Amber turned her attention to Ivan, as the other men laughed and gossiped about their friendship circles back home. Sandee attended the Chinese man with a construction job in the Middle East, who only seemed interested in the women on board and not the men.

"I'm so glad I'm here," said Ian. "I have been trying to get out of this wedding for one of my wife's friends for months. This was the perfect excuse!" He leant back to submerge his chest beneath the water.

"It's always the same," said Yohannes. "I don't want to be in a room full of people I don't know for the wedding of someone I don't care about."

Chrissie turned to face the one man that hadn't joined them in the tub. Shane wore the right clothes and said the right things, but he never quite matched the others' energy.

"Aren't you joining us?" Chrissie asked him.

"I prefer dry land," Shane replied.

"Kind of a weird thing to say on a yacht," Chrissie said, narrowing her eyes and playfully tilting her head to one side.

"I'm just here on business. That's why I stay at the inn at the marina." In the three days that she had spoken with Shane, he had given nothing away.

"What do you do for business?" Chrissie asked, brushing her hair behind her shoulder with the back of her hand. They kept saying they were here for business but they never seemed to actually talk business. At least, not in front of her.

He dug out a small nugget from his pocket and placed it in Chrissie's palm. She turned it over with her thumb. The nugget was barely the size of a marble. A small, polished hunk of gold that rolled around in the palm of her hand. She was aware that if this was pure gold, it would be worth a lot. "Keep it," he said.

"You don't want it back?" Chrissie asked, cradling the nugget as its cool, smooth side tickled the lines on her hand.

"No, I have plenty," he replied.

"Where did you get it from?" Chrissie asked, unable to pull her attention away from the small orb.

"I go down to South America and meet up with gold traders down there," he said. "We go down a couple of times a year and just scoop up everything we can."

"It's beautiful," Chrissie sighed, enjoying every facet of it. "Are you here to sell gold, then?"

The man smiled and hummed. "I'm here to make friends."

"For business," Chrissie clarified.

"For business," he conceded. "Friends who can assist with business."

"Why do you need assistance?"

"You ask a lot of questions."

Chrissie was about to apologise, but instead smiled and sighed, "You don't seem to offer conversation otherwise."

He liked her flirting. "That's true. I like gold. I like business. I don't like red tape. It's always good to have friends who can avoid the red tape."

"People with boats?"

"Should I call my lawyer?"

"What?" Chrissie was confused.

Shane laughed, "You're talking like a cop," he said. "Trying to get information out of us."

Chrissie smiled. "I'm not a cop," she said. "I just like talking to people."

"I know," Shane said leaning forward on his desk chair. "You seem like the kind of woman who wants to help people. Maybe you could help me?"

"Sure," Chrissie said with a shrug, unsure how she would be able to help him. She knew very little about business, and the longer she stayed on the boat the less she understood.

"Well, my company is opening a new office in London," he starts.

"London is so cool," Chrissie said, thinking about all the films she watched with her mother that were set there. Her mum would borrow old videos from her friends at work and they would eat popcorn and pretend they were at the movies. Floppy haired rom-coms where the problem was always which man was better for the woman.

131

"Yeah, well. It's been easy enough setting up the company," he said. "We didn't even need an actual office there to do that. But," he hesitates for a moment. "You know how the English are; all snooty and closed off." Chrissie nodded thinking about the rom coms.

"Stiff upper lip," she adds.

"Exactly!" Shane exclaimed. "Exactly! You get it!" He shrugs dramatically, "It's just been hard to find a way in with people. You'd think my gold wasn't good enough."

Chrissie smiles thoughtfully. There were no English people on the yacht. No one had even mentioned business in London, "Oh!" She cried. "Erm, the Russian guy, Ivan, one of his houses is in London. His father bought it in like the 90s, I think. So maybe they have business there… or maybe it's a holiday house," she began to doubt herself. "He did mention a Lord that was supposed to be here. I don't know if he's English, but he's a Lord, so he probably is, right?" She looks up at Shane.

"Probably," he said, considering this new information. "Thanks, Cassie."

She smiled, and didn't correct him. There was no point, he would only forget again tomorrow.

Chapter 9
Huddle

Some good days last a day. Some last a little longer. And sometimes the bad days seem to fall away entirely.

Or at least, that's what I've heard.

Mostly, my good days rarely last beyond a huddle; the informal, morning, team meeting in which a manager says something and I'm supposed to pay attention.

I should really work on my attention span.

While the huddle is sometimes a portal through which to dispense vital information on changes within the company, other times it is so teammates can 'catch up' with each other, but the vast majority of the time, a huddle is purely to reiterate something already known to the majority of the team. Already known, understood, recognised, comprehended, etc. The huddle is used as an official instruction or dissemination of information.

Like today.

For the past week there have been nightly updates on the coming storm. I believe they have called it 'Helga'. We had our first flurry at the weekend, and there have been constant reminders that there are likely going to be disruptions to traffic and commuters and **people going into offices**, yet somehow our particular office has avoided any internal messages advising us to stay at home.

That's not 100% true.

We did get a message about the underground car park being closed due to ice, but not even that was enough to stop them forcing us in.

After two years of working from home, you'd think they'd care less. But, no.

Did you get Jan's email? A message from Megan pops up on my screen. I have barely even sat down this morning. I'm trying to deal with system issues on Paul and Carlie's computers. I pull up my inbox and find that Jan wants us to huddle this morning. Now. Right now. She sent the message ten minutes ago, so obviously I was given plenty of time…

Stop moaning and just go downstairs.

I have now, I message Megan back.

Bring the temps.

Small rage, like a new mother—I've just got them settled!

It's not a Beast from the East but it's just as bad. A thick, flurry of snow blocks out the sunlight. The IT guys have gathered at the corner window to watch the road disappear from sight. Cars are already struggling to climb the hill. Pedestrians are battling against the icy wind, turning their faces, and covering them with pulled down hoods and pulled up scarves.

The first floor is almost peaceful. The phone line has eased off. It's likely the offices around the country have started to send their workers home.

Jan is already stood at the bank of desks, where all my team colleagues are half standing, half sitting, half somewhere in between[19].

"Thank you for joining us," Jan says. I smile and lean against the nearest desk as the temps awkwardly hover. "As I was saying, I'm going to be in meetings all day. We are keeping an eye on the weather and will keep you updated. You may see some teams starting to leave, anyone who can, will be asked to work from home."

It took her less than 30 seconds and she's gone, disappearing into a closed office with the other managers. It took us longer to get down here than it did for her to tell us nothing.

The temps wander back up to the glass box, but I hang back to chat for a moment. "How long have they been in there?" I ask Hannah.

"Longer than I've been in," she replies.

"At what stage do you think they'll send us home?"

"Ten minutes before too late," chirps Ben from across the divide. "None of the teams have been told to go yet. Only sales were told last night to work from home."

"Of course, they were," I mutter. I look over to Megan's screen, she has the Met office's live weather maps open on her desktop. "How's it looking?" I ask her.

---

[19] Bad maths

She um's and ah's with the authority of someone who opened the map first. "I mean, it's coming," she says, refreshing the screen. "It's going to hit us pretty much straight on."

"There been no indication of what time we can go home?"

Megan shakes her head. "Ben is watching the trains."

"Ben?" I ask, now fully in command of my control room and my minions with their very specific and weather-related jobs. Knuckles on the desk, leaning in and waiting for a response so that we can make a vital decision. Like I'm M or the director of the CIA.

Damnit, man, tell me about the trains.

"They're already running a reduced service after yesterday," he says as he swivels his chair to face me. "They are talking about the last trains out of central being around 3pm."

Good work, transport boy.

"The supermarkets aren't going to close until later this evening," says Hannah.

'As we all know, people who work in supermarkets, sleep in supermarkets and therefore don't need to go home,' I don't say, because I would sound ridiculous.

"Even the taxi firms are warning people that they might not be able to continue services," Hannah says.

The door to the managers meeting opens. Every head in the office turns to watch one of the managers come out and call over people by pointing at them.

"What do you reckon?" Megan asks.

I recognise a couple of people. I've babysat some of their kids.

"Parents," I say.

"Schools announced they will be closing early," Ben adds.

The people gather their bags and wrap themselves in coats, scarves and gloves before rushing over to the staircase down to the front door.

"The one time I'm jealous of the breeders," Ben mutters.

The rest of the managers break out of the meeting room and spread across the floor.

"We're keeping the office open until 2:45 and then everyone will be able to get their bus or train," Jan informs us.

The buses and trains are going to be absolutely rammed. Jam packed to the ceiling. Why, oh why, wouldn't you let us go now. By the time we get home we can log back on and finish off the day from there. What is the point of keeping us here, risking people not being able to get home?

I won't get an answer for that; we never do.

"What are you still doing down here?" Jan asks me.

"I was told there would be a decision soon, so I came to find out what it was," I lie.

It's not a bad lie.

She believes me.

Or doesn't care.

"Ok," Jan says. "You guys can't take the documents home. You need to finish typing them up and then secure them and the glass room and then you can go."

"What if that takes us beyond 2.45?" I ask, knowing full well it might.

"You'll just need to finish this before you leave," she says. "Or you'll need to come in tomorrow."

"The office will be open tomorrow?" What a shitty and pointless bluff. Tomorrow? When there are only supposed to be emergency and essential workers outside. Tomorrow; when there will be no buses and I live five miles away. Are you kidding me?

"We'll be done by 2.45," I say, not being particularly clear if I mean the work or people will be done. "Do you want me to let the one with kids know they can go now?"

Jan glares at me, "Not if they are temps."

Wow.

I manage to keep my eyes from rolling until I am walking away from her, but put no effort in hiding it from the other managers I pass on my way out to the stairs. I hike back up to the glass bowl. I feel a ball of resentment growing in my guts—it's not fair that people in the office with kids are going home, but the temps can't. That resentment is already gnawing away at me—that I have to be the one to withhold that information from the temps. What if they find out? I'm the bad guy? I don't want to be the bad guy! The sensation is rising up into my stomach. I'm getting a headache just thinking about it.

I hate lying. I hate stretching the truth. Not because I'm against lying on principle, and not because I'm particularly bad at it—I just hate the feeling of lying. Holding in that toxic secret of truth. It eats away at me until there is nothing left but an angry stone in the pit of my stomach.

"Hiya," I say, entering the glass box. "The office is closing at 2:45," I tell them. I almost leave it at that, but my stomach jumps up into my mouth and blurts it out anyway, "if you've got kids, you might want to talk to a manager, cos they are letting some people go early to pick them up and stuff."

I feel so much better.

"My kids are with my in-laws," says Rachael with a shrug.

"Paul?"

"His mum will get him," he says.

Never mind then. I tried.

We manage to get through the last box at record speed. The temps take a half hour lunch while I power through. At this speed, I suspect there will be a tonne of mistakes that I'll need to search through, but I can double check some stuff while we are working from home.

Oh, but I can't take the paperwork home.

Shame.

Absolute shame.

I start packing up the boxes and locking them away in the metal cabinets. At half two, I pack up the last box and put it away. The snow is now blocking out the view from the window entirely, and rather than flashing a brilliant white, it is dull, grey and worryingly thick.

By the time I grab my jacket and bound down the stairs, not trusting the lifts as the lights flicker, the temps and IT guys have gone. Account and HR on the second floor seem to have gone too. I see Frances at the front door.

"Are you the last?" She asks me, pulling on her fur-lined gloves.

"I think so," I say. "Both the second and third floors looked empty when I was coming down."

"I should have counted people out," she says. "There was some meeting hoohah on the fifth floor. I better go up and check."

"Will you get home alright?" I ask. I don't have any help to offer, but I should stay if she's got further to go than I do.

"No, no. You get off, now. I drove in this morning."

I don't have to be told twice. "Ok. Take care," I say with a concerned voice. I can't imagine driving in this.

The trudge to the train station takes almost ten minutes. The wind is pushing me on from behind, but that isn't particularly helpful when I'm trying not to trip over footprints left by someone ten yards in front of me.

The station master is stood at the door waving people in. "Last train," she calls. "Last train."

The platforms are full to the brim and ready to spill onto the tracks. People cram into every inch of it. The platform is open to the elements, a haze hangs over the mass of people as their outbreaths are heavy with condensation. Our bodies are scrunched so tight together that we keep each other warm, even when our faces are being pelted by tiny snowballs from the sky.

I usually hate the sensation of another person's warmth, especially that of a stranger, today I am a little glad of it. There isn't any snow on the platform, but there is a freezing slush that is slowly creeping into my shoes.

The last train is delayed by five minutes. Then another five. Frustrating, to be sure, but the staff keep announcing over the tannoy that "the next train is the last train out of this station and on this line. It **will** stop at every station along the line. Please be patient and fill up the whole carriage so that all customers can get home safely."

The train finally arrives and creeps slowly into the station. The crowd slowly packs into the carriages. The station master locks up the building, and joins us on the train, giving a quick thumbs up to the driver as they hop up into the remaining space by the door.

We are crushed into the carriage as the doors close. Every seat is taken, every inch stood on. The tables sat on to make space for more people. Bags are balanced on feet so they don't take up valuable space between bodies that could be used for breathing. The last chopper out of Saigon looked roomy compared to this[20].

The engine, with great effort and audible strain, pulls out of the station, hauling the weighted carriages and makes its way down the track to the next station, where, somehow, more people manage to pile in. The train then heads into the dark, underneath the city centre, ready for the long haul out of the city. There is a brief relief at each stop going forward, with a jostling dance as people make their way from the centre of carriages to the doors in order to get off the train. An odd form of Tetris; bodies gliding round one another unable to steer clear of personal space.

My cheeks begin to burn. I can see it reflected in the windowpane. There is no space to stretch my arms out or shrug off my jacket. Every stop at every

---

[20] A little flippant, but you get my point.

station brings with it a slight reprieve as the baltic wind wisps in with glacial snow.

I am tired by the time the train reaches my stop. I dance my way through the crowded box to the doors and am met with a glowing storm as I step off onto the platform.

Wrapping a scarf up around my head, I shove my hands in my pocket and slog through the building, blinding snow home. My shoes, not as waterproof as I'd hoped this morning, are heavy with frozen socks.

Holl is already there. All our blankets on a heap on the couch, as well as a duvet Holl dragged through from their bedroom.

"Mind if I join you?" I ask, removing my sodden coat and scarf and kicking off my shoes.

"Be my guest," they reply.

"What are you watching?" I ask as I find a pair of slipper socks in the recently washed laundry.

"Just catching up on the omnibus," they say. "You want me to change it?"

"I didn't say anything," I smile as I climb under the covers and am delighted to find a hot water bottle radiating heat. "What time did they let you go?"

"We got a message through last night," Hol says. "They keep you on till the end?"

"More or less," I say, pulling my bra out of my sleeve. "They kept us till the last train." I pull cushions in around me to block any chill making it under the duvet.

"Weatherman says it'll be a couple of days, at the very least. And the transpo-woman said not to expect buses or trains until the weekend." Holl turns the TV volume down a notch. "Are they going to make you work from home?"

"They were wanting me to go back into the office tomorrow," I say.

"The fuck?"

"They'll message us later on the emergency line to let us know the office is closed."

"Did you see the message from the landlord?"

Oh, God. What do they want? "No. What message?"

"We're at the end of the contract. They're putting up the rent."

"How much?"

"Another hundred."

My jaw strains against itself, as I tuck my face into my chest. The cold of my nose poking my sternum. "We really need to find another place." I mumble.

"We need to talk," Holl says hesitantly. A chill crawls up my spine. I unlock my neck and lift my head back up.

"What's up?" I ask, feeling the blood drain from my face.

Holl hesitates, but doesn't draw out the pause. They know my mind is racing through any number of possibilities. "Syd has asked me to move in with him," they say cautiously, waiting for my response before a beaming smile slowly overtakes their face. "He introduced me to his parents a few weeks ago, and it's getting more serious."

"Are you kidding? That's great!" I reply. "It's taken you too long enough."

"It's only been a year. We're not lesbians," Holl snickers. "We were never going to move in with each other on the third date."

"One time!" I say, mock struck. "And it was more like the fifth date… which was in the second week…" I trail off before brightening up my smile. "That's awesome though. Will you be moving into Syd's place, or…"

"Yeah," Holl's grin falters. "I'm not going to leave you out of pocket, but if the contract on the flat is up…"

"It's absolutely fine. I get it," I say. "I'll er…" I can't think of what to say that isn't based on how this will affect me. "What's, erm, what's Syd's place like?"

"It's right next to New Street Station, so perfect for town," Holl says. "It's an end terrace and the garden wraps round the side. His mum and dad live on the estate," Holl goes on in detail and I maintain my curated smile, nodding appropriately and making small, excited sounds at key details, but I feel a drop in my chest as I begin to worry. I can't afford this place on my own. It was sheer, dumb luck when me and Holl got a place together that we liked each other. Can I even afford a one-bedroom place by myself? Then there's bills and stuff on top of that.

I want to pull my phone out and start searching for places, but I won't do that in front of Holl, not when they're this excited.

"That sounds great," I say in a pause in Holl's description.

Electricity prices are going up too, so I need to keep that in mind. Even if I get a new flatmate, they might want the heating on all the time. Holl and I barely have it on in winter—though we will probably put it on over the next few days.

Holl is looking forward to using Syd's record player. I nod.

There's always single occupancy council tax… though I doubt it takes the price down that much. I could get rid of the TV licence, it's only Holl that watches terrestrial TV anyway. The licence people will send threatening letters and that feels like a lot to deal with.

The moment that Holl stops talking, I will bury myself in the duvet and search for options.

Knowing me, I won't make a decision until it's too late.

Chapter 10
Compassionate Leave

I set myself up on the sofa. Mouse plugged in and resting on the arm of the chair, the old headset dusted off and swung round the neck like a professional noose. Holl needs the table space with all their extra bits and pieces. I rest a thick hardback book on my thighs and balance the laptop on top. I start logging on to the remote system a good ten minutes before my shift starts, but the circling cog is still whirring around five minutes after.

Of course, there is a delay in logging on. God forbid the system actually works. It's not as though it's had plenty of practice in the past few years.

I'm not sure what I'm expected to do today. Should I hop straight back into my old work queue and pick up stuff from my actual team, or do they ('they' the great unknowable masters, whose every whim I am supposed to anticipate) want me to continue on the new account with some... I don't know, quality checks? Usually for those I'd be checking what was input against the originals. The originals are all locked up in the glass cage.

There are no emails waiting for me. nothing in the instant messages. I have a quick look at the last few forms input yesterday by the team. Everything seems to be complete—or at least, every field has been filled. I have no way of knowing if it is accurate. I sense check the dates of birth—none are obscenely old or impossibly young.

It's fifteen minutes past, and I get up to stretch my legs and put on a load of laundry on a long cycle before I commit to opening up my old queue.

At half past I get a call through from Jan. "Your old queue. Yes, that sounds fine," she says, distantly before her fire alarm goes off and she has to go supervise her teenager while he makes toast. "The office will be open on Friday; you'll need to go in then to open up. Frances is on annual leave, and John is off sick."

How am I suddenly the only one with a key? "That's fine," I say.

The weather actually, surprisingly, does improve, and by Friday the buses and trains are back on. I open up the office, turn off the alarm, and wait at the reception desk until a manager is in to reprieve me.

While it is quiet, and there is absolutely no one in to question what I am doing, I take the excess files from the glass room down to the mailroom to return to Ivan. We shouldn't be holding these documents, I'm pretty sure it's illegal that we have been holding these documents, probably more illegal that they were sent to us in the first place, but I am pretty sure that if anyone ever questioned us about them, I could use the defence of 'look at the number of boxes I had to get through'. Honestly though, I don't want to look at them, I don't want to hold them; I just want rid of them.

Basement level 1 is taken up by the mailroom. Incoming, outgoing. They are the first in and last out. Everything that goes through the mail sits in here for some part of the day before they are sorted, scanned and filed away.

They have the heaviest doors in the building, almost as thick as the external doors, and with just as many locks and precautions. By the buzzer next to the door are a number of wall mounted brackets holding dozens of differently sized and shaped envelopes, for all your posting needs. I almost take off a layer of skin every time I pass them to hit the buzzer to be let in. It really hurts, an' all. Pointy-out slither of stabby-metal catching the top of my arm—it would have my eye out if I were a shorter person. I can't see any blood this time, so it's probably just ruched the top few layers of my skin.

It makes sense to have the envelopes on the outside wall so people aren't constantly buzzing for them, but could they not be on a shelf or a table or in a cabinet?

I take a large envelope and place the wad of paper inside before I press the buzzer to be let into the mailroom. It takes a moment for the door to buzz open, but I'm loath to push the button again—I've been told off for doing that before.

Inside the mailroom, there is a huge machine constantly printing and packing envelopes with leaflets and booklets. On the other side, the mail is being sorted by a couple standing on opposite sides of a table who throw papers into tall stacks, while another runs each set into a scanner.

"Hiya Greg!" I call over to the mailroom chief. He smiles as I walk over to him.

"Hello! It's been a while!" I'm never entirely sure if Greg knows my name. He never uses it. But, then again, I don't come down here all too often, whereas we do talk about Greg upstairs. The Scottish madman with the greatest stories. On occasion, when things are quiet and we're bored, we'll send someone down with a letter to post recorded delivery just so that they can return with a new story about Greg's newest weekend adventure. For a man pushing fifty, he has some of the best dating stories I've ever heard. He usually breaks something on holiday—a phone or a limb. His opinions on politics and Love Island are legendary[21].

"I'm alright. How are you these days?" I ask, genuinely excited about his response.

"Oh," he says enticingly. "It's been an interesting couple of weeks."

"Oh, aye?" I encourage him.

"Did I tell you about catching my neighbour's diabetic poodle going through my rubbish bin?"

Gold.

"You did not," I say, brimming with anticipation from all the possibilities that this story will bring to my grim and boring day.

"I wish that was the whole story," he says, standing up from his desk and coming round to speak with me properly. "The poodle's name is Boudicca the Third. Boudicca the Second was a chihuahua-pug cross and I'm no gonnae lie, the Second was the cutest wee dog I've ever seen. Ears of a pug, snout of a chihuahua, tiny wee boxy frame. Adorable," he says shaking his head.

"It was a shame when the ice-cream van got her." Oh no. "Ah, no. she wasnae hit, it was this dog-snatcher who went around in an ice-cream van. They never found her." I am relieved? I think. "But Boudicca the Third is a scavenging wee tyrant who deserves to be shot."

Greg puts his hands up defensively. "You know me, I'm against any kind of violence. A true pacifist. But this shitty excuse of a dog pushes even my limits. My neighbour, the one with the hairpiece and a tattoo of the Queen, doesn't bother to put the dog on a leash. Whenever they go out for a walk, Boudicca the Third runs off and is halfway down the street before the big man has locked his front door. Last Thursday, right, my bins are out on the street ready for collection, just like every other bin on my street, just like every other Thursday, but the dog

---

[21] Two separate things there. He rarely comments on the politics of Love Island, though I am certain he holds opinions and would likely share them if he were asked.

can smell something in my bin. He sniffs at it, jumps up and tips the whole thing over. Bags everywhere."

"My carry-out shame for the whole street to see. And I know, I KNOW what he's after, because my brother-in-law brought me these god-awful candy-chocolates back from the states when he was over in Tam-pa, and they are inedible. But this dog thinks they are pure heroine and he is after them. He goes in sniffing them out and he gets into these candy bars, these 'chocolates'. This is the dog mind that did a jobby and smeared it all over my driveway when it had diarrhoea for a whole fortnight after finding a stack of curly-wurly's in the big man's garage and he had the balls to say I done it!"

Greg blows out a frustrated sigh, I am too engrossed to interrupt. "Big man sees his dog having these American candies and blows a gasket! I'm no even awake," Greg points at himself. "It's 6 am. I'm in bed with a woman I met at One Up Bar. He's effing and blinding like he's at the football. He chaps my door that early in the morning, he is gonnae see what he is gonnae see when that door gets opened, because I'm still asleep. I've been with a woman, so no, I'm no dressed for company at 6 am. But apparently, it's my fault that he's no kept his dog under control."

"What happened?" I ask, suppressing a smile.

"Right," oh, things are getting serious; he's brought out the 'right'. He stretches his back before slouching back into the story. His accent steadily grows more distinct the longer he keeps talking. "His dog's at the vet in a diabetic coma. My neighbour thinks I did it on purpose. Like I binned these 'chocolates' so that his dog would have them. He calls the polis. They turn up at my door at 10 pm. They say they came round earlier in the day. I'm at work! I'm no sitting on my backside at hame watching Kevin McCloud rip apart some poor woman's dreams on 'Grand Design' repeats waiting for the coppers to come round. I dinnae ken they were coming."

"They say that this neighbour of mine has said to them that I poisoned his dog and was 'publicly indecent' in the street. The bin bags are still in the street—the binman wouldnae pick them up. I took the polis out to see those candy bars in the street. Then they asked about my 'nu-di-ty'. I asked them what they sleep in when they have company and how they'd answer the door when some nutjob hammers on it at 6 am **in the morning**. They backed off after I said that, alright."

I am satisfied.

I love the image of two local coppers trying to speak to this enraged Scotsman, who is being nothing but civil with a strong, Glaswegian accent.

"What did your neighbour do?"

"He's no spoken to me since," Greg replies before softening his face. "I put it behind me. I don't hold a grudge."

I smile.

"What can I do for you today, Mrs?" He asks.

I hand him a thick envelope, "Recorded delivery, please."

"Do you need the reference number?"

"Please."

"Two seconds," he disappears off into a smaller room in the corner, coming back a moment later with a post-it with the reference number written on it. I'm holding a card in my hand, one that I need to post out to my friend for their birthday.

"That a private card you've got there?"

"Yeah," I draw the word out a little longer than usual. "Is there any chance I can leave it here? I've already put a stamp on it."

"I'm sorry, hen. They're cracking down on my taking in things like that. It takes up space or something."

My brow furrows. "That's alright," I say.

"There's a post box across the road from the front door. It looks like a bin, but I promise, it's a post box."

I smile, thank him, and wave goodbye with my card-hand. It's bitterly cold outside, but I can't be bothered going all the way upstairs to get my coat. I dash across the road, whipping my head back and forth to check for traffic as I go, and drop the card into the box.

When I get back up to my desk, the notification light on my phone is blinking. Missed call. I quickly check to see who it was. David, my cousin. It's not like him to call.

Hey, sorry. I'm at work. What's up? I message him and place my phone back on the desk as I pull out a sheaf of paper and start checking the quality of the temps.

It's been ages since I last spoke with David. I asked him out for a coffee a while ago, but he was busy.

When we were kids, David came to stay with us. His parents were going through a messy divorce and it was decided that he shouldn't be subjected to the bitter arguments and fights that kept erupting between his parents. Our mothers are half-sisters and we were the only ones in the family with space for him. Which, thinking about it, isn't the nicest way to be offered a home. My brother had a bunk bed, so the two of them shared that.

It was supposed to be a short-term measure just while the house was sold and his parents fought for custody. But immoveable lines were drawn by both parties and he ended up living with us for almost two years, moving to our school and coming on our holidays.

I remember we went to Spain one year and he jumped off a cliff and nearly caused my dad to have a heart attack! It must have been a 30-foot drop, but it felt enormous. He seemed to take forever to come back up to the surface, and when he did, he had to swim out to sea to find a way back up the cliffside. Eventually, a passing canoe towed him to a nearby beach.

We haven't spoken in years. I can't pin down exactly the last time we spoke. There hasn't been an incident or a reason, we just don't really talk much. I think my mum checks in on him. I normally remember to send him a birthday card. I did this year. I think.

I don't know why he's calling me though. I find it deeply settling when I get a call in my private life. That's a business-y thing to do. The expectation that someone would be available at someone else's priority feels deeply wrong.

The notification is flashing at me again.

Another missed call from David.

You alright? I message. Another call comes in before I have a chance to put the phone down. I answer it, "You alright?"

"Hi, sorry," a stranger's voice says down the phone. "Do you know whose phone this is?"

"Erm, yes," I say. "It's my cousin's. David."

"I'm sorry. I'm really sorry. I saw the whole thing," the voice goes on. I listen silently, unable to grasp what she's telling me, the words fly in through one ear and then fade away before I can comprehend them.

"Royal infirmary," I echo—it's the only thing that fixes in my head. "I'll meet him there."

I grab my bag and coat. I crash the computer rather than going through the rigmarole of signing out. I call Megan on her work line. "Tell Jan that I'm going to the hospital. My cousin's being taken in by ambulance."

I rush downstairs and go over to the main road to hail a taxi that is thankfully driving by. "The hospital," I tell the driver. "A&E."

The driver doesn't make small talk. I don't have any change. I ask him to stop by an ATM. "Don't worry," he says, turning off the metre. "This one is on me."

The kindness of strangers; I could cry.

He drops me off in the car park closest to A&E, right next to a line of ambulances ready and waiting for the call.

It's been a while since I was last in this hospital, visiting a friend who was getting over a serious virus, but I've never been in the emergency area, the brutalist addition to the gothic Victorian main building. It's quieter and stiller than I imagined. There are no paramedics rushing people through, no doctors running in demanding things or nurses rummaging through files. Instead, there is a receptionist taking people's details and a waiting room full of people, who are, for the most part, waiting patiently.

"Hi," I say as I approach the receptionist behind her flexiglass wall. "I had a call that my cousin was brought in. I didn't get any of the details. His name is David Clarke."

The receptionist takes a moment to check the incoming patients on her computer. "Yes, he's been taken down to surgery. There's no other information I can give you at the moment, I'm sorry," she sounds genuinely apologetic.

I suspect there is something else written on his file. "You can wait here, if you like. Or there is a family room that we can show you to. Is there anyone else that we should contact? Does he have parents? Siblings? A partner or children— anything like that?"

I shake my head, not because he doesn't have any, but because I don't want to trouble the receptionist, and I need something to do while I wait. "It's fine, I can contact everyone."

Welcome to the family minefield. Do not step on any previously hurt feelings or ongoing dramas. I write a quick message and copy-paste it to everyone individually.

The last group message was from my brother three years ago announcing the birth of his kid, and I shit you not, people were pissed he hadn't informed them individually. Like he was supposed to sit there and tell every single cousin, uncle and aunt that he'd had a kid. Why do they think group chats were invented? He has a baby now. He has other priorities.

I'm never quite sure if people are getting on at the periphery of the family. My immediate family is the least dramatic, but the further out you go the more drama there seems to be. Aunties that don't get along, uncles having affairs with in-laws, small crimes—usually theft. Daytime TV wouldn't be the same without us. For a while we were ITV's bread and butter.

David has been taken to hospital. He's in surgery. I'll message you and everyone else the moment I hear from the doctor.

I send a further message to my mum, checking that there aren't any new additions to the family, or anybody else I should be messaging. I learn back on the sunken sofa. There are several other people in the family room waiting for news. An elderly woman sitting with her rosary. A young, south Asian family gathered in the corner—a young boy getting everyone a hot drink. A man flicking through a magazine—but I can see his eyes staring through the pages.

My phone starts vibrating aggressively. It disturbs the others in the room, until I manage to quash its ringing and put it on silent.

I'm so used to sitting at bus stops and starting conversations, but I don't think I can do that here. I'm not sure whether it's me, the other people, or the place, but I just can't bring myself to even say hello. Not even to the elderly woman.

My mind floats round the hospital seeking out a distant room when a steady-handed surgeon is fixing my cousin. Their brow patted every so often so that the stern concentration isn't interrupted by drips. They split open the skin and search deep down for the source of a bleed or rupture. They stitch him back up, good as new.

An adult version of Operation, except, instead of the nose flashing, the monitors do. Elsewhere in the hospital, doctors and nurses make their rounds, orderlies maintain order by disinfecting and sterilising the wards, receptionists receive patients. Office workers contact patients to let them know when they need to come in for appointments and give out test results.

This would be a good place to work. Doing good work. Every aspect of the hospital is important to the running of it. every person having a particular role, a particular function.

I was good at biology in high school. I didn't take it any further than GCSEs, but I could have. Is it too late to start now? Go back and train. Or work in the

149

offices—I wouldn't need anything further for that. It's probably more or less what I do now.

A doctor enters the room. The room falls swiftly silent as we wait to see who she's come to see.

Me.

She asks me to come with her into the next room.

I don't remember what she said. I can't grasp the words as they go in one ear and rush out the other. She is kind. She waits for me to grasp what she's saying.

Would I like to see him?

I don't know how to answer that.

My body is rigid, pulled taught. Is it really him? How could this have happened? I don't understand. I don't understand.

Yes, I have to see him.

I message my mum before the doctor takes me down. I block out everything around me and focus on the bottom of the back of the doctor's shirt.

I've known people who have died, but I've never seen a dead body. My grandparents were neatly tucked into their coffins before the funeral. I've never seen an open casket.

We go downstairs, along a long corridor. My heart sinks and the only thing I am aware of is the rattle at the end of each breath, like a cold I'm not yet over.

He's lying on a bed, covered by a sheet, but his face and arms are showing.

Yes, it's him.

He looks empty. Expressionless. I can't rectify this body with the boy I knew. Even when he was upset or angry, he was always full of life. Mischievous and frustrating. He looks quieter now. Smaller.

My phone buzzes. My mum's response: *call your aunt.*

"I need to call his mother," I say and leave the room before I hand my phone to the doctor and ask them to call on my behalf.

I don't want to talk to Aunt Claire. I don't like Aunt Claire. I haven't visited her since my parents last took me when I was about fourteen. In my mind, she will always be the Trunchbullian figure from my childhood; enormous and overbearing.

But I know that her son is dead and she doesn't.

Anxiety and nausea flood me while I speak with her. I don't know what's happening to me. I can't focus. Can't concentrate. I feel as though I'm about to keel over at any moment and I cannot for the life of me retain anything said to me.

I can't do it. I ask the doctor to call her.

When I get home, I frantically speed clean the flat. My parents are on their way. There are other things I should be focused on, but right now, it's getting the recycling into the right bins.

They text me as they pull into the street and I put the kettle on. Upon entering the flat, my mum pulls me into a warm hug. "Is he really gone?" She asks. "I had no idea how bad it was! He never said!" She starts crying, and as if finally given permission, I start crying too.

*

Hours later, finally able to breathe again and talk without sobbing, I sit in the corner of the sofa, feet up on the rim of the coffee table. My dad has replenished the mugs each time the contents went cold and undrunk. He rustled up some biscuits (I suspect he brought them with him) and has put them on a plate for us.

"What's this?" My mum asks, leafing through the papers on the coffee table.

"Just something for work," I say dismissively.

My mum nods, respecting that I don't want to talk about that, or can't right now.

"You said Holl was moving out?" She asks, still trying to find something we can talk about without hitting David.

"Yeah," I say. "They're moving in with their partner."

"Oh, how lovely. Give them my best."

I nod.

My phone buzzes so hard it almost leaps from the table. Someone is calling me. No photo. I blink the water from my eyes and see Aunt Claire written on the screen. My whole chest collapses in on itself.

"Did she give you any grief before?" My mum asks. "Do you want me to speak with her?"

I nod. "The doctor called her."

"Ok," my mum says, picking up my phone and going into the landing to answer it.

My dad is still standing up.

"You can stay in Holl's room tonight…" I offer. "Their stuff's still here, but they're sleeping over at Syd's."

"We've booked a room nearby," my dad says. "We didn't want to crash in on you or put you out."

Exhausted, I slip off to bed, only to be woken the following morning by the pings of messages coming through.

Where are you? Jan's message reads. *You were supposed to start an hour ago.*

I message her back. explaining what happened.

I'll put on the schedule that you are on annual leave.

Compassionate leave, I respond.

Compassionate leave is for immediate family.

My fingertips are blue. My room is spinning.

He is immediate family, I tell her and put my phone on silent. I'm not interested in her reply. It changes nothing for the present, so why let it anger me.

A funeral. We need to arrange a funeral. I need to check in with my mum about what Aunt Claire said and what needs to be done. We need to arrange a funeral.

Rahmat and Maimunah

Masjid Fitri

Malaysia

"I don't understand," Rahmat said in disbelief, his eyes drawn down to the ground. His hands palm up in his lap, feeling heavy, uneven and painful. His usual quiet demeanour magnified to an alarming stillness his wife hadn't seen since his father passed away almost thirty years ago. "I don't understand?"

The weight of his question cradled in his open hands. Everything he worked for; all the hours of the days and nights in the months and years that he had poured his blood and sweat into and everything he had to show for it was gone. The overwhelming amount of time and energy that he had put in suddenly drained from his body and left him hollow.

He had dreamt, ever since he was a small boy, of making his pilgrimage. His grandfather had managed it, saving for decades on meagre earnings. His grandmother had put aside every spare coin, wrung out the very best deals with vendors to eke out just one more ringgit.

His father had done the same. Rahmat took after his father in many ways, quiet to the point of frustration, preferring to act and use actions to say everything they needed to express, but the one time his father had given him advice (advice Rahmat suspected had been given to his father by his own father) it was to marry a woman who will support you in achieving your aims.

Rahmat's grandmother was able to cook the most beautiful meals on the cheapest of cuts, his mother was able to repair any item of clothing. He had often heard rumours and jokes about mothers-in-law and daughters-in-law being unable to work together or see eye-to-eye, but his mother and grandmother had always worked alongside each other well and laughed together.

In Maimunah, Rahmat was certain he had found a woman he could love and build a successful marriage. She was smart and industrious. He had gone a step further than his father's advice—he had made sure that the woman he proposed marriage to shared his goal. On their wedding day, he had vowed to her that they would go on their holy pilgrimage together. She was as excited by that as the rest of the celebrations. Maimunah knew that Rahmat's father and grandfather had both taken their wives to the Holy City. It would take years, but she trusted that if the two of them worked hard enough, they too would perform Hajj.

Rahmat was a failure.

Maimunah, recognising her husband's complete withdrawal, took control for him. "How could this have happened?" She asked their financial consultant. "We have been saving for almost forty years! How is there now no money?"

"Puan," the consultant said respectfully, ashamed of the answer he was about to give. "The money you save with us is invested on the international markets to allow us to give you higher rates of interest on your savings…"

"So, how is there nothing?" She asked, her voice louder than even she anticipated. Loud enough to be heard in the corridor of waiting investors. "We sat in this office. We watched the video. You said that it was solid, that the government backed it! Why is there nothing for us? This is our year! We were going to go this year!"

Rahmat thought about the suitcase he had already bought. He had spent time picking something he would be able to wield by himself through the long airport and the enormous crowds. Their friends had gone a few years earlier and the weight of their luggage had been the only complaint. He spent hours speaking with the salesman, trying out the different types of handle and wheels. He had spent time with their clothes assessing how much space the two of them would need. Maimunah had watched him lay her best clothes on the bed and practise folding them down and measuring the space they took up.

"Puan, some of the investments did not perform as expected."

"It's all gone," Rahmat murmured into his hands that he brought up to cover his welling eyes. It had been enough. He had done it. He had enough for Hajj, all the flights, visas, meals and accommodation, with enough to spare for them to make a donation. They would complete their holy pilgrimage and that pillar would be complete.

"How could you have let this happen? How could the government let this happen!" She was beyond worrying about anyone's opinion of her, and spoke loudly and directly. "That man, that man ran this investment, he was… he was photographed with the prime minister! He was well-known, well respected. How is it just 'gone'?"

"I understand you have lots of questions," he says, toeing the company line. "We are still trying to understand what has happened."

"You don't know!"

"It's all very complicated."

"Was it corruption?" Maimunah demanded to know. "How could it not be? So much has disappeared!"

Being there, speaking with the consultant who did nothing more than confirm what Maimunah had already been told by her friend, Sitti, in the garden beneath the minaret earlier that morning. Sitti had run across the grass to her, eyes wide, her tudung pulled back by the torque of her fraught pace.

"Imai!" She had called out above the peaceful breeze. "Imai! Your Hajj savings!"

Maimunah had sat there, on a bench in the shade, unable to blink as Sitti had frantically recalled the events of her previous day with their consultant. The money they had been saving for their daughter's wedding was gone. Sitti had cried all night. Her husband had consoled her, but he gotten so angry he disappeared early that morning to demand something be done else he threatened to do something.

Maimunah had listened to Sitti and worry had metastasised in her stomach. Her husband hadn't placed their savings with the same adviser as Sitti, still Maimunah was concerned. Then Maimunah had seen Rahmat come out of the mosque. Face ashen, holding onto a wall as he put his shoes back on. His lips were drawn, his eyes staring off into the mid-distance. He had already heard. He knew then that his savings were gone.

They had crossed the city in the blistering heat, unable to find a cab to take them, only for it to be confirmed that it was all gone. Rahmat rocked back in his chair before letting out a sigh. Maimunah worried about his heart.

Their adviser didn't even try to convince them that corruption was not a part of it.

"Is there anything we can do?" Maimunah asked, but the adviser shook his head.

Their son met them outside the office, holding a cab to get them home. He was about to ask about their conversation—the news had already trickled down and now all of society knew and there were queues along the streets of people waiting to speak with their advisers—but he saw his father's face and beneath his breath, he whispered a word his mother didn't approve of. In this instance, and only this instance, she didn't chastise him.

At home, surrounded by her children, Maimunah could no longer hold back her tears. Rahmat went to lie down. He couldn't bear to be around his children and grandchildren. He just wanted to be a failure alone. He closed the door and sat on the edge of his bed.

Ever since hearing the news, he had felt a weight grown on his chest, as though someone was squeezing a band around him. His arms felt heavy and distant. The pain in his neck was overwhelming, throbbing so hard it made him feel sick. Beads of sweat covered his forehead even though the fan circled above him.

As he thought about his failure, his discomfort grew to such a point that he had to lay down on his bed and let himself drift off.

Chapter 11
1-2-1

I'm not back yet. In body, maybe—I mean I am technically physically in the office, but my mind is constantly drawn into the past. I keep having these feverish waking nightmares of all the happy times when we were children. Any time David was playing with my brother and I, every time we walked to school past the park on the canal. The slide was narrow and steep, the rusted monkey bars that tore up our hands and how we gripped each rail anyway. Dinners at the table. My dad asking us all how our days were. Playing in the backyard, skinning knees.

I haven't thought about these for months, maybe years. I had a happy childhood. David was right there next to me, playing the same games, going on the same walks, eating the same food. But it was different for him.

I keep trying to batter the thoughts away, trying to focus on the work that's built up in my absence. My 'annual leave'.

It only took a weekend to clear out his flat. Me, my mum and dad packing up possessions into boxes, but most of it was waste. Newspapers, junk mail, cans and bottles. Old takeaway boxes piled to waist height in the corner. I found some photos David had put in an envelope inside a photo album but had not yet sorted through and organised. An unfinished project that, from the style of the album and the dust on it, was a project he started years, if not decades ago.

We took a tea break to look through them. There was a photo of him and Aunt Claire, one with his father, but most were of us. Moments I had no memory of and had to work out the year and occasion by background clues and haircuts.

I bawled my eyes out.

I took the album and the photos with me.

It's sitting on my coffee table to complete.

But now, I am back in the office. The guys in IT have already asked me to smile more.

I came in to an email inviting me to a 1-2-1 with my manager—because I don't have enough to do in a day, and this will certainly be the cherry on a very disappointing and emotional cake. I pull the certificates from the online courses we have to take throughout the year. Additional training sessions I have attended. Evidence of projects I have worked on and feedback from those above me. Extra meetings I have attended and social activities; proof of my commitment. Statistics of the quality of my work. Comments and commendations from colleagues. I print it all and have it ready before I open any of the other emails.

Of course, when I open the other emails, I find I have been invited to two other meetings. One with Darren fucking Deal (not today, mate), and one to follow up on last years' failed Upgrade project. Both scheduled at the same time as my 1-2-1. I check my timetable for the day, and sure enough they are all somehow layered on top of each other in the same time slot—a feat of software engineering I wasn't aware was even possible. The words are all slammed together and written on top of each other.

I'm not even sure how that is possible. Normally the system rejects/**PANICS** when people try to layer activities manually, yet somehow the system has accepted and plastered these into the same space.

I message Jan through the internal messenger. It should pop up in front of anything she is trying to look at. She uses it when we are trying to work, I don't see why I shouldn't.

If you need something desperately, call me. If not send an email, is her response.

Excellent. We are both in good moods.

I call her.

"Yes, what do you need?" She clearly didn't read any of the messages I sent, or pay attention to the telephony course we all attended.

"Hi," I say. "My schedule is showing two other meetings at the same time as my 1-2-1. And my whole week is messed up." I screenshot the timetable and email it to her.

"What do you mean messed up?"

"I've emailed you a screenshot," I say. She huffs at me. "I have fifteen-minute blocks to do online courses, a three-hour meeting with Billie Magowan on Thursday…"

"Oh, just reject the other meetings for today and ignore it. I'll message Scheduling about the rest of the week."

"And…" I'm pushing it. "When should I take my lunch?"

A heavy sigh. "You've not got any lunch?"

"No."

"Just take it after the 1-2-1."

"Ok," I say. She hangs up.

I set out the work for the day with the temps. Now that all the clients are on the system it shouldn't take too long to add all the evidence and proof of their assets… as long as all those documents are in the original boxes we received.

Yup.

I ink out a checklist on the glass walls for what we can accept and what needs to be checked, and I give them a one-pager with pictorial-reminders of how to attach this to each client.

"What if what we have doesn't fit with what's on the list?" Carlie asks.

"Leave it on my desk and I'll look at it when I get back," I say. "I have a meeting now, if you need any more that box has them," I point over to the box on the chair. "I'll be back in a couple of hours."

I go down to the first-floor private meeting room—a smaller version of the third-floor box, lined up against a wall with a half dozen clone boxes. Glass on three sides, with the opportunity to look into the next space, frosted to shoulder height, giving at least the illusion of privacy, but through the frost I can see the movement of arms in grand gesticulation. To my right, there is no movement at all.

There are other 1-2-1s going on— 'tis the season.

I recognise the muted voice of the one on the right. He's a sales rep, though I don't know his name. I've seen his face at the bottom of an email blast congratulating him on something or other. A large account he landed that threw off the curve for his colleagues. He was riding high in the stratosphere. But I can hear agitation, a tightness in his voice. I think he has realised what happens when you fluke one year; they expect the same again the following year. He is frustrated, but even without words or sight, I can tell he's holding back. I can feel him shaking.

The sales rep has to do better next year, has to get more in, has to improve—increase productivity and income. It reminds me of that chessboard problem where you get a penny on the first square and two on the second, fourpence on the third, and so on and so on—doubling on each square until you have all the money in the world.

No business can increase forever. Nothing in business should.

The sales rep is worked up so bad he is vibrating, his chair tapping the glass as he rapidly rocks back and forth, trying to explain, trying to justify. The visible quaking, I saw Darren Neal do at the charity event.

He's not going to meet the predictions and goals for this year. How could he? One good year throwing his career off balance. He knows his good luck and hard work last year have fucked up the next few years. His commission and bonuses will bomb. He'll be living off basic.

That's not how sales works. I bet he hands in his notice before the next quarter. He'll easily get a new job with his stats and the company will lose one of their best, steadiest guys in the department.

Jan arrives. A wadge of paper and her notebook.

"Right," she begins. "How are you doing?"

I nod, raise my eyebrows and turn my lips inwards. How the fuck do you think I'm doing. I hope she can feel the cold stare I give her right in her soul.

Jan doesn't have a soul. She starts soliloquising at me. It's the same every time we have a 1-2-1. She starts telling me all sorts about her life and how the business is going.

"I see you're a bit behind in your PDP. Maybe we should go through it now, see if we can jazz it up a little?"

PDP. Professional Development Plan. The most useless exercise known to man.

I don't say anything. I'm nine years old watching my brother and David racing on a beach at low tide. She is going to talk about what she is going to talk about. I expect her manager has told her to focus on this. There is no way she uses the expression 'jazz up'.

"Are you listening?" She asks, pointedly.

The beach, the sand, the waves, and the seagulls fade away. No, I'm a bit distracted Jan. I'm burying my cousin in a few days and you've forced me back into the office to deal with this shit. So no, I'm not listening. Not really.

"I'm never sure what to put into it," I say.

"Well, it's about **setting goals** and then **prioritising** them and **measuring your progress** to make sure you are **on track** with your **desired outcomes**. Make sure you are **developing** yourself to your **fullest potential**."

She hits all the buzzwords. I'm pretty sure she practised that speech.

"Right…" I hesitate and say nothing more.

For a split second I think she's going to ask me about it. about the death, about the funeral. About the fucked up corporate policy that says we are not real family. She doesn't.

"Well, let's think it through. What would you like to be doing this time next year?"

Anything but this?

"I just want to do my job," I say. Jan hesitates before making a note. "Do it well."

"A promotion?"

I shrug. What would be the point in that? Where would I even get promoted to?

"Would you be interested in moving into another area?" Jan asks.

Hell no.

"I would consider it," I say.

"Well, how about we set that as your goal—to investigate other areas of the business and see if you can find something that interests you?"

I nod and hope she doesn't notice that I would hate that. Why isn't it enough to just do the job. I shouldn't even have to expand on that and say 'do it well', just do the damned job. It's not rocket science, and that's ok with me. I want a job that I just *do*. Nine to five, weekdays. Finish up for the night and go home to a warm house.

"You need to decide on how you are going to measure this…" Jan says encouragingly.

"Check the internal job boards and speak with people in those teams."

"That would be a good start," Jan says, making a note. "When you get back to your desk, make sure you add this to the online HR."

The OHR. My day gets worse and worse.

That seems to be enough for her on that subject, at least for now. She brings out the pay raise/bonus paperwork and I prepare myself for disappointment. It never seems to matter how well the company is doing, the pay rise is always pathetic and the bonus is usually enough to pay rent and bills for a month or top up the savings that get dipped into at the end of each month.

They have a new metric that they are very excited about for their sums. My manager explains it poorly. Though, to be fair to her, I've read through the documents and they make no sense.

Imagine, if you will, you are at the centre of a Venn diagram of various bonus and wage pots. Each pot is worth a different amount, controlled by a different business area and has different rules. Each business area prefers to keep the pot for their own people, though they are supposed to offer some for cross-department cooperation—they seldom do. When they do, it is usually to our detriment. You are pulled by the weight of your role, your competencies and execution of work, and then are placed on a sliding scale within your experience band. There is also a multiplier for each year of service (something measly and insulting—but more about that later).

Quality assurance is used to grade you within your team, and your role is compared to other companies in the financial industry currently hiring in the market to ascertain the average (they are shockingly unclear whether this is the mean, median, mode, or *other*), and then compare that to similar roles in non-related industries. Your goals are then taken into account—to see how much you have attempted to stretch yourself for the benefit of the almighty company, and how many of those goals you have actually achieved.

While this is not calculable nor devisable, we are assured that their calculations are fair and even across the board.

Hardy fucking ha.

Your manager also gets to weigh in with their opinion, which trumps competencies and statistics but not quality. You are then weighted by years—about 0.05% per full tax year for full-time employees and substantially less for part time.

At least, that's the first round of sums.

There is an additional pot for union members... though there are qualifications as to whether due paying union members get access to this pot. The pot itself is always contested, the union arguing that it represents all workers, and that the pot is ridiculously small, and the company arguing that only the staff that joined the union before the company rebranded (some nine or ten years ago) actually count as union members and are entitled to the pot.

Guess which side of the union line I fall under.

I've never understood how the company can treat us like this, but they do, and it doesn't surprise me.

The union pot can be rejected by a majority vote from all union members. There is an incredible amount of heel dragging during the second round of negotiations, so union members that do get considered for the union pot usually only get their raise/bonus a month or two later than the rest of us. Although it is usually a better offer than the rest of us get, it is still pathetic.

There is a third pot that we lowly floor workers don't get access to: the managerial pot. There are considerably fewer managers, but this pot is the largest by far. WE don't know how this pot is divided. Its documents are hidden behind privacy walls on the hub and we have no permission to view it.

I wonder if we could submit a request to view it. Like a freedom of information thing.

It's funny how no one ever gets a rise in line with inflation or the cost of living. It doesn't matter how well the year has gone, or how behind on targets every department is, it's going to be roughly the same figure each year.

Bonus time!

Yay?

Ha! Nooooo.

No, see, bonuses are based on two of the above categories—what you've done and what your manager says. the bonus pot is worked out based on how little the team fucked up over the year. You work in a strong/small team with few mistakes—that's great: big pot, few people. But oh! oh, no. You work in a shit team who haven't pulled their weight and you've been propping them up all year? Yeah, you get an even distribution of a shitty, shitty pot.

And if your manager doesn't like you? *shrugs* it's all at their discretion.

This, of course, is completely separate to what they will offer noobs when they wander in off the street as their initial pay is based on the needs and desperations of the company. Desperate for somebody, anybody, to warm a seat. Looking to backfill for an upcoming heavy season after a competitor has just gone out of business? Let's see how little we can offer.

You know what. Pay rise should increase with living costs. Bonus goes up with years at the company.

How fucking hard is that?

Oh wEll iTS Not aS SiMpLE aS ThAt—fuck off. If you spent less on bringing in outside people to analyse where you could scrimp and save, you could pay us properly and not admit through numerous articles that you encourage literal belt-tightening and offer directions to food banks.

We aren't stupid. We know where the money goes. Some of us need to heat our homes.

Temps get paid through their agency.

Contractors… no idea.

"Have you seen the stuff on the hub about help with financial worries?" Jan asks me.

"Turning the lights off while you're brushing your teeth," I mash advice. My brain suddenly switches on a memory of being seven years old and brushing my teeth with my brother and David after a special school assembly telling us how to save water for the environment.

Jan frowns.

How can you tell us how wonderfully the company is doing, how much we're made, how great we are doing in our sector, across all sectors and how happy our investors and the stock market and whatever else is going great and then turn around and tell us to 'tighten our belts'. That year after year we are able to afford less and less.

"Ok," she says, passing over a letter with my bonus and raise. "Because you are working within expectations, this is what your share comes to. Just sign and date it."

Do I have a choice?

"Why am I only 'within expectations'?" I ask, while school report cards come flying at me. The ones that said I was never living up to my potential. That I fell short of perfection. Never quite good enough. As an adult, I have many theories as to why the teachers thought that I was always capable of so much more. I suspect it is the same with the office. I am not visibly struggling, and therefore there must be more I am capable of.

"That's just what the stats say," Jan says leaning back in her chair.

I'm balancing on a branch of a tree, holding on to the twigs around me. The boys are on the ground waiting for me to jump onto the trampoline.

I push the papers I printed towards her. "I disagree." I haven't done this before and my heart is beating in my eardrums. "As well as my ordinary work, I've worked on three projects this year. I have helped train and mentor new staff. I am currently working on a project that's for an 'extremely important' client— which suggests I was put on the project because I was the best person for it. The most competent. I have done plenty of things that aren't included in the stats. I've worked extra, unpaid hours to maintain my position. I have highlighted and corrected mistakes created by people and the system. I feel that shows a dedication and commitment to the company beyond 'within expectations'."

Jan stares at me. I'm going to be sick. I've never spoken about myself or my work in such a positive way or for quite so long. I can feel my cheeks flush with embarrassment. I may have overstepped here. Surely, they must have already taken all this into consideration when they make these decisions on how to grade people—that's what the managerial input is for.

Except, Jan is my manager… so…

There is static building between the two of us. I am suddenly conscious of all the muscles in my legs tensing and shifting, ready to bolt out the door.

I break first. "What happens if I don't sign it?"

I half expect Jan to shrug, to tell me it won't make a difference and sign it or I can't leave this room. The two of us will be stuck in here forever. An eternal battle of wits.

"It goes back to HR with your comments," she says. "And mine."

"I'll write up my position when I get back to my desk."

"Ok, just make sure it doesn't affect the work you've got to get through today."

That's a low blow. With my timetable as screwed up as it is—no one knows how much work I should/could/would have done. I'm focused on this now. I can't get any less[22].

"The funeral's on Thursday," I say as I stand up and leave.

---

[22] Or can I?

Chapter 12
Housekeeping

Bukowski's Burger BOGOF Friday, a culinary institution, which depending on who takes your order, can sometimes stretch to three, sometimes you share and fill up the rest with side dishes. Chunky chips are good. Beer-battered onion rings too.

I like Bukowski's. It's close enough to the office that you can get there and back within a lunch hour, and it's just out of the way enough that it's never busy during the week. You have to go down an L-shaped back alley to get there, and down some shoddily welded stairs. The interior is dark, I couldn't even tell you what colour the wall is.

Above each table is a hanging light with a low watt bulb, just enough to see the menu. The edges of the tables are chipped. The leather seating in the booths is ripped. There are framed photographs on the walls, but unless you are two inches away and concentrating hard it's hard to make out who is in them in this low light.

It isn't the cheapest bar in town, that honour goes to the oddly named, poultry themed, Cock-tails which is clearly a front for money laundering—there's no way that all drinks are £3, and sometimes you don't want to drink surrounded by barn animals. But Cock-tails doesn't sell food, and that is where Bukowski's beats it. Every day of the week there is a different offer. BOGOF Fridays is the best one.

Hannah and Megan are treating me. They heard about the incident in the 1-2-1; Jan has never been particularly subtle. Apparently, she was telling one of the other managers about it over the phone, a stage whisper loud enough for everyone at the bank of desks to hear.

Megan goes up to the bar to order, while Hannah starts to tell me all about her university plans. She seems to have her shit together much better than I did when I went. She's even picked out a course based specifically on the hiring outcomes for her desired profession, little weirdo, instead of studying what interests her.

I've always been divided on university. I love learning. Loved learning? Still love, perhaps—if I had the energy for it. I didn't go to university with any specific career in mind and chose to follow my interests rather than anything I was actually any good at. I think part of that was being able to accept failure if it wasn't something I was particularly good at to begin with.

I also blame Time Team and The Mummy for encouraging me to take two semesters of archaeology.

No regrets.

I would have liked to walk slowly across a damp moor with some geophysics device, using a digger then trowel to draw back the soil before getting into the trench with a small brush. Looking for evidence of pre-roman settlement. Cursing the weather when it inevitably turns on us. Hurrying to cover the trench so it doesn't wash out, then racing across a field to the prefab to have a builder's brew to warm up my hands before sifting through the archaeological evidence and buckets of spoil.

A nail. A roman nail. Some pottery and charcoal. Extend the trenches! Let's see if we can find a nice piece of jewellery or a scion or some religious earthenware to date our site. Holes that housed huge beams of wood to support a maybe iron-age structure.

I would always be clamouring for funding for the next expedition. Whoring myself out at university events. Never quite safe with employment. Probably having to go into the cut-throat world of academic work and doing self-financed digs in the summer holidays.

Also, Baldrick wouldn't be there. I think that disappointment alone would kill me.

If the Detectorists had been in my childhood, I would have asked for a metal detector for Christmas. I could probably still get myself one.

Hannah, though, has a plan. A focus that I didn't and still don't have. Hannah knows what she wants to be when she grows up. I, a good decade older, still don't. While I have no intentions of going into primary education (surrounded by multitudes of small children *shudder*) I do envy Hannah's conviction. She has taken her time to work out what she wants to do and is determined to now do it.

Megan brings our drinks over. "Three burgers, but we had to pay for a side of chunky chips and the salad will be… 'minimal'." She joins us in the booth.

"Have you decided which uni or college you are going to? Or are you looking at the course first?" I ask Hannah.

"I'll be staying local," she sips her drink. "I can't risk going to another city and not being able to afford rent and stuff. I've got my savings, but I don't want to spend it all on rent." She places the glass back on the table. "There's one in southside that has really good graduate employment rates, so I've applied there."

"What qualifications do you need to get in?" Megan asks.

"The evening course I'm doing at college is good enough. I have one more project to do, and another exam, and then I get my results and will hopefully get in," Hannah says quietly. I smile kindly. She works bloody hard on those projects and always gets top marks, but she panics in exams and runs out of time. I think she worries her answers don't sound good enough, even if the answers themselves are correct. She took time off before the last exam to do a load of practice papers. I expect she'll do the same again for the next one. "What about the internship?" She asks Megan. "Did you hand in the application?"

"What internship?" I've missed something by not being at my usual desk.

"There's an opening in Marketing," she says. "Jan suggested it to me at my 1-2-1 last week. They are taking on a group and it's open internally."

"Paid?"

"Unpaid," she admits. "But if it leads to a job in what I want to do then how can I pass up the opportunity?"

Urgh.

They could at least pay you for the work you're doing.

"What was the application like?" I ask. I've seen the hoops that need to be jumped through for the lowest ranking temp admin job, I can only imagine what is needed for a department as fickle as Marketing, who are constantly putting up adverts hiring people.

You'd think they'd know how to entice the right person for the job.

"Usual CV stuff. Answer some questions. Then this weird hybrid IQ test."

"Weird how?" Hannah asks as the waitress arrives with our burgers. Hannah and I tuck in.

"The first part was like a knock off IQ test, but then there was a load of multiple-choice questions like: How do I decide when to stop working on a project? And; what are the main challenges to how we will market things in the future? But you aren't given any space to type, you have to pick one from a list."

I grumble through a mouthful of burger, expressing my agreement that that is a weird way to do those kinds of questions.

"I managed to get my answers short enough in the free text boxes. They gave you less characters than a tweet."

Fewer.

Oh, shut up.

"I had to miss out loads though. And I didn't have time to answer all the questions. I know I could do this internship and work in Marketing; it was just a really annoying application."

"Who's looking at the applications?" I ask after swallowing my bite.

"I don't know," Megan looks at me quizzically, tilting her head backwards and to the side as she frowns. "How can you tell?"

"When they put an application form on the internal system it adds a code at the bottom for the person that put through the request. The internal job posting is then copied and pasted onto the external board, so they usually include that note at the bottom."

Megan and Hannah look surprised. "It's the first three letters on the surname, first initial, the number if there's more than one person with that name in the company, then a letter code for the department, followed by an office number."

"How the hell do you know that?"

"Oh, the shit I pick up," I say nonchalantly, "I recognised Jan's handle when she was looking for new team members, and it just kind of snapped for all the others."

Megan brings up the screen shot of the ad she has on her phone. "Warphr01. Some HR dude/dudette down in London."

"Huh," Megan looks down at her phone. She places the phone screen down on the table. "How was the funeral?" She asks carefully.

"It was…" I'm about to say 'fine', but I can't say that lie today, not about this. I swallow my words. "As funerals go, it was…"

No. I can't say it that way either.

"Bad," I say. "It was bad."

The two of them look at me. With one word I've shattered the whole atmosphere.

"Did something happen at the funeral?"

I shake my head. Family was family. My aunt and uncle sat at opposite sides of the chapel, refusing so much as to look at each other. Aunt Claire weeping loudly throughout the whole service, my uncle thanking everyone as they left. No one was told how he died, though of course rumours fly about. Just before the service began, Aunt Claire pulled me aside to say that there wasn't any need to spread hurtful comments about the way he died. I wanted to tell her that I wasn't spreading hurtful comments. He lost a battle with illness.

It wasn't pretty. The only other funerals I've been to were for elderly relatives, people who had lived long lives and had all these markers and milestones. David was cut off in the middle. He cut himself off.

I don't want to think about it, but enough time has passed to make it all uncomfortable. Fortunately, it is nearly time to head back to the office, so we concentrate on finishing our burgers.

*

I find Holl at home, packing up the last of her stuff. They've paid rent till the end of the month, and I didn't want them to feel rushed packing and leaving, but I did put up an advertisement online seeking a flatmate. Holl described me, which was useful because they made me sound not half-bad to live with, and I described the flat as honestly as possible, taking into consideration that the letting agency has been saying for a couple of months now that they are sorting out the mould in the bathroom. The bedrooms are only big enough for a bed and maybe a wardrobe, but the living space is nice and furnished, so that's a plus, right? The furniture's not particularly new, but it's solid.

Holl helped me vet the responses that came in.

People with pets were a straightforward 'no'. They clearly hadn't read the ad. If we had been allowed pets, I'd have had a cat by now.

One person described themselves as a 'little bit OCD'. They went straight into the 'no' pile. We would drive each other mad. They would constantly be tidying up behind me, and I would be pointing out the OCD is a serious condition and not a personality trait.

There was one woman who sounded really nice, but for some reason she included a photo of herself on holiday in Spain in August—wearing a thick woollen jumper. Heating prices are already skyrocketing on our minimal usage.

If this person is that cold, mid-summer in a hot country, I can only imagine them at Christmas, or the next time the Beast hits.

I sent a few responses offering to show people round the flat, but so far none of them were suitable.

One of the men that came to visit seemed genuine and funny. At first, at least. We had a cup of coffee while he had a quick look around the bedrooms (both bedrooms), and then went through each and every kitchen cabinet commenting on the tins and jars. At the end of each room, he would hum and then look up at the ceiling before moving onto the next room. After viewing the entire apartment, and walking round it twice, he commented that he would be happy to pay more for his share if that made things easier for me. I politely turned him down. I don't know what that was about, and I don't want to.

There were two other evening viewings set up for the day before the funeral, and it was too late to cancel by the time I remembered.

The first didn't show up, and didn't message to say why.

The second gave a long and overly-detailed ramble about having to move out because his current flatmate is psycho who won't let him in her room.

I said I'd let him know.

Then I lost his number.

I can't be bothered looking through responses tonight. I'm wiped out. All I wanted was a couple more days to myself to get my head on straight, but there wasn't enough time for me to take a few more days off work. Holl brings me a cuppa.

"You look beat," they say. "Are you sure about this party next Friday? We can always cancel, or do it another time."

I shake my head. "I'm just tired. Friday will be good. Just what I need."

*

Friday was not what I needed. Saturday morning is proof of that. If I could groan without moving any bones or muscles, that's what I would do. But I can't. It's getting light outside my window, but my eyes remain stubbornly shut. Whatever time it is, it's far too early and I have a hangover to sleep off. If I remain very still, my body sometimes doesn't feel like a boat listing over, taking on water and ready to sink to the bottom of a very shallow sea. Every breath I take fills me with nausea. I can hear a distant bike rumbling. The stuffy air tastes of other people's sweat. I should open a window—but that would mean getting up and the motorbike would be louder.

A heavy lump falls across my torso. The shock wakes me. My eyes shoot open and I look down to see an arm pinning me down.

Who the fuck is in my bed?

A gentle snore from the pillow behind me. I roll over slowly, cautiously lifting the limb to create as little disturbance as possible to the sleep man.

Oh, no. No, no. Bad-bad.

The urge to vomit is overwhelming. Beside me is one of the sales guys from work. Where the fuck did he even come from? How did he end up at the party?

Not the right questions. Not the right location. I need the bathroom.

Disturbing the sleeping body as little as possible, I slide out from under his arm. Placing my hands on the floor and crawling like a naked crab away from the bed. With my feet on the floor, and knowing that any sudden movement would a. wake him up, and b. cause me to vomit, I continue my crab shuffle to the door, picking up a long t-shirt off the floor and jamming it into my teeth as I go. A quick check into the hallway to make sure no one is sleeping there (thankfully none are) and I shuffle out and pull the t-shirt over my head before I silently close the door behind me.

Standing upright, I have the sudden, demanding urge to pee. My legs, not entirely awake, stumble across the hallway and into the bathroom.

Sitting on the toilet, I clear the sleep from my eye and try to wake myself up. Itchy skin. My throat is dry, it hurts when I swallow. Some half empty beer bottles stand on the rim of the bath. I pick up the closest one and sniff it.

Seems legit.

I take a swig of flat beer with a small, solid surprise that hits my tongue. I immediately stick my tongue out and remove a cigarette butt.

It could have been worse.

I empty the bottle into the sink and rinse it. I fill it back up with tap water. That tastes worse. I swill the water round my mouth so it at least no longer dry, and spit the liquid out into the sink.

I flush the loo and wash my hands and face in the sink, cleaning away fag ash.

Eugh. I catch a glimpse of my face in the mirror. Panda blotches for my eyes where the mascara and dark eyeshadow blend together in an unshiftable stain. I search through the bathroom cabinet, still chock-full of Holl's bottles and batches of stuff. There are some wipes stuck against the back of the cabinet. I'm not sure how long they've been there, but they'll do. Out of their packet, they are dry and scratch at my skin. I push through, scrubbing my eyes 'til they are red raw.

It now looks like I have an infectious disease rather than two black eyes.

I'm not sure which is worse.

I don't want to look at myself any more.

What's the name of that sales guy? I think he's married. Divorced?

I didn't make a bad decision when I was drunk. I didn't make any decisions.

Now's not the time to justify and… my brain can't even finish that sentence.

I retrieve a pair of shorts from the hallway cupboard. I threw the drying laundry in there yesterday just before everyone started showing up, shoving the clothes horse in so I didn't have to bother with folding and putting things away.

Now in a state of semi-dress, I step into the kitchen and pour myself a mug of milk, all the glasses sitting on the side ready to be washed. I steady myself against the kitchen surface for a moment trying to cough out the frog from my throat and remember the sales guy's name.

Steve. Probably.

The real issue is getting him out.

I could set the fire alarm off and push him out the bedroom window. There's a fire in the kitchen, please auto-defenestrate by the nearest glass portal possible. I'll be right behind you.

He might see through that.

I could always set fire to the kitchen…

The office has called, I have to go to work? No. He'd never believe that.

Your wife called!

Again, still not 100% sure he has a wife. I can't even look him up on social media to find out.

Jim?… John?…

I could leave. That would be easier. It's his flat now. He can deal with the mould and the flatmate search. I will walk out and not stop until I hit a country where my t-shirt and shorts make sense. Somewhere warm. Somewhere it rains but only at predictable times of the year.

I live on an island. I would have to swim at some point.

If I make enough noise he might wake up and leave on his own accord.

I want my space! ARGH! Can he not just leave?

Marin Petrescu

Carwasher
S.W. England

The post was waiting for Marin when he returned to his lodgings in the back upstairs room of the redbrick house halfway down a one-way street on the outskirts of the city. The thick, crisp envelope he received had a logo on the front that Marin had seen on some of the shops on the high street. He hadn't been inside, but there was a cash machine on the wall outside and he assumed it was a bank.

He stripped off his sodden wet t-shirt. Worse than the soapy water that came from the hoses and buckets was the cold drizzle that was pervasive over the city that he had come to work in. He had changed his shirt after work, but needed to change all his clothes again when he got home. He hung his t-shirt over the cold radiator to drip dry before picking up a jumper that was loose and bulky. Marin was glad he had followed his mother's advice to bring warm clothes to the UK. The damp, draughty mid-terrace was somehow colder than the old farmhouse he grew up in. At least there he was able to feel the warmth of the open fire his mother built every morning.

For a room shared by three men, it was meticulously clean, and that was not in small part due to Marin's attention to detail. He had been a packrat his whole life; and this drove his mother and his wife mad. He was certain that while he wasn't there, they were going through his things together, having a good laugh at his expense and throwing out all the bits of paper he had accumulated over the years. He still had his school books in a box at his mother's house. He should have checked for any old English grammar books he had at school—not that he got to speak much English. Everyone he knew here came from the same 50-mile radius back home.

Every piece of paper, every letter, every receipt he had received since he began on this endeavour was filed neatly away in the suitcase under his bed. The

174

other two men currently residing in the same room were thankfully ok with his incessant need to tidy and clean. A stark contrast from the previous roommate who would loudly, and frequently, even angrily, attack Marcin's need for order. Commenting to everyone who passed through the hallway that Marcin was impossible to live with, and a nightmare to share a room with.

He picked up the envelope from his bed and went through to the bedroom at the front of the house to speak with the one person who had studied English before he came to this country. Gabi spent most of his time outside work lying on his bed messaging his wife and daughter, checking in with how his daughter was doing at school and how his wife was decorating their house. He occasionally went to the pound shop to pick up a book to post to his daughter to help her practise her English.

"Eh, Gabi!" Marin called as he entered the room, receiving a sleepy grunt from Nicu, an older gentleman, who was trying to sleep on the upper bunk. Nicu turned to face the wall and began to snore. Marin lowered his voice to ask, "What's this?"

Gabi put his phone down on the edge of the bed. "Bank," he confirmed, ripping the envelope open and pulling out the letter. "You have an account," he said, scanning through the highlighted sections in the letter. "Congratulations."

Marin studied the welcome letter.

"Here is your account number," Gabi pointed to the long number that ran across the top of the page beneath the address.

"And this number?" Marin asked.

Gabi shrugged, "se spune 'fel cod'. The bank's number, I presume."

"How much money is in there?" Marin turned the letter over, not able to see any numbers and hoping that the figure had been written in words.

"It doesn't say."

"Ok, ok," Marin nods. Finally, a bank account. He would be able to see the money come in. He had hoped for a card that he would be able to withdraw his money that he could take over to the bureau to transfer the money back home. He knew that that wouldn't be for some time yet. He would still have to pay off his flights and housing. He didn't have the exact figures for that, but Ionut and Dana had told him not to worry, that he would be able to pay them back in no time and make plenty of money to send home.

There were often warnings spread throughout the villages back home, tall tales of almost fairy tale quality of villains that would snatch kids and sell them in the UK. Marin was careful with his choice, but his choice to come was set.

Gabi read his mind, "Don't worry, I am already sending money back to my Livia and Sanda. Another year over here and the house will be done and I will be able to go home and set myself up with my own garage."

Marin nodded. "How are they doing?"

"Sanda is growing up. She goes to school this year," Gabi said, turning his phone so that Marin could see a picture of Sanda with a new backpack. "she says she is excited to learn English so she can come visit. She wants me to take her to Buckingham Palace!"

"Can you take me too?" Marin smiles wryly.

"One day," Gabi laughed. His phone begins to ring. A videochat. Marin backs out of the room to give Gabi some space, but Nicu grumbles loudly, and Gabi goes down to the kitchen with his call.

That wasn't the only letter that Marin received that week. A series of letters with different brand logos arrived. He opened each one after he arrived home and swapped his wet top for a dry jumper. He brought them through to Gabi to translate. Echo Financial, Icso Holdings. Letter after letter after letter.

"Spam," announced Gabi, flicking through the papers and booklets that were received. "It's just junk. Throw it out. I got loads of letters when I first moved here. I spoke with Ionut when I first got them. He said the banks send you loads of stuff, all these accounts they are trying to sell you and all these little extra things that you don't need. Then they sell on your information on and so you get a load of letters from other financial places."

Marin nodded, unconvinced, and folded all the papers over to slot them back into the largest envelope. He took the papers back to his bed, and carefully stored them in his suitcase. He wanted to ask someone about them, maybe reply to some of the thicker ones, try and call up the company, maybe there would be someone he could speak to. But he worried that he wouldn't be able to understand them over the phone; he found it hard enough face to face.

Chapter 13
Gate

TW: SA, SH

I am woken by the incessant chirping; a mechanical bird trying endlessly to get my attention. The blue-light notifications trip over each other to alert me of the incoming, until finally the whole room is bathed in light from the tiny blue bulb.

It's 2am.

I actually went to bed early. I mean, not massively early, but earlier than usual. I made myself a hot drink and didn't stream anything—which took a lot of effort. And now, less than two hours into my sleep, people are BLOODY MESSAGING ME. the fuck? The fuck, guys? It's past midnight. Stop pinging me!

Blinking sleep out of my eye, I open up the texts that are coming through. From work. From the emergency line. I batter the words into focus, but my tired eyes and the brightness of the screen fight against each other and it remains blurry.

I put my phone on silent, place it back on its rest on the bedside table to charge, and roll over to go back to sleep.

Whatever this is, I will deal with it in the morning.

Turns out I didn't put my phone on silent. Instead of cycling through the options towards silence, I stopped too early, and the damn thing nearly vibrates its way onto the carpet.

Message.

Message.

Message.

Ignore it.

Another.

Ignore it.

Ano… fuck off. Like actually fuck off. I pick up my phone to shut it off entirely. The sheer number of messages coming up on my screen are jamming it. Time was that you could flick the battery out of the phone and force it to turn off, but the metal bracket holding it all together makes that impossible now.

A bright light pierces my eyes, and Megan's face turns up in the centre of my screen.

I audibly growl.

But it's Megan. I am awake.

"He, are you ok?" I ask, answering the call.

"Have you seen what's happened? It's all over the internet!"

"It's 2 am, Megan. I'm asleep."

"This is bad. This is really bad," she mutters. "It was on the ten o'clock news! Didn't you see it?"

I open my mouth to protest, because who the fuck watches the ten o'clock news? But she keeps going despite my non response.

"It's crazy, like actually crazy!"

"Why? What happened?" She can tell me. I'm not keeping my eyes open and scrolling through messages or googling whatever was on the news. I am warm and snug in bed. I went to bed freezing cold. I am not moving for anything.

"Soanso has been arrested," she says, her voice switching pitches as she speaks—half an excited high pitch squeal then flicking down to a low conspiratorial frequency: which is a lot to do in four words.

"For what?" I ask, only half-interested.

"Everything!" The pitch of her voice strikes my eardrum with a sharp, painful strike, I jerk my head away.

"You're going to have to be more specific."

"It was on the news. It's going to be in every newspaper!"

"For the love of God, Megan. What the fuck did he do?" I yawn and groan.

"Ev-ry-thing!" She draws out the word, somehow emphasising the whole. "They're saying he took bribes from everybody. There's a Saudi Prince, a Chinese billionaire, a Russian oligarch," All the typical Bond villains. "They're saying that he only went to the House of Lords when they were voting on things that the people were giving him money for—bribing him to vote in their favour." She's reading these directly from the article she has probably already sent me.

"This surprises you?" It's too early for politics. It's too early cynicism.

"He was on that island with that billionaire. There are all these women coming out to talk about it."

"We knew this, Megan," I say. How is anyone surprised by this? We literally kept that man away from Hannah. We all knew his creepy vibe. So, he's finally been arrested. Good.

"He's been embezzling from that charity. Hardly any of it went to where it was supposed to go. He's got all these ties to kleptocrats," Megan goes on, rushing through the list at top speed. "He's been taking backhanders. The papers say the cops are investigating all the businesses that he works with. All his images have already been removed from our website."

My mind drifts off. It's too early and none of this is news. How anyone could be surprised by any of this is beyond me. I am fairly certain that the newspapers have had these articles for years and have just needed the excuse that the person in question has been arrested. Isn't that how it usually goes? An open secret. A super injunction. How can anyone be surprised when we've heard this story a hundred times?

"You there?" Megan asks.

"Sorry. I'm just…" I whisper through a yawn. "I'm tired. Can we talk in the morning?"

"Set your alarm clock an hour earlier; they want us all in the office."

"When did they say that?"

"The message came in about an hour ago."

"They can fuck off then."

Megan cracks a tapered laugh. "All right then," she says. "I'll see you when I see you."

"Night," I reply and turn my phone off.

Even though I fall asleep immediately after hanging up, it's a fitful sleep with no rest and I am more tired than I was during the early morning phone call.

I go through the messages from the emergency line—the official one that is checked twice a year and used for the sole purpose of weather updates[23]. Yes, they want us all in the office for nine. I grab some clothes from a washed pile I haven't put away, grab my bag and check my phone, purse and keys are in there, then skip out the front door 4 minutes after waking up.

---

[23] The only exception being a global pandemic, when it was used daily for the first two weeks and then they grew tired of it and left us to work in peace.

I try to wake myself on the bus, widening my eyes and flexing my fingers. I was working from home today. I was going to have a lie in. For the first time in ages, I was going to have a relaxed breakfast as I logged in while still in my fleecy pyjamas. I went out to the shop specially to pick up mushrooms and sausages. Instead, I am sitting on a fifty-minute bus next to a middle-aged man who hasn't showered, wearing the wrong bra with the wrong top[24].

I can feel the scratch of an uncut label rubbing through my skin. I really want to itch my scalp. I was going to hop into the shower at lunchtime. My hair doesn't look greasy yet but it's not hanging in its usual way and I know that if I itch my head, there will be dandruff. There will be a patch of hair sticking out at a different angle that will be noticeable.

Maybe the timing is a coincidence, but I blame Soanso for this. Sure, he probably didn't get arrested purely to mess with the one day I have this month working from home, the one day that I plan a late shower, but by heck, it feels like he did.

I open up my phone again and bring down the hundreds of app notifications onto my screen. Close to a thousand messages overnight. I wonder if anyone at the app's company noticed a thousand-fold increase on messaging in the small hours between these very select groups. I wonder how many of the other companies Soanso stuck his thumb in had the same panic.

Every chat thread that anyone from the office ever added me to is flooded with notifications. The manager has set up another team thread for disseminating information specifically about this. The party line. Not many people have responded to the manager chat, so most of it is a Q&A with Jan replying that she'll check with corporate. It is basic. It is careful. It is considered.

No press, she instructs. *Do not speak with anyone from any newspapers, tv programmes, radio programmes, or any other people wishing to spread any information about this!* (On pain of death I presume). *Please allow all comments from the company to come from the Public Relations team.*

It's not very interesting. I scroll down past the mega chats with hundreds of messages each—the ones where someone has dumped everybody from the office in and then everyone dumped everyone they knew in it.

I delete these groups. It would take an hour to sort through the messages. Most of it is going to be people repeating the same questions, same answers, same comments. The little insight it would provide, wouldn't be into the case

---

[24] My bra. My top. In case that wasn't clear.

itself, instead I would have the briefest of gazes into the workings of my colleagues' minds—and no one wants that.

I scroll down to a chat simply titled 'GATE', a group that Megan has set up for Ben, Hannah and myself. The core group. The people I would usually hang out with in the office. I open that chat first.

Oh. Oh, it's all a lot worse that I thought it was.

Ben has dumped in a load of links to various newspapers. I start with the more reputable papers, but trash rags—fear not, I'm coming for you later!

I recognise the by-line of the first link, I think I follow the guy online. Graham Bolt. All the commentators I follow always comment on and send out links to his articles. He's won awards for his reporting, like proper awards, not pat-on-the-back ones.

'...charges brought against Lord Soanso are still forthcoming, contacts within the justice system advise that this case is complicated and that victims, now in retirement, are now coming forward with statements that they were molested in their teens. Soanso was only a matter of years older than his first alleged victim, and it appears that the age of his victims has seldom fluctuated since.'

I hate when they say 'alleged'. I get the whole 'innocent until proven guilty'. But the only time I see the word's 'alleged victim' is to do with sexual assault—even when there is proof an assault took place. It angers me in my core. We, as a society, do not believe women.

Or men, it seems. Graham Bolt goes on to talk about the *allegedly* assaulted men.

I know it's probably a legal thing. I know that the paper is covering its back. I know there is a lawyer hidden away in a room somewhere offering advice on terminology to use, but you know what; there is clearly enough evidence for them to publish this. There are women, and men, coming forward with credible stories and evidence, so no. Soanso may be the 'alleged' abuser, but they are not the 'alleged' victim.

Maybe some English graduates, ones that specialised in linguistics, should come up with a whole new phrasing. Sure, have a list of rules, but keep them up to date.

'...relationships with various foreign political figures (whom we are unable to name) as well as international businessmen, oligarchs and billionaires, are being examined under a microscope. As many of these people are foreign nationals who are not resident in the UK, investigators are speaking with officers in jurisdictions across the world.'

'...Currently, over 30 women and 6 men have given evidence and at least one note from a woman who died from self-inflicted wounds which detailed an experience with Lord Soanso when they met last year at a charity event in a church near the Lord's home town.'

'...Forensic accountants are currently scouring Lord Soanso's finances, and investigators are currently trying to gather documents for the offshore bank accounts that the lord has.'

I'm not even halfway done with the article. My eyes skip from one paragraph to the next.

Fraud, bribes... embezzling from a charity for cancer-stricken orphans... a real-world comic book villain if ever there was one.

I turn off my screen and stare out the bus window into the darkness. It's late in the year, and dawn won't be for another hour. I try to rest my mind. Try to stop it whirring over everything that I've just read, stop the thoughts tumbling over each other trying to get my attention. Let out a steadying breath and get a nose full of my bus neighbour's body odour.

The office is in uproar. Managers sequestered away in one of the glass bowl meeting rooms, trulling round in circles, too pent up to sit down. Strategizing. Writing notes on a large paper notepad that has been turned to face inwards so that none of us lowly plebs can see what they are planning. One of the tech-savvy managers hunkers over a laptop—typing rapidly and nodding as she takes comments from the other managers. She hands Jan her lanyard who sees me at our bank of desks and waves me over to the glass door.

"Can you go print these off?" She asks, thrusting the lanyard into my hand. "Just print it and bring it back to me." She turns back to the room without waiting for a response. I dump my bag and coat at an open desk.

"Could you log in for me?" I ask Hannah who is already opening up her queue of work. Hannah smiles and I go wend my way through an office-full of colleagues whispering lascivious gossip round the banks of desks.

No one is waiting for the printer. Sometimes you come over and there is a long snaking line of people who are impatiently waiting for a big job to be finished.

Waving the manager's card over the sensor, dozens of documents pop up on the tiny display, all dozens of pages long and with multiple copies ready to print. I select them all and wait for the printer to whir into action before grabbing a cup of water from a nearby water fountain and leaning against the cabinet that houses the printer paper.

As each set of documents is out, I start collating them on top of the printer, God-forbid a manager arrange the documents to print in a prepared order.

Don't be that person. It's a stressful day for them.

I have a habit of reading and scanning any and all words that my eyes come across. I've always been like that. It's not a nosiness thing, I do it regardless of what is written, what it's written on, where it is or where I am. I can't help myself. The internal procedure documents are nonsensical at the best of times, but I still try to read them. When we are given them to read, I skim over them a couple of times (far more than what most people do), but never manage to get a grip of what I'm reading.

They seem to be written in a specific, jargon-juiced way, that are completely illegible and in no way reader-friendly. The amount of business jargon and un-glosseried anagrams, as well as renaming staff as 'employees', 'colleagues', and 'readers' means I'm never entirely sure if they are talking about me.

The last page shows that this particular internal procedure document was updated this morning, though it doesn't say what has been updated. Usually there is a table on the last page that says what part has been amended, when, and by whom. The paper I am holding is still warm, and only has the date of change.

I have a quick look at the title. If memory serves, when Jan gave us the rundown of the procedures so we could answer three questions about it and sign a document, this procedure is about releasing confidential information outside the company. There was a-whole-nother scandal a few years back when a guy in one of the offices down south.

The next set of documents are copies of emails from corporate with information on what is expected in the next few days, and comments that the next few months may be difficult for the business and that management should quietly prepare for the worst while corporate investigates internal accusations and concerns.

Neither the accusations nor concerns are named. Lord Soanso's name isn't even mentioned, just some obscure reference to the 'recent incidents' and 'current events'.

Should I be reading this?—probably not. Not that there's any details. But clearly the company at some high enough level is concerned enough to send this information down to floor managers.

Investigate what? What accusations have been made? Surely these must be older than the hours that have been since Lord Soanso was picked up by the police. If they knew, maybe they were the ones who informed the police, and kept the brand name out of the paper.

Last week. The email is dated last week. They knew this was coming. So why not take the photos of Soanso off the internet before today? Why not have us a little prepared?

All these questions churn in my head, and I reject each one. I want to believe that this company would do the right thing. I could maybe even reason my way to believing that they only kept the photos online so as not to leak it to Soanso that he was under investigation. I want to believe that. I want to believe it so desperately that I am collating together emails that clearly suggest that this isn't the case. Emails that advise *keeping a lid* on the whole thing, from a corporation that wants to *keep it all under wrap*.

Only about half the documents have printed. I search for paperclips in the cabinet, and find them in a scrappy cardboard box. I clip together the email trails and lie them down portrait over landscape.

More emails from third party business. 'Friends', if the company had such a thing. Companies that worked with my own. How much business has been dirtied by his shitty paws? Who's going to investigate all these comments? Are they going to make us do it? We don't have training for this kind of thing.

Oh, Christ. They're going to give us training on it, aren't they? A two-hour online session with someone reading off a one-pager. They should be bringing in professionals, people with expertise and knowledge of whatever fraudulent crap he's been doing. Police officers who have nothing better to do than warn teenagers off the steps in the centre of the city. Here is something they can do. Here are the true criminals, the real villains, destroying our society.

Are management going to tell us about even half the stuff in these printouts? I doubt it. Should I be keeping a copy?

That's an interesting thought.

My torso tenses as I breach the conundrum. These emails and documents are not mine. They don't belong to me, and I have no right to them. Except that for some bizarre reason, Jan trusted me to print these out. More fool her. The information in these emails shouldn't be hidden though. Their content affects everyone in the office. It affects far more people than just that. What if I tell people about things and they are fixed without having an effect on us? What if they bring in professionals—what if the only reason they bring in professionals is because of the pressure that the office puts on them.

What if, even after telling them, no one in the office cares?

I need a sounding board. Someone to take this through with. Megan will tell me to toe the company line—not your emails. Not your business. Hannah wouldn't get why I'm stressing out about it. Ben… would go off on one for ten minutes and then start a revolution and there would be no way to call him off. I can't run it past Jan for obvious reasons.

Would that just be me passing the buck?

Should I be looking through all the stuff that came through for the new account on paper. I saw several sales reps round Soanso at the charity event—should I speak with them and their admin?

They aren't going to bring in outsiders to investigate this. there is too much at stake. External investigators would stick their nose in every puddle and the company would never willingly allow that. I know this. It would be costly and interrupt work. Having us do it would be cheaper and keep everything neatly in-house. They wouldn't have everyone work on it, only people like myself, Megan, possibly even Ben, and our equivalents across the other teams. But would we really know how to 'investigate'. Perhaps they'll bring in people from *customer relations* (i.e., complaints) to do a deep dive on a couple of cases. Then again, Complaints usually contact us when they don't understand something.

Halt on all recruitment, I read in the next batch of paper. *Ongoing assessment of current staffing levels.* That hits me in the gut.

I can't say anything about that. It would cause a panic. Gossip breeds so quickly. There are already so many rumours going around, I would just be adding to the noise, and if they knew it came from this, an email between the CEO, CFO and all their minions, it would have an authority that I don't have.

No. I don't want to worry anyone. I don't want to add to the gossipmonger rumour mill. I have nothing important to add that isn't already being said on some chat.

After delivering the stack of printouts to the managers, I log on at the desk. I have multiple emails from Darren-fucking-Neal asking me to call him as soon as I can, and several missed calls from him.

I log into the phone and label myself as making an outbound call.

There isn't the flurry of calls I was expecting. Clients and customers aren't making hurried calls to check on their account. There's that to look forward to this afternoon. As soon as someone puts two and two together and posts it online, we're going to be inundated with people asking questions we don't have answers to.

I feel a migraine coming on.

I set up the call, and ring Darren.

"Why has it taken you so long to get back to me?" He demands to know.

It's twenty past nine.

"Things are a bit busy here," I say blandly. "It's like something big has happened."

He doesn't take the bait, which is a shame; I'm pent up and ready for a fight.

"I just want to see how things are going with the account," he says. *The account*, like there is no other.

"I'm not on the account today," I say.

"What?" He seems genuinely surprised by this. Did no one tell him about Soanso? Is he the last person? "What do you mean?" He screeches.

"Well, the managers want people to be available to field calls today. Tomorrow as well, I suspect. So, people on special projects, including *the account, have* been pulled back to the general phone line."

"That's not good enough," he spits. "They can't do that. You have to get back on the account. It needs to be sorted out as soon as possible!" He begins to trip over his own words.

"You'll have to take it up with a manager," I say.

"*You* need to speak with *your* manager and get her to put you back on it."

"My manager has told me that I am taking calls today. This came from her manager…"

"I don't care who's told you to do it. You need to get back to work on my account," his voice grows louder and sets my teeth on edge. "You can't do this to me! Ivan Ivanovich has expectations."

"Do you want me to call Ivan Ivanovich and let him know what's happened and why I am unable to work on his account today?"

There is an angry silence before Darren-fucking-Neal lets off a string of expletives.

I'm glad I'm recording this.

I hang up on him.

Fuck you, Darren.

By lunch time the slow trickle of calls has swelled into a deluge and I am lost on every one of them.

The managers, still huddled in their glass think tank, haven't come out to advise us. When one of the senior administrators from a team on the other side of the floor tapped on the door to ask, she was told, in no uncertain terms, to not disturb the meeting. The large screen in the corner has been turned on and set to the news. The banners running across the bottom of the screen keep hinting upcoming revelations on the story. People and companies that are involved. More high-powered and wealthy individuals refusing to comment.

Apparently, he's talking. Soanso's talking and taking them all down with him.

I can't tell if this is some altruistic move, a realisation that he's done wrong and wants to expose others like him, or whether this is purely some sort of plea bargain to save his own skin.

I'm kidding. I know which it is.

"They've put a statement on social media," Megan says, ducking beside me to be hidden from managerial oversight. I keep looking at my screen so as not to draw attention to her.

"What does it say?" I ask, barely moving my lips.

"Between the lines—it's got nothing to do with us, we hardly know the man."

"We just like hanging out with him at sporting events and charity functions," I add. "They know that they can't pull down all the photos off the internet, right? They only have control over what's on our site."

"Unless they get internet providers and search engines involved," Ben says under his breath. "They could pay to sweep it to the bottom of a search."

"Has anyone picked up on the post yet?" I ask.

"The only comments are from people with a half-dozen followers," she says. "And that one guy who messages everyday saying we stole his money."

"Did we?"

Megan shrugs and rests her knees on the floor. "He made a claim, it was denied. He put in a complaint; it was denied."

"Anything from the charity's PR team?"

"Their website is down for 'maintenance'."

I scoff. Of course, it is. "Is there any news on how much he's stolen?"

"Not yet."

"And the other accusations?"

"Lawyers saying unsubstantiated and that he's helping the authorities in any way they need," Megan shifts uncomfortably. "At least the media is saying the accusers are credible."

"Plus, he's creepy," I say.

"Plus, he's creepy," Megan echoes. She lowers her voice to barely a whisper, "How's Hannah doing?"

"Quiet," I say. "Maybe we should take her out for lunch? Change of scenery?"

"Sounds good," Megan says, straightening up and walking back round to her seat.

I can't shirk the worry that I should be looking into my regular cases and making sure none of those have been tainted by his involvement, but I can't help myself. I start with the company I know has ties with him.

Ivan Ivanovich Ivanov. It sounded fake when I first heard it, but what do I know? I once knew a Tom Tompson IV, Dr Grimm and a Stacy Stacey, so who's to say what makes a name real.

I look up Ivan Ivanovich's company on the government's official company registration webpage. There is nothing beyond the very basic, required information. Ivan Ivanovich's name, an address, and the date the company was formed. I searched for Ivan Ivanovich and find a few more companies. Some active, some not. All registered to the same address. I search by the address and crash the system. It appears that there are many, many companies registered to that address. Somewhere in the thousands.

That doesn't seem right, somehow.

It's probably one of those office spaces—the ones in the centres of big cities where small companies and one-man-bands can rent out a room and it has all the amenities and security of a much bigger enterprise. I had a friend who worked out of one of them a couple of years back. It had a really nice canteen. Much nicer than ours. The food was a bit more expensive, but not prohibitively so. And the chairs were proper comfy, not the school dinner chairs that we have.

I look up the address of maps—but it starts to hone in on the arse-end of nowhere. A home-county hamlet surrounded by greenbelt.

There is no giant workspace here.

The website for the holding company itself is down and, surprise-surprise, is 'undergoing maintenance'.

I find a bunch of articles in a language I can't even guess at reading, that have photos of Ivan Ivanovich. I run them through an online translator that throws out a blurry story of political intrigue. I think.

The translation is really bad.

I've read enough. This is clearly about the person I know as Ivan Ivanovich (though in the translation, the name also appears as Ivan Pavlovich—same guy? Different guy? Who knows). He has a direct relationship with Soanso, they went to that charity event together.

The gibberish doesn't help, at least not me, not now, to understand what is going on. I know Ivan Ivanovich was at the charity event, and he spoke with Soanso and I'm pretty sure he also spoke with Darren Neal.

It was probably nothing. Networking. Boys in the boy's club.

I jot down the website address on a post-it and stick it in my pocket.

Nobody has noticed I'm not on the phone. The managers are still holed up in their meeting room. Blazers and jumpers hanging on the backs of their chairs. Damp foreheads. Wiping the sweat away with the back of their hands.

I told them those rooms get hot.

We shake the rain off our coats when we get to Bukowskis. Half-price pizza on a Thursday. We usually get two mediums to share. It's not the best pizza in the world (it's not the best pizza on the street), but they've managed to keep their prices low in spite of everything, so it feels rude to complain.

Rumours are that the bar is a front for smuggling drugs.

Good for them; diversifying their operation. Especially in this economy.

Megan goes up to the bar to order our food, and I am left with Hannah staring glumly at the table, scratching the side of one thumb using her other, irritating her skin into a hot, red burn.

"You alright?" I ask quietly, not wanting to shake her too vigorously from her thoughts.

She hums and nods but says nothing.

"You want to talk about it?" I gently push.

"About what?" is her answer.

"He was a creep and he liked being around you."

"Nothing ever happened," she whispers defensively.

I don't tell her 'it could have'. In the office there were always people keeping an eye out for her. But at the charity event, in a corridor that was unguarded. "I know nothing happened, but he clearly…" I flounder, unable to adequately express what I mean. Yes, we were there for her. One wrong day, one bad turn— it's not worth thinking about, but she clearly is. Hannah is shaking her head away from the conversation. Kind and thoughtful, I don't think she wants to lump herself with the others who were physically assaulted. The women and men he was able to get at. "We should have said something to the police," I say.

"The police know," Hannah whispers. "Ben sent a load of articles to the group chat. There were complaints about him going back decades. They always know, and nothing happened."

I clench my hands into fists, trying to warm the tips of my fingers by pushing them into my palm. "I wonder what made this time different?"

"Nothing," Hannah's voice seems to distance itself with every new word. "He hasn't been charged with any of that. Not even for the embezzling stuff. Not yet, at least. They're only holding him on tax avoidance."

"Really?"

Hannah nods. "They were talking about it on the TV when you and Megan were getting your coats."

Megan has our drinks, but has read the table and is holding back for a moment.

"When we were at the gallery, and Soanso was trying to talk to you…?" I leave the question open for her. Her gaze shifts away and the corners of her lips pull down. "Hannah?" I urge softly.

"Nothing happened. Not like that."

"But… something happened?" I ask.

"No, that's not," her eyes snap up to reach mine. "that's not what I meant. He didn't do anything to me. he didn't say anything. He was just a creepy old man."

I hold her gaze for a moment. I'm not sure whether I should push her any further. I nod and back off, "Ok."

Megan brings over the drinks and manages to break some of the tension by swiftly pivoting from the reason we have gone out for lunch, and instead asks

Hannah about her application to uni. Within moments, all the discomfort has been leached from the table and I am able to join with the conversation again.

"When do you get your results?" I ask.

"Next week," she grimaces. "I'm getting nervous about it."

Maybe that's where her mind has been today. Maybe it's nothing about Soanso at all.

"You've done your best," Megan says, brimming with pride. "What do you need to get in?"

"A distinction," Hannah says. The smile on her face subsides. "I need to have aced pretty much everything on those last two parts to get in."

"I'm sure you've done it," I say. She works hard and almost constantly. She spends more time in the library than I ever did. It's not a comparison, just an observation. She works so hard to get what she wants. She will make an amazing teacher.

"I'll be right back," says Hannah, waving her hand towards the loos. The ones in Bukowski's are comfier than the austere almost clinical toilets in the office. Less clean... less hygienic, sure... but nicer in all the ways that seem important in a pub. The walls are papered with posters from the live music events going back decades. I sometimes get lost in them when I'm taking a pee. All the forgotten bands, the ones that fell apart and, in the end, amounted to very little except a memory of a once possible trajectory.

Now that I have Megan alone, I bring Soanso back up.

"You know the project I'm working on?"

"Vaguely," Megan admits. I smile a little—I always suspected she wasn't listening when I spoke. Either that or she is playing dumb for my benefit, allowing me to speak about it in depth.

"It's one of the ones that was started with a Soanso introduction," I say. "I think I should be looking into it; you know. I already thought it was dodgy as hell so..."

"So, look into it," Megan says, ripping into a pizza before the poor server has had a second to put it down. She doesn't sound like she's encouraging me. In fact, almost the opposite. She sounds resigned to the fact that I'm going to do it anyway. It's true, I never can leave things well enough alone.

"Do you think there will be somewhere to report it?" I ask. "I mean, shouldn't they already be looking into it?"

"Maybe they are," says Megan, taking a large bite of pizza and squashes it into her cheek before she continues. "It's the first day. It might be that that's one of the things the managers are doing in that room. Trying to work out which accounts are tainted by association. What they need to pull and investigate."

"That would make sense," I don't tell her about the printouts—though I probably should. The conundrum rears its ugly head inside mine, but I stamp it down. I've already made my decision on that. Remembering that I haven't given Megan any money for our food, I hand over a tenner. "But, Soanso's name isn't on the account. I don't think there's anything that matches him to Ivan Ivanovich."

"Ivan Ivanovich?" She questions the name.

"CEO of this investment firm. They're the one that's setting up the account," I say. She raises an eyebrow and continues chewing.

Megan knows how much I hate feeling useless. This is the first time I have been in the eye of a storm that has hit. Somewhere I could actually do something tangible to help.

"Make sure it's not just cos you're on a crusade to kick a creepy, old man when he's down," she warns.

"He's not some bloke whose house has burnt down, or who's got a flat tyre or something," I chide. "He's a bad guy."

"Inno…"

So help me, you say 'innocent until proven guilty'… "We met the fucker. Are you telling me that you think he might be innocent?"

Megan rolls her eyes and wobbles her head non-committedly. The door to the toilets is opening.

"Did you hear back from the internship?"

"I didn't get it," she says curtly. "Not enough experience."

"I thought the point of an internship is that it *is* the experience."

"Apparently not," Megan clearly isn't interested in speaking about it further. It goes some way to explaining why she's in a mood. We eat in a bubble of silence. It feels like it's my fault. Pushing people too far. Not respecting boundaries. I think I have ruined lunch.

"We should get back to the office," says Megan, taking a last sip of her drink. I rock back in my seat to get some momentum to stand up. As I lean back though, I catch a glimpse of something on the floor. "Is that yours?" I ask Megan. She curses under her breath and picks up her purse.

As my mother would say, Megan *would lose her head if it weren't screwed on.* She buys nice bags and fills the bags with nice trinkets, and then anytime she places it on the side or on the floor, she is bound to lose something. Something will silently topple out and get lost under a chair or table, or by the bathroom sinks. And even though Megan knows that this happens, she is never aware of it happening and so I take it on myself to check her and ensure that nothing is missed.

Of course, I'm not always there. There have been many mornings after midweek nights out, I've bumped into Megan coming out of a pub as I'm on my way into the office. At first, I assumed she was an alcoholic unable to get to work without a drink or two inside her (I can respect that), but no. She would be picking up a purse, a phone, some expensive lipstick or perfume that was missing from her handbag. Sometimes she would wait until the end of the day and go knocking on the doors of bars as they begin to set up for the night, in hope that she would be able to find her lost possessions.

Fortunately, and rather amazingly, there weren't many times that things were gone for good. She either found them at the table or they had been handed to someone behind the bar.

A brief respite, some hope for humanity.

Hannah and Megan walk in front of me back to the office.

I'm going to report my account to the whistleblowers' hotline. Regardless of what's going on in the managers meeting. Regardless of what happens in the police investigations. I am reporting it. The whole, gnarly mess.

"Hey, I'll catch up with you two, I just need to make a call."

They look back at me for a second and nod and continue on into the office.

I cross over the street and stand beside the post box. From here I can see not only the office, but the road in both directions. No one can overhear me. no one can sneak up. I find the whistleblowing number and call it from my mobile.

I am on hold.

I am on hold for a long, long time.

It starts drizzling again.

Just when I'm about to hang up, a bright voice rings out in my ear.

"Hi, you're through to the whistleblowing hotline voicemail. Please leave us a message and contact information and we will look into your corner and get back to you. All information will be treated confidentially. You do not need to leave your details; however, we will be unable to contact you for more information or with updates if you do not."

I'd rather not leave a message. I know their calls are recorded, like ours, but a voicemail seems worse somehow. I leave it though. I go through all the details I remember, all the things I found weird, all the justifications I made to myself, and then I hang up. It's done.

My hands feel a lot colder than they did when I started the call.

When I get into the office, I head up to the fifth floor and pick up my notebook and slip it into my bag.

I'm just taking my notebook home. My notebook. There's nothing suspicious about that.

Chapter 14
Occupation

It's the weekend. Forget about work. Forget about everything. Just have yourself a lovely weekend. Go fishing in a dating app and after finding someone who didn't hit any of the big red flats or hard no's, I agree to meet her at Bukowski's, which happened to be halfway between our homes. She told me that she knew the place well and a part of me wonders if we've ever bumped into each other while drinking there. Maybe we both attended the same gig, or sat to eat at neighbouring tables

It's unlikely, but I like to think of the how beautiful that coincidence would be

I had promised Holl and Syd that I would meet them for the protest Syd has organised. I message to let them know that I might be late, and might have a date with me.

Protesting on a first date—I think that could be fun and good and respectable, couldn't it? The two of us marching hand-in-hand with placards raised above our heads, leading the chants—demanding justice.

Ok, to be honest, that sounds more like Holl and Syd. That works for them, and hey, it could work for me too.

I grab an umbrella for defence against the promised rain later on today, and I head into town early to pick up a nice top to wear. It's been a while since I bought myself something new, and this seems like as good a reason as any. My wardrobe bursts at the seams, and my previously favourite dating-top, one that was pretty and shaped me without splurging out the sides, had a tear down in fabric under the arm that finished as the fabric rose onto the bust.

Gutting.

I hop on a bus into the city centre, to go find myself something nice (and at this point in the month, preferably cheap) at the Meadow Weir Shopping Centre for my date.

I hate shopping, even at the best of times. Clothes shopping especially. Standing in the centre of a department store, I am completely overwhelmed by the vast array of colours and patterns. Perfume samples being sprayed at me and clogging up my sinuses, and then trying to find anything I like, in my size, in a texture that doesn't offend my skin.

I just want soft clothes. Is that too much to ask?

I pass a boutique that I read uses child labour, another shop who's bougie CEO is a TERF, yet another shop that uses designs of a Nigerian woman without payment or credit. Narrowing down the shops I want to buy from. I just want to be able to buy a top. One that looks nice, has fewest air miles and where the designer, seamstress and shop assistant are paid a fair wage.

There is a small shop, down one of the department stores cul-de-sacs, that has a poster in the window saying 'ethically sourced'. Small print directs me to a website.

Looks legit.

That wasn't sarcasm. It actually looks legit.

Inside the shop, instead of photos of models, there are pictures of the clothes journey and the people who make the clothes. There is a picture of the founder, who looks awfully familiar, but I can't quite place where I've seen her before. The fabrics are soft, the patterns pretty. Each label says eco-cotton and regulated factories. This sounds good. Looks good. I feel happy to spend my money here. *Prudence Designs*, the clothes are a little more expensive than elsewhere, but I easily justify it to myself, this is the kind of place I want to buy clothes from.

I find a top in the sales rack. A soft, dark blue, fitted top with white embroidery and three-quarter length sleeves with tiny white buttons and small fabric loops. It's a size too big but when I try it on it hangs nicely. I consider trying on a few other things, but the woman in the cubicle next to mine grunts as she pulls something on and tells the nearby shop assistant that it *is* her size, that she shops here all the time, before she bursts into tears and storms out of the shop.

I've been there.

But, sod it. I'm done. I'm just going to get this one. After paying and leaving by the nearest exit, I am out on the street and able to breathe unperfumed air again. It's only about an hour before we agreed to meet, so I nip into a coffee shop to have a drink and then change tops in the toilets.

Not the other way around. I learn from my mistakes.

I make my way up to Buksowki's and take a seat at one of the few empty tables. The waitress drops off a couple of menus and takes my drink order. During the week I only ever have a half pint at the most, usually cola, but the weekends are a bit fancier than during the week—everything is full price, and the menu is a little bigger than it is Monday–Friday. Megan once told me it was because it's a different fella that runs the kitchen on the weekend. He runs a canteen in one of the bigger buildings towards the centre of town during the week, but he likes the creative freedom his weekend work gives him.

I'm not sure I believe her, but the weekend menu is certainly different and a little more… playful? I'm not sure if that is the right word, but the food is definitely unlike anything at any of the other pubs in town, unlike any restaurant. Not the food itself, not even the presentation, but I suspect the chef is playing in a different spice box.

My drink is brought over to the table. I check the time on my phone. It's only just reached 1 o'clock, the time we said we'd meet. I take a sip of my cherry whisky sours and settle in. She'll be here in a moment.

I wait.

Ping. *Sorry I got caught up. I am on my way now.*

I wait at the table with the reservation card. There aren't any windows to look out of, because we are below street level, and I feel like I'm intruding when I look around at the other tables, so I look intently at each of the posters hung up on the wall. All the musicians that played this small venue and went on to their success.

Ping. *Mad traffic. I'll be there soon.*

The bar hits capacity. Plates brought out from the kitchen, the scraping of chairs and tables being rearranged for a turnaround.

Ping. *I'm sorry it's taking so long. I'm just down the road.*

I wait.

The waitress comes over. "I'm really sorry," she says. "The couple that booked the table after you have arrived and it's their turn." She is genuinely apologetic, squirming her torso and wringing her hands. "There's space at the bar, if you want to wait."

"Yeah, of course," I say. Who am I to stand in the way of someone else's date? Words come spurting out as I get my bags to gather and move my drink to the stool at the bar. "Yeah, I'm sorry. I can move. That's fine. Don't worry." I smile. She smiles back, relieved, and welcomes the couple to what is now *their* table.

"Do you want another drink?" The barman asks.

"Please," I say, tapping the rim of my short glass. "Same again." I take a look at the bar menu. I have been ready to order for almost ninety minutes. I check my phone. Nothing. Stuff it. "Can I order some food?" I ask.

"Sure," the barman says as he places a fresh drink on a new napkin in front of me. "What can I get you?"

"The fake fish and chips," I say, before remembering to add, "please." He nods and goes to put the order in at the till.

No messages.

The food arrives.

No messages.

She's not coming. I resign myself to that reality.

There are, I reason, maybe three things that could have happened which would result in her not turning up:

Firstly, she has a good reason. She was crossing the road and was hit by a car. Touch wood, that didn't happen. If it did, she wasn't hurt too badly. Maybe she was hurt just enough to be dazed and some kind passers-by insisted that she should go to hospital. She had her phone in her hand at the time and it was smashed into the asphalt and that's why she isn't responding.

One of my great-aunts was waiting at the altar and got mad at her fiancé when he was late. Turned out, he'd been mugged on the way to the church and had been giving a statement to the police while being patched up by a paramedic. What I'm saying is, these things happen and it became a charming story that would be brought out at every family gathering, because my great-aunt was so angry at her wedding thinking that her fiancé had stood her up that she picked a fight with a bishop.

She, of course, won that fight.

What idiot bishop suggests that if a bride smiled more then maybe her fiancé would be there to marry her?

I digress.

Second reason my date hasn't turned up is because she was never coming. This was a ruse for some game she was playing with her friends. They arrange dates and never show up. Never leave the house. Just see how long you can get some poor sucker to stay waiting. They have a board that they chart up their successful non-encounters—names and pictures of all the men and women they'll never sleep with because the game with the bezzie mates is far more important than meeting up with the person that they arranged the date with.

I agree, it's something you're more likely to find in an American Teen TV drama about frat boys, but their dominance over our culture would suggest it's plausible.

Unlikely, sure. But plausible.

Thirdly, and what I assume is most likely, she managed to get to the bar. She looked in at the door and saw that I was the only person sitting by myself and made a judgement call that I was not her type.

Despite the accuracy of the photos on my profile, despite our banter, I am not the person for her. She had one look at me and was put off by what she saw. Nothing in the world would entice her to stay for a single, polite drink before her phone rings and—oh, no! There's been a terrible accident. Her nephew is stuck down a well and she is the only one with the necessary climbing gear and skills to go rescue the poor chap.

You know—bow out gracefully.

This has happened to me before (not like that exact same scenario, that would be weird, but being stood up). I am certain it will happen again.

I eat my tofush and chips and leave.

We aren't going to be marching arm-in-arm down Station Road towards the court house. At least, not today.

The walk back into town through the industrial estate is mostly down narrow pavements. High stone walls and narrow passages that are half-blocked by metal bars, forcing people to zig zag their way into the alleyways. The bridge runs over a canal which crosses over a railway. Layers of the city pile up on top of one another. Even though I'm feeling down about being stood up, I still enjoy the mash of history here.

Nothing can take that away from me. my shoes clacking over the cobblestones my great-grandparents wore down. Canals that their grandparents walked down. I'm not even sure if my family's history with the area goes back that far, but it certainly feels like I could turn a corner and bump into people in clogs and shawls leaving through a factory gate.

I like the sound of my shoes on the cobbles. I could probably walk in rhythm and tap out a tune. There's no one around, and I am carrying an umbrella… I could probably knock out a fair rendition of Singing in the Rain.

When we were kids, my brother, cousin and I would come into town on the weekends, sneaking onto the trains and getting off a stop before the barriers to walk the last half mile into town. The money saved from that would be spent on video games or some drinks from an off-licence. I'd come in with friends and go shopping at the Palace, a mess of alternate, low budget, independent stores housed in an old storehouse, the name of which had been lost to the elements so that only the word 'Palace' remained. I hung out with a group at the steps to the library by the fountain right at the heart of town. We were never asked to move on, but we were aware of cameras and a high-pitched whine that seemed to emanate from the walls around us.

As we got older, we would come into town for the music and after finishing whatever Saturday jobs we had, we would sit in a pub garden nursing each pint for as long as we could before admitting defeat and going up to the bar to get another.

This still remains my policy for buying drinks.

I message Holl as I cross over the canal and walk down the towpath past the garage, then I unwind my earphones and plug them into my phone so I can listen to Syd's podcast and get up to date with the protest.

I never really 'follow' the news, or any particular news stories. I couldn't even tell you the first time I heard Max Dunnings name. It was all over the news at one point when I was a kid, my parents vaguely remember the circus around his arrest, and even when his appeals were announced on the local and national evening news, I was only half aware of him.

The police commission came to the conclusion that while Mr Dunning was imprisoned on false allegations, supported by untested (and sometimes outright faked) forensic evidence, with no eye witnesses, due to political motivations, the state decided there was no reason to inform Mr Dunning or his legal team that there were failures and corruption within the system that meant the integrity of the conviction was flawed. Prosecutors wanted to avoid a retrial at all costs.

No, I heard that right. I didn't realise it was **that** bad.

It shouldn't surprise me (it's a shame how often I say those words), but it does. I still have that certainty that I live in a decent world. That certainty is chipped away every time I open my eyes.

Mr Dunning sat in his prison cell, unable to afford a lawyer to keep fighting on his behalf, the only possibility of overturning his conviction was with the public release of the police commission's report.

The commission itself is an independent body that was set up to investigate complaints made against the police. However, the current independent commissioner, Carl Westbrook, is a life-long friend of the current commissioner of the police, John Ellis Cook—they went to the same schools, attended the same clubs and attended each other's weddings as groomsmen—this was surely an oversight.

Syd's voice drips with sarcasm.

So, when it came to this report, and seeing his friend's name plastered throughout, knowing that this would be an end to the career of the highest-ranking member of the police and possible include investigations into every and all cases that Cook touched to ensure that no other case had been so egregiously handled, no other investigations were made. No other reports written. Not only was Mr Dunning kept in prison to save a man his pension, but others were not investigated. The men were already criminals in the eyes of the law, regardless of whether they were guilty of any crimes.

Mr Dunning has finally been released from prison. Almost fifteen years to the day since he was initially sentenced in the same court that he now walks out of a free man. His compensation? Less than £17 for each day he was denied his freedom. His parents and two sisters died while he was in prison. Mr Dunning's son is now a grown man with his own family. His wife remarried.

There are others who are still locked up. Others who declare their innocence, and are not only ignored but whose innocence is actively covered-up. Why? Because we expect those charged with murder to proclaim their innocence, we expect them to lie. But when those in power have been found lying, we have a duty to listen to those declarations, they have a duty to investigate and we have a duty to give back lives that were taken unlawfully.

A beep comes through with a message from Holl, they are passing the courthouse and are on their way to the town square. I'm only a few streets away from the square.

Lastly, we have a duty to hold those in authority to account. No police officers have been reprimanded or fired for their participation in covering up the original crime nor the report that came out four years ago. No one has been arrested for these crimes. The system is rotten; the bad apples have soured it.

I take my earphones out as I walk through a small back street that lies at an angle to the square. At its mouth, I come to an abrupt stop. A police van is parked up on the kerb and a group of officers are standing on the pavement just in front of it. They are chatting intensely, and notice me.

"Where are you off to, love?" One asks, as a few of them turn to face me.

None of your business, I want to say. "Just over there," I timidly say instead. "I'm meeting some friends."

The officer looks me up and down, judging me, considering something. I'm not sure what. Maybe my clothes and general appearance. We don't normally see them in force unless it's match day. The old derby games can still get rough. But there isn't a game on today, and I'm not in a football shirt.

He hasn't responded. Neither have the guys either side of him. I'm not sure if I can go. Why shouldn't I? I'm doing nothing wrong. The men just stand there looking at me. the muscles in my legs strain as they try to move without my permission.

"Alright then," he finally says, and I walk down to the traffic lights rather than crossing straight over the street. Three more vans are parked up before I reach the crossing. All big, white vans. All the officers stood waiting. As I wait for the green man, I surreptitiously photo the line of vans and send the photo on to Syd.

On the other side of the crossing, a counter protest movement has formed. They are against police reform as it just panders to the woke, and they are against the early release of prisoners.

I'm not sure that's an appropriate slogan today. I'm not sure they got the message about Mr Dunning's case.

The people standing there are exactly who I expect to be standing there. Blackshirts.

Over the road and across the square, I can see the front of the march. A few hundred people have already turned the corner and are walking down the short street into the square. Leading the group are the national and international charities that have taken interest in the case.

The big players in the field of Human Rights with their highly recognisable brands. Mr Dunning and his family, front and centre, calling through a loudspeaker. Local BLM and NGOs and civil groups like Syd's who did the organising. A couple of politicians, some up from London for the day, and even one of the local councillors are chanting along with the strong mass of people that are behind them.

Placards waving in the air, handmade and defiant. A detailed painting of a uniformed pig snug in the lap of an ex-prime-minister. Flapping red flags. Voices demanding justice. Demanding reparation. Demanding parliamentary inquiry. Echoes of the cries across the Atlantic: Defund.

Many in the crowd are chanting, and although there are many chants that start off and slowly fade as the crowd passes, one sticks out.

No justice, no peace.

What more needs to be said?

I mean, lots, obviously. But that just encompasses what's needed and what's promised. The chant lives on, echoed at several points down the moving crowd. We will keep demanding justice until there is justice. We don't want scraps to be thrown at us like a bone.

I wait as they all turn into the square and begin to gather at a bandstand in the centre. The leading body waits in there for the rest of the square to fill up. The people around me, although shouting against injustices, are in a pretty good mood. Not happy-smiley, but positively defiant. Hopeful, even. Ready to demand a world we've been told we already live in.

And it does fill up. I hadn't expected so many people, though I probably should have. It's a huge story. People filter through the spaces and a dense pack waits for the speeches to begin.

Holl waves me over. "There are a lot more of them than we expected," they say, casting a wary eye over the police officers who are now standing facing the square.

"There's counter-protestors over there."

"Oof," Holl scoffs, not looking away from the cops for a moment. "Couldn't care less about them."

Syd has set up speakers on the bandstand. A generator is chugging away, firing up the system, Syd picks up a microphone and greets the crowd with a hesitant but firm mic check.

"We are here today," Syd says. "To demand that the reports written on the corrupt officers be released to the public, so that we, the public, may scrutinise the conduct of these officers and the administration that directs their actions. So that lawyers might use the information to overturn wrongful convictions of the innocent. So that we know who it is that is wielding the batons against us."

There is a cheer from the crowd. From the corner of my eye, I can see the police line-up.

"We have marched past Watermere Street Courthouse today," continues Syd. "The same courthouse that Mr Dunning here was handed a life sentence that was based on lies and the concoction of evidence. The same courthouse that rejected every appeal, even those made after the commissioner's report was completed. It wasn't until after that report was leaked to the press that Mr Dunning was made aware of the despicable way his case had been handled. That the family of the victim, who believed that the true murderer was in prison, was informed that they had been lied to."

"There is no justice here. Today we gather and we march to show those that we have elected to power that there is pressure here. That we expect our elected officials to hold office honourably. To instigate integrity into the positions that they hold, because for a long time now there has been none." Syd takes a breath and allows a moment for the cheers to die down. "We demand accountability when the system and the people in the system fail. We demand integrity. We demand justice!"

A cheer followed by clapping. Syd hands the microphone to Mr Dunning to allow the man to speak on his own behalf. He is quiet, and his voice is lost in the static, but those who marched with him and stand with him hang onto every softly spoken word.

"I was betrayed," he tells us. "When my mother and father came to this country all those years ago, they believed in British justice. They believed that here, our family could live in peace and that we could use our hands to build a good life. Yes. I have been freed from that lie," he says sadly. "I want to thank all of you who stood with me over the years, and everyone that helped me and believed me, even when I didn't believe in myself. And everyone here today who wants to know if there are others like me, and I think there are."

He's finished; said everything he wants to say, and I suspect many people in the crowd, want to make it all better for him: the man who lost everything. Syd smiles kindly at Mr Dunning, nodding encouragingly as the microphone is passed on to the next speaker. Although I can't see what's being said, I know Syd is asking if Mr Dunning wants to stay in the band stand or come down away from the limelight for a moment. He does. Syd flashes up a couple of hand signals to another member of his organisation before leading Mr Dunning off the stage.

"They used to use walkie-talkies," Holl informs me. "But the hand gestures are much more effective and don't rely on batteries. I think most of the gestures are from Hong Kong, but they've added in their own signs for other useful things."

"Hong Kong?" I ask.

Holl hums, "The NGO had a conference of protestors last year sharing all their knowledge and skills. It was fascinating."

"How did I miss that?" I ask.

"It was before Syd and I started dating."

"Still, it sounds like something I would have enjoyed."

"There were Hong Kongers, Americans from BLM and Me Too. UKBLM. Two Saudi women from their driving campaign, and a couple of Iranians. It was huge."

"That no one heard of?"

"That you never heard of," Holl corrects me with a nonchalant shrug, but then concedes. "They do need to work on their communication."

"How was the march?"

"Good. We went down and passed Watermere Street Courthouse. We put in our request a couple of days ago to view the documents under the Freedom of Information Act. They're trying to put a stay on it because they think it could cause civil unrest and a dissatisfied populace."

"They think?" incredulity dripping off my tongue.

"Hmm," scoffs Holl. "We're just getting warmed up."

My attention is caught by an excited ripple that runs down the police officers waiting at the edge of the square. Standing a little straighter, wringing their hands round their batons, shifting their weight from one leg to another. An officer from the beginning of the wave, who I suspect must have come purely to give information to the officer at the end of the line, retreats. He goes back to the car on the corner to sit in the warm front seat and speak privately on his phone.

Holl sees it too.

The officers take a step towards us. One long line of repeating uniforms, masked behind riot gear.

And I feel a crushing weight wrap around my chest.

The MP is giving their speech now. A rallying call. And while I am sceptical of any politician throwing their hat into a ring like this one (being likely as they are, to take credit and use the event to their own advantage), I am grateful for the official support that they bring to the event.

As they speak on past injustices, the crowd of protestors becomes ever more aware of the officers slowly, steadily, moving in. Their boots cross the road and reach the pavement that rings around the square.

Syd finds us in the crowd, "I've seen Mr Dunning and his family off," he says, his attention also taken by the officers. "The PMs just made an announcement," he stands up on a raised flowerbed and throws up instructional gestures to a recipient on the other side of the square. Syd comes back down to our level. "They're all around us. Our protest is no longer legal."

My head is full of fuzz. "Not legal?" I ask. "How can it not be legal?"

"The PM held an emergency meeting. Our protest is not in the public's interest, and so they've given permission to the police to shut us down."

"They can't do that!" Holl exclaims. "We have the permits for this!"

"Permits have been voided. I need to let people know." He turns squarely to face Holl and rests his forehead against theirs. "Be safe," he says quietly.

Holl closes their eyes. "Go," they tell him.

I am committing a crime. I didn't start out to start a crime. It wasn't one when I started doing it. I don't think it is a crime, or shouldn't be one.

Syd has climbed back up onto the bandstand and informed all those there, including the MP, that they are now involved in a criminal act. The MP holds the microphone done by his side as he listens carefully to Syd. There is a brief back and forth, and as they discuss what this means and what they should do, the crowd, almost in unison, notices the police separate around the beds of fauna and reform into a long impenetrable line that now stabs into the crowd's comfort zone. I can feel their presence brush against my skin and it unnerves me.

The MP picks up the microphone, but words are lost as the crowd's voice rises and cries out in protest against this new edict. How is this fair? How can the great 'they' take away our right to protest? To protest against a system designed to be wielded against us. A system that so easily hides the truth. A system that protects itself and not the people.

I am angry.

I am scared.

I want all this to be over.

The protestors that form the edge of our group, link arms. The politician calls for calm and peace, imploring the officers to stand back and allow us to leave the square. The officers already have their marching orders, and they tighten their grip on their batons.

Metal fences that cordoned off parts of the square that were to be repaired, are handed down the line to brace the front to place a physical barrier between us two groups. I help one be lifted over the crowd to the line of people between me and the police, now mere yards away, rushing forward to pull at the arms of those placing the barrier down.

One officer grabs hold of the teenage girl next to me and tries to pull her over the barricade. She cries out as he pulls on her arms and shirt, ripping it, to drag her over the metal fence. She begs them to let go, she tells them they are hurting her. As the officer grapples with her, he releases her shirt for the briefest of moments, and without a thought, I open my umbrella in his face as the people behind pull the girl to safety.

To safety.

Away from the police.

For the briefest of moments, and in a clarity unparalleled in my life, I lock eyes with an officer who tried to take the girl. I recognise the look in his hooded eyes. The determination. A hunter with prey in his sight. Without breaking eye contact, I step back and disappear into the crowd.

The square shrinks, I can feel it in my stomach. A switch at the back of my mind is flicked and I am suddenly aware of the exact dimensions of the world I now inhabit. My world has shrunk down to a single square in a small city surrounded by a force that is hostile to me. That force stands as a homogenous block between me and the world. A single slab that has the authority to take me away for standing and speaking with my friends.

Words of peace and justice are trapped within this kettle.

The crowd raises a unified voice of defiance, demanding the officers admit if they saw the report. Did they know the officer that raped and murdered that poor girl last year? Did they know the officer that killed that black boy in police custody? Did they know the officers that shared gifs and memes to celebrate the deaths of the immigrants in that factory fire?

Do they still talk with those officers? Do they still go down the pub to have a cheeky pint? Do they go to each other's garden barbecues?

One cry rises out above all the others until it is shouted by the entire crowd, a demand made by the entire crowd, as though a promise:

If one bad apple spoils the barrel—burn the barrel!

Nasrin Munshi

Seamstress

Splendid Garment Factory, Bangladesh

"What's your name?" Nasrin asked as she and her daughter weaved through the morning traffic, laced with cabs and bikes on their way to the factory.

"Hamida," Nasrin's daughter, Inaya, replied.

"And how old are you, Hamida?"

"Eighteen."

Nasrin nodded at that, "don't forget it." She waved to the doorman as they approached. "They are very strict on age," she told her daughter. The two of them slow down as they reach the door. "Hi Firoz, this is my niece," she told the guard. "She's getting a job here today." Firoz smiled welcomingly.

"Could you show these two the way up?" Firoz asked gently, pointing to the two workmen approaching carrying fire extinguishers.

"They have finally bought us extinguishers?" Nasrin asked as her reply.

"I think they are second hand from an office block a couple of kilometres west of here," Firoz told her. "The back staircase is blocked at the moment, but there are more men coming to clear that away today."

"So, we are expecting *visitors*," Nasrin says, conspiratorially lowering her voice.

"Surprise inspection," says Firoz, matching her intonation. "Tomorrow's surprise."

Nasrin rolled her eyes and tsked under her breath. "Come on, then," she said to Inaya. "Let's go up the front stairs."

The two men with the extinguishers followed Nasrin through the ground floor shopping mall, past the staircase labelled 'Splendid Garment Factory' where two men on step ladders used a tin of old white paint to fill in the cracks in the walls, and round the street food vendors surrounded by a dense mass of people wanting to grab some food before starting work for the day. Nasrin pointed out the best place to go for food at lunch time.

At least here in the factory, Nasrin would be able to keep her daughter away from trouble. It wasn't that Inaya caused trouble, far from it, she was a kind and sweet child who studied long and hard. But she was a child, and Nasrin's estranged husband often forgot that. He had come round to the house when Nasrin had been out and told Inaya of the marriage he was arranging for her. One of his friend's younger brothers. Luckily for Inaya, he hadn't taken her then and there, and so Nasrin had spent every moment since then with Inaya close by.

"He doesn't live with us," Nasrin told her daughter sternly as they took the staircase up to the factory. "He doesn't pay anything into this family, he does not get to decide this for you. If he tries to take you, you kick and you scream. I don't care if the whole neighbourhood hears it. I don't care if everybody knows our business. I don't care. You will have options and choices in life. If that means work for now and go back to school when he has this idea of marriage out of his head, so be it."

Nasrin's husband hadn't spoken to her directly. They had been estranged so long that Nasrin was fairly certain they had passed on the street a few months ago and he hadn't recognised her. Instead, her husband had sent his sister to reason with her.

"She is fourteen years old," Nasrin had said to her sister-in-law. "She is too young to marry that man."

"You were fourteen when you married," Sumaiya reminded her.

"Yes, so I know what I'm talking about! She is too young!"

"He is arranging this for his daughter, like any good father would."

"Good father?" Nasrin had scoffed so hard it hurt. "Good father! He hasn't lived with us since she was three years old. He can't even come here to speak with me himself!"

"He knows how you are," Sumaiya said while waving her hand dismissively. "He is doing this for Inaya! She needs to be married before something happens and we can't find her a husband."

"She is a good girl. Nothing is going to happen."

"You cannot be there to watch her all the time!"

Was that a threat? Nasrin had thrown her sister-in-law out at that moment and knew that she would have to keep an eye on all the other members of that family in case they came by to take Inaya.

This—bringing Inaya to the factory and getting her a job—this was Nasrin buying time. For now, that was enough. In the autumn, Inaya would be able to go to the scholarship school, and there she would be safer. At least that's what Nasrin hoped.

The manager took Inaya into his office and Nasrin sat at her workspace and began to serge the pieces of soft, navy-blue fabric right-side together. She expected the interview to take little more than a few minutes, but almost fifteen minutes passed, and Nasrin began to get nervous. She tried to think of things to do to keep her mind occupied while her only daughter was out of sight.

"Sir!" Nasrin called over the supervisor. "I only got 3000 takas this month, but I worked twenty days, not fifteen."

The supervisor shrugged, "maybe you were docked for being late?"

"I wasn't late," Nasrin answered. "Not once. It should be ৳4,500."

"They won't have made a mistake," said the supervisor.

"Who can I ask about it?"

"You can talk to the boss," the supervisor said, pointing to the office. He stepped back, but not wanting to leave the conversation like that, he pointed at her workspace. "Make sure you clean that up and get rid of those scraps. The business lady from England will be here tomorrow and this place needs to look its best."

"Is that why Dipak is painting over the cracks in the back staircase?"

"That mouth of yours is going to get you into trouble," the supervisor said as he left.

Inaya came out of the office and beelined straight for Nasrin.

"How did it go?" Nasrin asked over the top of the tapping machines.

"I can start the day after tomorrow," Inaya said.

"Sit down," Nasrin instructed her, pulling up a stool so they could sit side-by-side while Nasrin finished off the intricate pattern on the blouse with white thread. "The day after tomorrow? Did you stick to the information on the card?"

"Yes, I did," replied Inaya. "He said I looked younger than my picture, but that I could work here, just not tomorrow."

"Good," Nasrin smiled as she breathed out a sigh of relief, content with her plan to outwit her husband. "Good. You can sit with me today and I'll show you what I'm doing here."

Chapter 15
Brainstorm

All the crap that usually rests on the coffee table is unceremoniously dumped on the floor. I'll tidy it up later.

That's not true. That pile will sit there for several weeks. I will step over it each time I go to sit on the sofa and every time I get up to make a cup of tea or stretch my legs or open the door for the postie. That pile might just live there now. Forever. That's where it belongs.

I open up the remote access to the office on my laptop and check my emails. An acknowledgement sits there from the whistleblowing team.

Thank you for calling... and investigation has been opened... we will look into this...

The ball is rolling.

It will probably roll backwards and crush me—but it is rolling.

I need to lay this whole thing out, map it out fully and understand exactly what is going on.

I take all the names of people I noted from the applications and list them all on a blank piece of printer paper.

What else have I got?

Addresses. Or at least the mid-terrace in Bath and the company house address that broke the government's own online portal.

The names of the advisers—the head honcho, Ivan Ivanovich. Some of his employees notes from the files—I have them all stuck in the back of the notebook—keeping them safe and together. I read through them all. Names that mean nothing to me. Solitary names like Kostya, Ionut, Dana, Timur, Dorinel... the list goes on and I have nothing more, no surnames or locations, that I can include in a search, so these names are just names—but maybe to someone else they might mean something more.

I have bank numbers. I take the sort code—the rest is bunk. Though most were taken out in clumps, meaning large portions of the individual account numbers are similar, I don't feel comfortable writing them out on another piece of paper. I write comments and directions to the account numbers, but not the numbers themselves. That's a line I won't cross.

It's quiet in the living room. Unbearably quiet. Every time a pipe growls, a piece of wood flexes or a car rumbles outside, I am put on edge. I turn on the TV and put it on the repeats channel.

I google the house again, and take a screenshot of the map. Is there anything else I can find out about the house? I run it through google, but beyond finding the last time it was sold, there is nothing. I run the investors' names and find social media for most of them, or at least I think I have, because none of them seem to be from the UK. In fact, the more I look, the more I find that many of them only lived here for a few months, around the time that the bank accounts were taken out and then they went back to a small region in Romania.

I don't hear Holl until they appear beside me at the coffee table.

"What's all this?" They ask.

After a small heart attack, I answer them, "Just investigating." My voice sing-songs over the words, as though it's just a game I'm playing. They pick up one of the handwritten notes I've made and turn it over to read the back.

"No, seriously," Holl says. "What is this?"

I heave myself off the floor and onto the sofa. Maybe Holl needs a distraction from everything that is going on with Syd and the lawyers.

"I think the account I'm working on at work is doing something illegal," I say. "And I'm trying to work out what they are doing."

Holl places the paper back on the table. "Have you reported it?" They ask, pulling back their hoodie to reveal a new pixie cut.

"Nice hair," I smile. "Yeah, I've reported it. I just need to look into it."

"Because you don't think they will?" Holl joins me on the sofa.

I hesitate for a moment. I was relieved when the email showed that they had opened an investigation, but did I believe that that would actually do anything? "No, I don't trust they will." It's the first time I've said that out loud. "I think it'll be hushed up to save the company face."

"What kind of crime is it?" Holl asks.

"Some sort of money laundering," I reply. "I'm just trying to work out what they're doing and how."

Holl turns the list of names towards them so they can more easily read it. "What do you think is going on?"

Do I have a fully formed theory yet? Do I need one? It's not my job to work out what is going on, but I just can't help myself.

"I think that someone is using the names of these people that come to legally work in the UK to open bank accounts, and then they're moving money between these accounts just below the threshold that the banks would take notice of, and they are making the accounts look active. Then they are using these accounts to join an investor… or the investor is creating these accounts to make it look like they have more backers with more money to invest? Maybe…" I drift off. Unsure of what I'm saying.

"I don't think the people whose names are on the accounts know that they have these accounts. I don't think they know someone is investing money in their name. I think the investment company is a scam to get money into the UK and they are laundering it through us so when they get pay outs it's clean money."

Holl isn't following the mess of an explanation I'm making. "I think someone made a lot of money somewhere, and they are using this company to launder their cash. I think this company has done it before under lots of different names. I think…" I run out of steam, and think nothing else.

"I can make tea," Holl says. "I don't think I'll be much good at anything else."

"How's Syd doing?" I ask.

Holl shakes their head, "not great."

I haven't seen Syd since he was taken away by the police at the protest. I keep trying to block out the rest of what happened. I've been to protests before. I've even been kettled at protests when I was at uni. Once we were occupying this unused building at the university, using it as a study space with a soup kitchen for students that were struggling.

We had to take it in turns to sleep over in groups because the principal kept trying to shut us down. His students couldn't afford to eat because rents were so high, there was one guy who slept there regularly because otherwise he was on people's couches. I never had a couch to offer—the landlord turned our living space into a third bedroom and never told the council. We couldn't tell the council, because it was the only place we could afford.

Syd is waiting in a police cell to be charged. Waiting, somehow, indefinitely. In their infinite wisdom and haste to create a new rule, the lawmakers had missed out several fairly important parts of legislation—which included, but was not limited to, failure to define the length of time a person could be held. The lawyers that work for the same company are working round the clock, but even things that felt slow-moving were now stubbornly stuck.

Holl puts on a brave face. They know that Syd will be out at some point, but they aren't even allowed to see him. No one is.

The initial protest was relatively short-lived, but since then there have been numerous 'gatherings' and 'vigils' (we don't call them protests—not that the police or authorities care). Most are shut down within a few hours. There were twelve last night, all across the country.

Hundreds of thousands of people in total, marching silently, some holding candles, some with tape across their mouths. I've seen the local papers pick it up, but nothing national. Nothing on the news. One guy called into a radio programme but his call was quickly shut off with "I'm sorry, we seem to have lost that caller. Anyway…".

I went to the vigil outside the police station, but we were moved swiftly on. The new law includes protests at police stations. I can see the logic, which is always the worst part. I understand why it could be a good law. But I can also see how it's being used in practice. That scares me a little.

Another week passes. Another weekend. Slowly at first, and then all at once. I'm back in the little glass box, this time by myself, running checks on the data entry. It's impossible to tell when all the details look the same and, for the most part, are the same.

It's been a fortnight since I called the whistleblowing hotline and I haven't heard anything back. Should I be calling them with my understanding? I told them everything when I first called, but I've been thinking about it now and I have some theories.

The information on my screen keeps blinking in and out of focus as I wonder what has been going on at whistleblowing. I reread a single data point six times because I keep forgetting that I've already checked it—oh, sod it. I'm never going to be able to concentrate at this rate, I might as well call through and see if they have an update.

They actually answer this time.

"Hi, I'm calling about a message I left the other week," I give the woman on the other end my reference number from the acknowledgment email they sent me. "I just wondered if there was an update on anything…" I flounder, but get my query out.

"Yep," comes a crisp confirmation. "I have a note here about this one. It came in this morning, bear with me," she says. I hear her nails tap on the keyboard. People walking past the glass box distract me. their innocent glances into the box as they pass. The chance encounters of our eyes meeting. I feel guilty every time our eyes lock. "Yes," the woman continues. "After thorough investigation, we have found no evidence of illegal or immoral action on the case that you called about."

"I'm sorry, what?" I've surely misheard her.

"The investigation is complete. A report has been made. Nothing has been found."

"The investigation only started two weeks ago? No one's even come round to look at the paper documents."

"Investigations can take different lengths of time based on what the allegations are and how much there is to look into."

"But you haven't looked into it," I think I said the 'you' a bit too harshly. I don't mean her specifically.

"The investigating team will have done all the necessary checks from here and only do an onsite visit if they deem it necessary."

"But…" What can I say? What words can I say to make this clear? "It is necessary. All the information came in on paper forms?"

There is a silence on the other end of the phone and a short sigh I recognise as someone reading through notes on a screen.

"I can see all the checks have been done and marked on the system, and then there are managers who have signed all that off."

Checks? The checks I am doing now?

"What do you mean checks? I am doing the checks now—nothing has been signed off by my manager," I tell her.

"Someone else must have done it," she says. I look around my tiny see-through cage. There's only me. There's no one else.

I open up a client's profile and look through the back system to find the checks completion to prove that it hasn't been done. To show that no one there has looked into this properly and they need to come on a site visit. But there it is, smugly glaring at me from the screen. A small tick next to the checkboxes.

Who the fuck has done that?

"Hello?" The woman from whistleblowers calls down the line. "Is there anything else I can help you with?"

"I don't understand," I stutter, unable to get the words through my brain fog. "I am doing these checks. I am doing them right now. I haven't ticked any of the boxes. I don't know who has. I'm the only one working on this."

Silence at the other end of the line. "Hold on," she says, and places me on hold.

Is there a way I can see who has checked the box? I know there is a log for everything done on the front of the system, anytime someone views it or changes things like contact details or surnames, but for the back office... I don't think there is. I check the log anyway. Maybe whoever ticked the boxes messed about with something on the front system. I check a couple of profiles, but find nothing.

"Hello, again," the voice rings out.

"Hi," I say.

"I've spoken with my manager here and he says that as a manager has confirmed it, there's nothing more to look into for this investigation. He suggests that maybe someone did overtime at the weekend or something."

So why am I doubling up work by redoing it?

Thinking about it, I haven't seen Jan yet this morning. So maybe she just missed telling me that I don't need to do it.

"Is there a way to log that I still think someone needs to come and look through the paper documents?"

I'm testing the patience of the woman at the other end, I can tell.

"This call is recorded. I can send it on to the team that investigated and log it with the report that we have filed." She sounds really unhappy about that. Like I'm causing a fuss over nothing. Like I am messing her about. "You should go check that this wasn't done by someone else."

That was a little aggressive.

"Which manager signed it off?" I ask.

"I can't give you that information."

Well, who the fuck am I supposed to check with. She can sense my hesitation.

"We can't release that information. There is a multi-disciplinary team that are involved in these investigations, which includes whistleblowing investigators and a select group of people that are from the types of teams involved. A report is prepared and we file it with an external body."

"But they didn't go through the documents…"

"It wasn't deemed necessary."

"Is there anyone else I can speak with?"

"When I put you on hold, I was speaking with my manager."

The Karen within me demands to speak with the manager, but I suppress her. There is no point.

"I could raise a complaint for you?" She offers. I know the complaint will do nothing in this instance. That the decision made already will be upheld. I know that there is nothing I can do.

"No," I admit defeat with a quiet voice. "Thank you." I hang up.

I open a profile I know is riddled with fake information. Information I was going to need to send back to Ivan Ivanovich to get further details. The same street address as all the others. email@email email address. 00000000000 phone number.

The box has been ticked.

The box to confirm that we hold all the correct information for a client has been ticked. They didn't even bother to change the obviously fake.

And then, someone signed off on it.

Not me. Sure as hell, not one of the temps—they've never even seen the back system. This tick box. This one small visually insignificant box, has just approved the client—all the clients, authenticated them, allowing them to go forth and invest.

This is not good. This is very 'not good'.

I screen shot and I print it. I don't even know what I am going to do with that. I don't even know who I could show that too.

An email pops up on my screen from Jan asking us to gather at her desk as soon as possible. I go via the printer, folding the warm paper and shoving it in my pocket. The IT guys are making their way out for a smoke, pulling a lighter from a small gap between the desk and the cabinet that rests underneath it.

I am the first to arrive, even with the furthest to travel. Megan and Hannah are still milling over after having locked their screens. Jan ignores us and keeps tapping away at her keyboard until everyone is gathered.

"I know a lot of you are concerned with everything that has happened in the past few weeks. We, as a company, are trying to make decisive but not rash decisions," Jan keeps looking down at a notepad of her perfectly rounded letters. They are written too small for me to see what's coming.

"There are some things that need to be treated as more urgent than others. There are going to be some immediate changes that will be going into effect almost immediately. It only affects a couple of people in our team and I'll be talking to those people today. Don't worry," she says unconvincingly, pulling her lips back into a tight smile. "It's not all bad."

It must be bad. She's telling us not to worry.

"If you go back to your desks, I'll email the people I need to see with the times that I want to talk with you. If you haven't received an email in the next five minutes, nothing will be changing for you."

I need to pull her aside before she does all that. See what she wants me to do today, seeing as the checking I was supposed to be doing has already supposedly been done.

Jan turns back to her desk as I hover. "Actually," she tells me. "Do you want to go wait in the small meeting room there, I'll see you first."

I look over at Megan for a hint, but she's already disappeared behind her computer.

I go over to the small meeting rooms. The only free one is the one on the end. I go in, leaving the door slightly ajar, and wait for Jan. The last time I was in one of these rooms, my old manager was letting me know I was switching teams. The last time they had a proper reshuffle was a couple of years ago, and to be honest, they are overdue one.

Jan enters and sits down across from me.

"Right," she says. No song or dance, "we are going to have to let you go."

What?

"With all the adjustments going on, unfortunately, we need to lose a few people, and you will be one of them."

Why me?

My voice is small and distant and barely breaches my lips. Telly snow and white noise. I don't hear her. Her response is long winded and full of tangents.

"What did I do wrong?" I am in shock. Tears roll down my cheeks, burning my skin. "I don't understand."

"Good news is, you'll be on garden leave for your notice period—so you'll be paid but won't need to come into work," she smiles. I think she is trying to look kind, but it comes off as tone-deaf.

"Is this because I reported that account to the whistle-blowers?"

Jan's mouth crimps shut. She leans away from me, closing her hands over her belly.

"It can't be about that," she says. "That's not something that would happen."

Linguistic gymnastics. Saying something without saying something. I can't tell if she did that on purpose. It's a bit of a risk if she did.

"How many people are being let go?" I try to sound firm but surprise has gotten the best of me.

"For now; you," my manager answers. "But we are at the beginning of restructuring and things will be clearer later down the line if we need to let others go. We're mostly just moving people around."

"Except me."

"Except you."

"What happens now?"

"You just need to empty your locker and hand in your card."

"Right now?" I ask through a stiff jaw.

"I think that's for the best," Jan says, not unkindly.

I can't move and for a moment I think I've forgotten how my legs work. My breakfast churns in my stomach. My hands feel cold and I keep trying to trace back the events of the past few months to work out how I got to this point, but my mind jumps all over the place to things that are completely unrelated and I can't reel it back in, no matter how hard I try.

Jan, acting sympathetic, stays with me.

"Did you sign off on the whistle-blowers report?" I ask with a wheeze.

Jan shakes her head and looks down at the table between us. "No, it wasn't me," she says.

I regain myself. I empty my locker. I hand in my pass to the security guard at the front desk. No one even knows I'm going. They don't notice me leave. There's no more than fifteen minutes between our conversation and my flagging down a bus home with a bag-for-life filled with the junk that accumulated in my locker over the past five years. My head hasn't caught up to my body yet and I sit lifeless on the bus.

"Cheer up, love," a man on the bus takes one look at my forlorn expression "might never happen."

I burst into tears. He backs off quickly.

Serves him right.

I have to give my body instructions. I have to order myself to move. My body divides from itself.

I don't understand. I just don't understand what I did wrong. I did everything I was supposed to. Everything I was told I was supposed to do.

Tears are running thick and fast now. No matter how full the bus gets, no one wants to sit beside the sobbing woman.

My anger grows overnight. A dozen messages from people in the office asking me where I am and what's happened.

I don't answer.

I don't know what to tell them.

My notes are on the coffee table where I left them.

*

It's all organised now. All the bits of paper that I had all the notes I took. The crumpled piece of paper in my pocket that almost went through the wash, all smoothed out and filed in order. My notebook tucked under the elastic band wrapped around the binder. I didn't know where to take it except here, no more than a hundred feet from where Syd is locked up.

There was a trembling sense of uneasiness when I came to the realisation of where I had to go. Even now, sitting on the grey plastic chair in the waiting room, being watched by the desk sergeant, even my shortest breaths are shockingly bold. I wasn't sure what to say to the officer who, from behind his shatterproof glass, asked what I was there for. Financial crime, I guess.

The clients are fake. I know this for sure. Or at least haven't provided accurate information which means that they are as good as fake. You can't have a large group of people with supposedly that many assets with no social media, or professional websites, or proof of where they got their finances. Even the business that submitted the account has next to no online presence, and the company is registered to an address that is clearly fake or purely for legal purposes. And the man that runs it is clearly friends with Soanso—a predator and conman. And the company I work for—worked for—has avoided any scrutiny of them or their clients.

I should know. I should have been the one to scrutinise them.

It's like I'm missing this whole long chain of events of why this is happening. It must be money laundering; I can't think of any other reason a company would be this shady. The money must originate in some sort of dodgy or illegal business. I don't think I'll ever get to the bottom of that—but someone should. Someone needs to look into this. Someone needs to investigate and work out what happened.

I tell the officer I speak with that internal investigations at the company were bungled. That they were too quick and didn't consider any of the information I uncovered. That I went up every avenue internally. That I tried.

I don't know why that seems like the most important part to me. I'm tired of thinking about it, of saying it—*I tried. I tried* to do the right thing—at every single turn. I did what I was supposed to do and it got me fired.

Not that the company would ever say that. I'm still waiting to hear back from Ben about what the union has to say, but I doubt it will be good news.

Not that the officer believes me. I am some lunatic ex-employee. I have made the whole thing up to get back at a company for firing me.

I tell him I wasn't fired. I was let go.

He doesn't care about the nuance.

The longer I sit with the detective the less sure I feel. Not less sure of my findings, or myself. My low opinion is cemented. After reaching rock bottom, they have pulled me through the crust into the mantle, and I am less sure of them. Of the police. Of the company.

I leave the station in shame, feeling like a liar attacking a well-respected company that followed all necessary procedures, a company that knows what it's doing.

I go past the courthouse and sit in the square unsure what to do next. The binder and the notebook lie in my lap. They didn't even make a photocopy.

What now?

What do I do now? This, surely, is as high as it goes.

I don't want to go home. It's empty and cold, colder than outside. I can't talk to my friends; they are at work.

The thought of calling my parents briefly crosses my mind, but I'd have to tell them that I don't have a job and I don't want to get into that conversation with them until I have a new one.

Could I go directly to Soanso? Surely, he'd be able to fill in some gaps. Or talk to the team investigating him? Surely, they'd want to know about the things I've found.

Maybe I can get my fifty quid back from his fake charity's event.

I know I'm not getting that back.

I've already mentioned Soanso's name to the officer I spoke with. He wasn't particularly interested in what I had to say about him, but maybe the prosecutors would be. I don't even know how I would get in touch with them.

I tug the font of my coat forward and around me. I opened it to sit down comfortably, but now all the warmth has escaped. I should really eat something, but I don't want to waste any money, so I just sit and feel the wind blow through my coat and chill my bones.

The longer I sit without eating, the hungrier I feel. It builds up like an anxiety, a worry that I won't have food again.

Hours pass. Dogs are walked. People going into work pass me by. A small gaggle of children on leads are led through the square, herded by a group of women from the nursery. Maybe I should work in childcare. A soother occupation, one with timetabled walks and snack time.

Who am I kidding? I'd be rubbish at that. I don't have that nurturing intuition or the desire to play with small children all day. I'd love it if I did.

When I do stand up, I find I am frozen solid. My muscles feel swollen and stuck in place. I have to crack my bones to stand up straight.

I cross over the road to the newsagents, and pick up a packet of crisps and a can of the cheapest larger they have. At the counter there is a wire hanger carrying all of today's papers.

"Hiya, love," says the woman behind the counter. "You want anything else with that?"

I look through the front pages and find one that still mentions Soanso's case (on page 18). I add it to my shopping and pay the woman behind the counter.

Back on the bench, I turn to page 18 and read the by-line: Graham Bolt.

Ok, Bolt. Time to find out who you are and if you'll listen.

I scour for a phone number for him on the website, but finding none, switch over to his twitter and send him a direct message.

I have worked at Ieso Financial and Wealth Management for five years. I have some information regarding Lord Soanso and his interactions with this company. Please contact me for more details.

Is that enough? I'm not going to spend forever writing a detailed report with my thumbs on my phone.

I skim through the rest of the paper. Same old, same old.

Maybe I could work for a newspaper. They must need secretaries/admins—I could do that to start with. I could start off in some office taking calls with tips and typing up reports to pass on to the journalists… I don't know if that's how it works—but one day, all the journalists would be out and they would need someone to quickly meet up with the secret informant. I, being the only one in the office, am tasked with this.

The cafe that the information suggests is secluded and run down. One of the long beam lights hangs out of its socket and flickers while we sit at a table beside a mildewy wall. They look anxious, nervous, barely touching their coffee in a dull, beige mug. They ask me if I'm ready to listen, that nobody ever listens. They surreptitiously hand over a manilla envelope with papers and a CD. Old school. I open it a little to peek inside. Watermarked, letter-headed. Official documents.

Where did you get these? I ask.

Where do you think? He replies, cosying his hands around his drink. *I have to go. They'll find me.*

He's paranoid. They sometimes sound paranoid on the phone, but it's different seeing it in person. His eyes flicker between the doorway and the window hatch to the kitchen. He gets up.

Wait! I beg. *Please wait. What is this? What have you given me?*

He looks down at me, wide-eyed and deadly serious. *Enough to change the world.*

He pulls his arm from my hand and turns up the collar of his anorak and pulls down the brim of his hat as he steps out onto the slick-wet street.

It wouldn't be like that, of course. It would be sitting in an office, arranging meetings for one of the journalists or 'content creators', working the internship on the side only to be told twelve weeks later 'thank you for your work—it's good, really it is, but we've no space for another writer at the moment,' as they welcome someone in through the door.

I'd get bored and apply to other jobs, using the strength of my internship and the fact that I was currently working at a paper. I would start applying for jobs with 'competitive salaries' only to find they were anything but, and needing three years' experience for an entry-level position, benefits include comprehensive *blank* and generous *blank*, family friendly, etc. etc.

They'll want people who 'thrive' on tough deadlines—preferring speed over content. Oh, ever-more content. Content to drive people to their site. Content that rates celebrities and tantalising clickbait that promises to surprise me. Nothing of substance.

The ones with substance and support retain their writers, I naively assume. At least until the paper goes under.

There's no reply to my message.

It's too cold to sit still. I walk around aimlessly, giving in to my whims of which direction I should go. Blown about like the leaves falling from the tree, hitting the ground and then being swept up into a low spinning tornado.

By the time I reach home there is a message waiting for me from Graham Bolt.

Thank you for your message, please email me full details.

I get out my laptop, crack my knuckles and type up the longest, fullest explanation I can. I add in all the details I can remember and date. I note the types of documents that came through. The piles of boxes, how unusual this was. I even detail my situation. Dates I did things. What I did, where I turned. How I was the only one to be 'let go' in the restructuring. How all that happened right after I spoke with the whistle-blowers. How my union was now involved. I write about the time I saw Ivan Ivanovich at the charity event, the charity being the one under scrutiny.

By the time I'm done I'm exhausted.

I boil the kettle, but forget about it as I sit brimming with nervous energy.

Chapter 16
AOB

It takes a few days for Graham to get back to me. After a polite introduction, the email is a short paragraph long and my heart sinks at the length of it.

Thank you for getting in touch and sending the information about the suspected financial scam. We at the Meadow Weir Inquirer do rigorous research on all leads that are submitted to us. Unfortunately, there just isn't enough information in your email for us to use what resources we have to investigate any further. As there is nothing concrete in your findings, and as there are no original/copies of original documents or indeed any proof at all that this relates to Lord Soanso, we are unable to take you at your word that there is a scam taking place or that there is anything that links with previous articles I've written on the subject. As this would be a minor scam compared to the major scandal and criminal case being brought against Lord Soanso, we would not be able to justify dedicating space in our newspaper even if...

At this, I stop reading.

He would need bank statements. The ones that show the money moving round. He would need photographs of the events showing Soanso and Ivan Ivanovich—the ones taken down from the website and staff events board—things that, if they do still exist—are in an office I no longer have access to.

There's no way I can get them.

Is that it? After everything, is that it? Does it just end? I've almost pieced together the whole thing. The whole crime. And no one cares.

I lean back into the sofa. The muscles in my jaw and cheeks tense painfully, and a tickle starts in the bridge of my nose. The corners of lips pull down and tears come and a breathy, hoarse whine.

What do I do now?

What is there left to do?

I lie in state waiting for something, somebody or even anything or anybody to just pull me out, because I am sinking, alone in a flat I can no longer afford, let go from a job I hated, and disenchanted with a world I believed in.

Maybe David was right.

Don't go that way.

Just cry. Rebalance. Let everything inside, out.

Every time I reach out to my phone or laptop to start sorting out my life the unbearable weight of everything I have to do crushes me. I try to sleep, but even if I do manage to drift off for a few moments I am trapped in a restless dream. Dreams that offer joy, and nightmares that no longer scare me.

What if I don't find anything? What if there are no places to rent that are suitable or affordable? What if the people that respond to the flatmate ad are much the same as the people who respond to online dating?

I get a message from Hannah; they have finally been told what happened. Or, at least a portion of it. She asks me to come in for a leaving do they are planning—as though I chose to leave.

Friday.

Ben can pick me up on his way in.

I want to tell her to fuck off. To tell her I didn't leave, I was booted out. I want to tell her that I am not coming. I want to tell her about everything I've done in the past few days since being frogmarched out the door.

I don't. Of course, I don't. I tell her I'll see her Friday.

I wash my hair and blow dry it. Pulling myself together, starting with my hair.

I actually start to look forward to it, in a weird and perverse way. I miss the people I work with, even Carol.

Ok, maybe not Carol.

I know Hannah has booked us some booths at a swanky wine bar that half of us can't afford, but we will rely on the kindness of strangers, and the guilt or benevolence of managers keen to win us over before their performance feedback forms are collected next month.

Not that I have to care about that anymore.

I pull out my one nice dress, the one I last wore to the charity event. It feels tighter than the last time I wore it, still swings at the bottom, though. Resigning

227

myself to the fact that it's the only thing I have and I can't afford to buy another, I put it on and grab a clutch that Holl left behind and hasn't been back to pick up.

I receive a message from Ben saying he's outside.

"I need to stop off at the petrol station," he says as I open the door to the sharp, almost piercing scent of Ben's aftershave. He's wearing a skinny suit, not quite what I expected, not what he would usually wear to a leaving do. But, then again, we are going to a wine bar up at the top of a hotel, with 360° views of the city. Just like me in this ridiculous dress, he has dressed for the occasion.

"Apparently there's a deal on at the old pump down on North Road. My dad asked me to pick some stuff up. Normally it doesn't make much of a difference. But if you buy enough petrol, you get a percentage off in the shop and well, he needs some petrol for his mower and antifreeze and that. It'll only take a minute or two," Ben says apologetically. I shrug. I was only half listening.

He pulls into the pump and asks me if there is anything I want from the shop. I shake my head before the voice in the back of my head reminds me, I haven't brushed my teeth. "Gum," I say. He doesn't hear. He's already opened the boot and taken out a petrol can.

It does only take him the couple of minutes he promised. Soon we are on the one-way system making our way through Friday night traffic. It's already dark out. No stars though. They never quite pierce the light pollution from the lampposts.

We park underneath the hotel, and take the lift up to the top floor. Hannah is already there. She bounds over to meet us at the bar, brimming with excitement.

"I may have taken advantage of one of the manager's offers," Hannah whispers to me, deviously. "He said he'd pay for the deposit. Which means," she grins so infectiously I can't help but mirror her image. "There's about a hundred quid behind the bar for the first drinks and only we know about it." she lets out a high-pitched squeal of excitement. There are two empty cocktail glasses already at one end of the booth.

"I did not expect this of you," I return his mischievous energy. "I am thoroughly impressed."

"I'm handing in my notice!" She says, unable to hold back her news any longer. "I got into uni. I start in a couple of weeks!"

"Well done, you!" I say as I hug here. She deserves it, she has worked so hard to pass her exams. "We need some prosecco!" I flag down the barman and order us a bottle to share. "Are you excited?"

She's beaming, unable to contain a smile. "Beyond excited!" She says. "I don't know what I am! I can't wait, I only got the email at the weekend. I wanted to tell you straight away but I didn't want to… And now I've done it here…" her face falls. "I'm so sorry. I didn't mean to do it here."

"Hey," I say as I watch her mood plummet. "Don't worry. I don't mind!" I put a comforting arm around her. "We all have to move on at some point. I'm happy for you!" The barman cracks open the bottle for us. Two glasses stand waiting for us. He pours us each a glass. "I'm very happy for you. You've worked that hard for it, you deserve to get what you want!"

Hannah restrains her smile but perks back up.

"Here," I say, handing her a glass. I then raise my own. "Cheers."

She shyly clinks my glass. Ben joins us with his soft drink. "I'm going to stay at home," she says. "I can't afford a flat, at least for now. And I can't afford student halls. But it's only for now."

"You're going to do great," I tell her, already halfway through my second glass. "You're gonna study and then get a great job. At least your course takes you straight into employment. You'll be able to afford a great place to live and you'll have a fantastic life ahead of you."

There's still a part of me that believes that.

Maybe this is the second bottle talking, my words are slurring together and I'm repeating myself and the only place where I'm clear and make sense is in my head, but Megan arrived a glass or two ago and she still hasn't said 'Hi'. She's sitting at the far end of the table, not even in the booth, about as far away from me as she can get.

I lift the bottle of bubbly off the table to offer her a glass, but she shakes her head to decline my offer. All sorts of people from the office have arrived, every one of them commenting that they'll catch up with me soon, but all of them sit around the chair and form their own small conversations.

The lights are dimmed and the music cranked up.

"I finally got a response from the union," Ben shouts in my ear.

"About my termination?" I ask.

He shakes his head. "No, they've only just got back to me about the Smartcards. I emailed them about you on Wednesday—I don't know when I'll hear back." I sigh. If he's only just getting a response about the bloody cards tracking our every move, then I imagine it will be months before they get around to little, old me.

"What did they say about the Smartcards?" I ask for no more reason than to be polite.

"They say it's an overreach. Serves no purpose to the security, safety or smooth running of the business. They're going to challenge the use of the technology and the lawyers will be looking into legal action that can be taken on our behalf. There was a vote put out by email on Thursday to see if people would be interested in industrial action if the company insists on continual use of the cards."

"They voted no, didn't they," I say.

Ben nods. "There's another company," he tells me. "I can't tell you which one, but the union has discovered that this company installed eye-tracking software, so not only can they see that the person is at the desk, but also whether they are looking at the screen, and where on the screen, and how long they need to look at the screen to do a task," he finishes his drink. "They timed how long it took people to do things. How often people looked away. They could tell how long people chatted to the colleagues sitting next to them, who initiated the conversation, stuff like that."

"Creepy."

"It's fucking ridiculous," he says. "They declined industrial action too." He shakes his head. "I don't get it. I don't know why every waking minute of our lives is being monitored by these people and why no one wants to stand up against it."

"Right?" I chime in, but let him go on with his ramble.

"They control your every move, every habit. You can't leave your work space. You are forced by this tiny, invisible shackle to sit straight at your desk, to stare at your screen, to obey the great corporate overlord. I don't get it—why aren't people angry? Why do we just accept that this is what it should be like. That this is what work should be like? That we should expect the very worst that corporations have to offer? You know," he interrupts himself before I can respond.

"I bet that the person who invented the technology in smart carts did it for a really good reason. Like a really, nice reason. Like they just wanted to follow penguins, or whales or something. Or like the guy in that film about a twister…"

"*Twister*?" I offer.

"Yeah, that *Twister* film. We could have all these great insights into the world. And instead of watching us going to the toilet or kitchen every few hours, we'd get to understand penguins or polar bears or whatever."

"You know, if you want to have a drink I can get a taxi home," I offer.

"But we don't use it for that. Some parent company bought the rights to it— they just flat out went, 'you know what, we can sell this. Companies will want to see what their people are doing'. And they were right. They were fucking right."

I nudge my glass over to him. "Have a fucking drink," I say. He thanks me and knocks back the glass.

"Another bottle?" He asks.

I nod.

Down at the far end of the gathering Megan feigns interest in the conversation between two people I don't recognise. Which is odd. Odd that I don't recognise them, I mean, seeing as this is supposed to be *my* leaving do. She is actively listening, I can tell. Not engaging, but nodding at thoughtful points and encouraging them to speak. I can't remember if we did that at the telephony workshop or whether it was the course we went to before that. Making the right noises while on the phone to show that we are listening.

She looks dead behind the eyes though. Maybe she's just bored stiff. The man next to her hasn't stopped speaking in ages. I can't catch what he's saying; the music is too loud and he's too far away for me to watch his lips.

"I asked if you could have your job back," Hannah says, her bottom lip quivering. "When I handed in my notice, I did ask if you could have your job back." She stares down at the table, sad and sorry at the same time, needing me to know that she tried.

"They're probably at full headcount," I remind her sarcastically. And she smiles in relief.

"Still," she says. "I'm sorry. If I'd handed my notice in earlier it might have made a difference. It's just I didn't find out my results until after…"

"It's alright," I gently interrupt her. "It is what it is. It wouldn't have made a difference."

Hannah notices that I keep looking over at the other end of the table, and for a second we catch Megan's eyes looking back at us. An indescribable emotion across her face. Her brow and forehead rigid, her upper lip stiff. Her eyes keep darting back to us even as she faces her companions.

"Megan got that advertising internship. That's why she's sat down there with them," Hannah tells me. "Those two next to her are setting her up with a remote desk in our office and she'll work down in London a couple of days a month." Megan's eyes meet mine but swiftly avoid maintaining contact and shift down to the ground. "I'm sure once you've got yourself sorted, we'll all be in a much better place than before," Hannah says. She means it too. She genuinely means it.

"The internship?" I try to remember our conversation from Bukowski's. "I thought she wasn't accepted for it? or am I misremembering that?"

Ben hands Hannah the new bottle, he's brought over his own glass to join us. Hannah pours me a drink.

"She wasn't accepted originally," Hannah says. Ben looks quizzically. "Megan's internship."

"Ah," is all he says.

"Jan told her that day you were let go."

I look over at Megan again. She feigns a smile that curls up her lips into her cheeks and stops there.

"She didn't have enough experience," I whisper aloud. "She didn't have the right certificates. They told her she would need those first. Why would they change their minds now?"

"I can't hear you," Hannah says over the music.

My brow begins to furrow. It intrudes on my vision. I watch Megan shift uncomfortably in her chair. Squirming under my gaze. Air rolls over my tongue as I breathe in through my ajar mouth.

Why didn't Megan say a proper hello when she arrived. Why is she sitting at the far end of the table, as far away from us as possible? As far away from me as possible? Does she feel guilty, like Hannah does? I mean, she has the job she wanted. Restructuring worked in her favour and she feels like it's unfair to me. She should be celebrating her success with her friends—with us. We have a bottle we are clearly sharing and we toasted Hannah's success, it's not like I'm putting a downer on the night. But, maybe, it doesn't feel like success. Maybe because she was rejected initially and then only taken after restructuring, she feels like an imposter, like she doesn't deserve it. Maybe she did something she's not proud of to get the job?

I chuckle at the thought.

And then I stop chuckling.

Megan tucks her hair behind her ear and gets up from the table. I follow her into the toilets and wait by the sinks and mirrors.

What if, and bear with me, Megan was the one who ticked the boxes. She has access to that system. She has the authority on the system to check those boxes. A manager says 'hey, we just need you to…' and she does it. Did they offer her the internship upfront, quid pro quo or did she negotiate for it? Does she feel guilty after the fact because I lost my job? Does she even link those two events together?

The door to the stall opens and we stand looking at each other.

I guess I have some questions I need answering.

"Hi," she says, taken aback.

"Hi," I say, coldly.

Avoiding looking in the mirror, she comes over to the sinks, places her handbag on the floor and washes her hands.

"Congratulations," I say. She looks at me, though her eyes barely go above my waist. "I heard you got the internship after all."

She squirts soap onto her hands. "Yeah," she says brightly, pushing the tap down and rinsing the soap off her hands. "I'm lucky they reconsidered."

"That's good," I say with a steady voice, betraying nothing. "I thought they didn't accept you because of lack of experience, wrong certificates or something."

"Or something," she repeats. "Someone dropped out last minute, so they had a space."

I hum. And, without a hint of challenge, I say, "You ticked the boxes." It isn't an accusation. Just a statement of fact. I'm letting her know I know. She freezes. "There aren't many people that have access, so…" I trail off. Leaving her frozen with water dripping from her fingertips, until she bursts back into movement; flicking the excess water from her hands and pulling paper towels from the wall. "Did they give you the internship before or after you falsified documents?"

"Falsified documents!" Megan scoffs. "What are you on about? Do you hear yourself?" She sticks to well-worn phrases and begins to stumble over her words. "I didn't do… they didn't…"

"Did you even bother to look at the shitty excuse for evidence they sent in? That they expected me to approve?" I am incredulous. "Did you open any of them boxes and look at the nonsense that was sent us?"

She won't even look me in the eye.

"Were you on the team that investigated the whistle-blowing tip?" I ask. She purses her lips and turns away from me to throw the paper towel in the bin. "They didn't ask me, cos I was the person on the team so it could only have been me that reported it. So they asked you. Who told you to tick the boxes?"

Her mouth clamps shut. She isn't going to say anything on the subject. Which, in of itself, says enough.

"Did you know I'd lose my job?" I ask.

"No," she says firmly. "I didn't."

At least that's something.

"But you had to know they were asking you to do something illegal?" She clams up again, refusing to say anything more. "Did you even stop to think how fucked up this whole thing is?" I am angry now. The words come out with vitriolic spit. "There is something illegal and immoral happening and you… you just ticked the boxes. Like it was nothing. Like the whole of our job meant nothing."

"You're overthinking it," she says, grabbing her bag off the floor and trying to shrug me off with an unconvincing smile. "It's just a job."

"It was."

Her face hardens and she storms out of the toilets, back into the bar, leaving me in a muffled echo chamber, thinking everything through.

The pocket of her handbag is still broken. On the floor beside me, next to some empty sweet wrappers and receipts, are her lanyard and card. I tidy it up. The receipts and wrappers go into the bin. My initial reaction is to storm back into the bar, slam the card onto the table, smash some glasses and be kicked out. but the stab of betrayal is still fresh in my back and a plan is forming in my head. Wordless, without vision, drawing in every minute detail I have seen at that place until all of a sudden it is fully formed and ready to implement.

I wrap the lanyard round the card and tuck it into the waistband of my trousers. I walk out into the bar and over to Ben.

"Hey," I say, smiling. "I think I left my purse in your car, can I get your keys just for a second?"

He hands them over without a thought and I go down to the carpark under the hotel and take the petrol can from the boot of the car, placing it into a bag-for-life and draping my jacket over it. At ground level, outside the front doors there are a group of smokers. Carol's there, taking long smoky puffs.

"Hi Carol," I say as I approach her.

"Hi!" She replies enthusiastically. "I'm so sorry you're leaving us. I'm going to miss you!"

That's right, Carol. This was my choice.

"I'll talk to you properly inside," I promise her. "I have Ben's car keys—he's up there, but I have to meet a friend to give her some stuff she left at mine," I lift the hand with the bag as proof of this. "Would you mind giving Ben his keys? I don't know how long I'll be."

"Of course! Of course!" She chimes. Taking the keys from my outstretched hand.

"I'll be back in a bit," I lie.

"We're going to miss you," she repeats as I turn my back.

I stride with purpose down the road and cross over at the lights. The hotel isn't too far from the office. With each step my resolve strengthens. I reach the door and open it with the key I forgot to return. I punch in Frances' code to turn off the alarm, I wave Megan's lanyard over the censor to enter. I walk up the main staircase, checking each floor as I go. All the lights are off. The soft whoosh and whine of the computers are now silent.

The glass room, so quiet and exposed. I half expect I'll have to smash the glass door with one of the trinkets from the IT desks or with a fire extinguisher, but I quickly realise that no one even bothered to lock it.

After all the grief I was given about keeping the documents safe!

I take the box of 'evidence'—the stuff that has never been checked and only looked over by me. I skim through the papers and find the chunks of financial and company records that are the most damning and stack them in a neat pile by the box. Content with the documents I have picked, I leave my shopping bag and make my way down the back flight of stairs all the way down to the mailroom at the first basement level. As always, by the door, there are large envelopes already stamped. I take the largest envelope there and scribble Graham Bolt, c/o Meadow Weir Inquirer on the front. I leave the letter on the front desk while I trudge back up to the third floor.

I consider taking the lift, but knowing my luck, I would get stuck in it, and that would defeat the point of all of this.

Back at the glass room, I pack up the boxes and drag them over to the lift to take them down. I care less if they get trapped. I tap the ground floor and jump out before the doors close on me.

Taking the can of petrol, I unscrew the cap and begin to dribble the foul-smelling liquid over the paper and computers in the glass box. Then at the IT desks in the main office, and out towards the front stairs. I slide my hand between the IT desk and the cabinet sitting underneath to pick out the lighter there and pocket it. I walk down the front staircase allowing a small trickle of petrol to follow me.

As I pass the community board, I snatch the photos from the charity event, still pinned up there, pointless and forgotten. I'll put them in the envelope.

On the ground floor, I put the can down beside the staircase and light the bottom stair. It takes a moment for the fire to leap up onto the next stair, but it does. And then to the next. slowly crawling back to the glass box.

I claim the boxes from the lift, using the sack barrow at reception, I wheel the boxes out of the office and across the street. I slip the envelope into the post box and place the boxes around it.

The fire is spreading. Speeding up. I can tell it has climbed all the way up to the top of the atrium from the way the light plays on the glass roof. I can also see where it has made its way into the third-floor office space.

I place my bag and jacket on the kerb and sit to watch the fire grow.

The first alarm, barely audible, cries out weakly. Soon, all the others join in. within seconds, every single one of them is blaring out.

The fire has caught on the other floors too, I can see its growth fanning out from the atrium until the whole building is burning bright.

A window smashes. I have the sudden urge to take a photo of this. To share that photo. Something that would be attention grabbing for the front page of a newspaper. Flashy.

I take my phone out and balance it against the box behind me, camera front facing so I can see what's in frame; night sky, burning building, me in the foreground. I make sure there's no flash on and then set a countdown. I stand up and take my place in the shot, just to one side, looking up at the burning tower. I wait until I hear the click of the photograph and then return to the kerb to check my photo.

Yes. That'll do. I look quite good surrounded by fire.

I post it on every account I have, and then email it to Graham, telling him to look out for the documentation in the post, and then I log out of everything, and delete all my apps.

I place my phone in my bag, close my eyes and stretch out my legs, allowing myself to bask in the warmth that emanates from my work. Calm washes over me. Every muscle that has wound itself tight around my core slowly releases with each breath. I listen to the crackling fire licking through the shattering windows and feel a sort of relief. A relief that I have done everything I could do.

Maybe, and I know this is both unlikely and maddeningly optimistic of me, but just maybe, people might pay attention. The police will have to investigate, or at least people will ask them questions. The paper has to print something. The company has to make a statement or do a proper investigation, otherwise people will ask what they aren't saying.

I'm not mad. They'll likely sweep it under the same giant carpet they always do. But a burnt-out building is harder to hide and big enough to make people look twice.

I'm an optimist. Who knew?

I'll just wait here for the blue lights to come and get me.